TWISTED MAGICS

J. C. JACKSON

SHADOW PHOENIX PUBLISHING

Twisted Magics

J.C. Jackson

Copyright © 2016, 2019 J.C. Jackson

Published by Shadow Phoenix Publishing LLC

ISBN-13: 978-0692699706, 978-1-7322835-1-0

Cover designed by J. Caleb Design

 Created with Vellum

1

THE SMELL of burnt paint and heated metal reached my nose. The fire from the explosion quickly died off, but the smoke was still thick. I heard the air ventilation system working hard to clear it out.

How many more times today was Lockonis going to make me do this? I was getting tired - I did not usually cast such high energy spells. Tucking a loose strand of dark auburn hair behind my ear, I looked back at the fiery redhead. My boss stood there with her arms crossed, analyzing my last cast.

"You're still over-thinking it, Ketayl," she told me. "You're an expert on arcane theory and these manipulations should be second nature to you. Remember what the Magus said: you're an Arcanist so you don't need to think your way through the spell like a traditional mage." The slightly taller Elven woman walked over and turned me back toward the target.

I stiffened up at her touch. She could have just signaled me like before.

Lockonis was not an Arcanist, but being a former Warmage put her as close to one as any traditional mage could get. She somehow understood my abilities better than I did.

I rubbed my eyes. The lighting in the large underground practice bay was starting to bother me or maybe there were too many colors swirling around the room from all the casts. Being able to see the arcane had its problems. Especially when there was an overload of information floating about - all the colors from the casts telling me something different. Reds and oranges dominated the area with arcane text lazily swirling about where each one had exploded. Arcane mites had started feeding off of the oldest ones, but it would be a couple of days before they would fully break down the arcane remnants.

This last cast had been more powerful than any previous. I was a lab tech, why did I need combat training? Why did Lockonis have a thing for fire-based spells?

I knew the answer to why I found myself in here once a week - as an Arcanist, casting helped me retain control over my power. I did not need combat training though.

Before Lockonis could say more, her phone rang. She pulled it out of her pocket and walked a few yards away.

I closed my eyes and tilted my head toward the ceiling, recovering some of my arcane energy. The bun on the back of my head felt like it weighed a ton. I had shed my large gray sweater earlier since my casts had heated up the practice bay quickly. The loose black short-sleeved shirt, jeans, and light boots I wore started to feel a bit too warm. Even though I got cold easily, I would happily deal with the snowy weather outside right now.

"I'm going to have to cut our session short," Lockonis said, walking back toward me. She still held her phone in her hand. "Why don't you go take a break and then head back to the lab. And a real break - at least an hour."

Glancing at the time, I could take an early lunch and be back in the lab shortly before noon. I would stay later tonight to make up for this morning. I did not need much rest anyway.

I bowed deeply and collected my things, putting my sweater back on. In the process I stopped to fix the diamond-shaped insignia pin on it - one of the its edges had gotten caught between the weave. The pin held five different-colored gems set in gold with a highly stylized "AC" keeping them in place. It looked a little dusty from the morning's exercises. Thankfully there was not another Arcane College mage around to give me a hard time about it.

I grabbed a quick lunch, only taking up the hour by checking the messages on my phone. Evidence from a new case was coming in with arcane components. I grinned in excitement because despite being classified as an Arcane Investigator, I got little work for it. Lockonis had also trained me to handle to normal workload in the lab and while those presented interesting puzzles, I found it rather routine work.

There was another message about having skipped my scheduled physical training time yesterday. I skipped those as often as I could manage. I did not know why it was mandatory for everyone. I found it as much of a waste of time as combat arcane training. Though I would never voice my opinion on either.

It was time to get to work and I hurried off to the lab where I quickly lost track of time with the new case.

THE ARCANE MITE under the microscope probed its surroundings. The specially-lined case kept it fed and visible. This one was collected at a crime scene that the field agents suspected was a poor assassination attempt of some politician or another.

I had long since given up caring about those details. What I really wanted to find out was where the arcane mites came from: they appeared within a few minutes to an hour after a spell was used and consumed the arcane remnant.

My own personal theory was they primarily existed on a level I could not see - their young feeding off the remnants, but what was their role beyond that?

Without taking my eyes off the mite, I scratched down its approximate age on a notebook to my right. It gave me a rough time-line for when the spell this one was gathered from had been cast. It was on its final stage and would disappear soon. Thankfully this was the last one.

I jumped and nearly fell off my stool when the phone rang, breaking the silence.

Moving to answer the phone, I saw a momentary reflection in a glass cabinet door. The woman had gray, bloodshot eyes and dark auburn hair falling out of its bun. The extended points of Elven ears made her hair stick out funny.

Realizing it was my reflection, I ran my hands over my hair to get it into some semblance of order. I rubbed my hands on my white lab coat before finally picking up the phone on the third ring.

"Lab," I said. My voice sounded tired even to my ears. I tugged on my sweater, straightening it out before rubbing out some of the creases in my jeans.

"Ketayl, my office. Now."

I stared at the handset, which gave its waiting tone. I easily recognized Vince's voice.

Vince was the Director of the Terran Intelligence Organization, making him the highest boss I had to answer to. The abrupt tone was typical of him, given how he interacted with others, but he usually treated me differently.

His distrust of the Arcane College, which I came from and was a liaison for, was well known. It had been a while since Vince looked at me with the same disdain and his sudden change of tone surprised me.

I gave him an estimate this afternoon on when I would have a preliminary report ready. There was not a huge rush on this information. Normally Vince would have come down himself for an update or sent Lockonis to help me.

Without bothering to take off my lab coat I grabbed my handwritten notes and the few printouts from the tests I managed to finish. I stuffed them into a folder quickly and glanced at the time.

I stopped and stared at the clock to make sure I read it right. No wonder I was tired. And hungry, given that it was nearly 0200 and I had been processing evidence straight through since I got back from lunch. It was a bad habit of mine when I got a new puzzle.

Clutching the paperwork with one arm, I rushed through the hallways in the underground maze which connected along the massive walkway bordering the hanger below. As I half-jogged down the walkway, it sounded like someone was working down there, but I did not have time to satisfy my curiosity of what would be going on at this late hour. When the Director says jump, well, the rest was a commonly known phrase around here.

I hit the button for the elevator a little harder than I intended and then shook my hand from the sudden sharp pain. I was usually much more patient, but then I usually did not have my boss calling me in the middle of the night either. Granted, I normally kept more sane hours than this, preferring the quiet of the early morning.

I worried there had been some development in this particular case which required a rush on processing the remaining evidence.

Some things plainly could not be rushed, but explaining that could end up being a losing battle. I had taken care of the time-sensitive evidence at least.

I jogged down the hallway as soon as the elevator doors parted enough to allow me through. I opened the door to the reception area more forcefully than I planned and tripped, dropping the folder I carried.

Quickly collecting my scattered files, I was surprised to find the Director's assistant still here. Fletch was a young Human man with brown hair which always seemed to stick straight out over his forehead. He should have gone home hours ago. He worked furiously at his computer, muttering under his breath.

Brown eyes caught mine and he jerked his head toward the door to Vince's office.

All the energy from the rush to get to Vince's office changed to uncertainty. I did better when I knew what I was walking into and had a chance to prepare. I pulled my lab coat tighter around me with my free hand.

I always felt I had to push hard to prove my worth. That if I did not, I would be sent back to the Arcane College. I was not sure after having tasted what it was like away from the hard, stone walls of the Arcane College that I could go back.

I looked at Fletch, who only paused one hand from typing long enough to point toward the door, exasperation plain on his face. The door in question opened before I could move.

"Good, you arrived first," Vince said. "Fletcher, hold the next one until I'm ready."

Despite his pale complexion and thin frame, I never doubted the tall, dark-haired vampire's power. The only trouble was I often forgot he was actually a vampire. He looked like a normal Human in his early thirties, when in reality, he was old enough to have long gotten over the "allergies" other vampires had, such as sunlight.

Vince sat down at his desk and signaled to one of the dark green chairs in front. "Sit. We need to talk."

I walked forward through the doorway slowly, tucking a stray lock of hair behind my ear and looking around nervously. Little had changed since the last time I was in here. The grand mahogany desk sat to my right, putting Vince's back to the large windows. A black inbox was piled high with packets of papers. Computer, phone, even pens sat in a very specific order which never deviated. Books and binders adorned the massive bookshelves making up the wall opposite the door. A screen hung on the wall opposite his desk with a smaller conference table between it and his desk. Two of the chairs from the table were the only things out of place.

The sound from the screen on the wall to my left was low, but distracting. He had the news on every time I came in here. I briefly caught a glimpse of a blown-out building and wondered if I would be getting evidence from that. Maybe Vince wanted to tell me I was getting a priority change, but normally it would have come through as an electronic request.

Watching news reports always seemed surreal, but perhaps it was because I spent my time holed up in the lab. I never connected with the actual crime scene.

Taking a seat in front of his desk, I mentally ran through what information I managed to get from the evidence so far, organizing it into some kind of a report. I wished I had at least taken the time to get the paperwork into a less chaotic format as I took some level of pride in presenting information which could be easily followed.

The perpetrator used a strong spell to freeze and then shatter the lock on the door...

Vince looked at the packet I held. "Didn't honestly expect you to have this much already. This case isn't why I called you in though."

There went the mental report I was putting together. Now I was back to being completely unprepared.

Vince sat back in his chair, his body visibly relaxed. It made me nervous. If I was not in here for this case, then why? Was it because of my training session with Lockonis this morning?

He stared at me for what I was sure was far less time than I imagined before speaking, "I'll admit, you've sure as Hells surprised me. I get cornered into taking an Arcane College mage and I honestly didn't think there was a single forward-thinking person among them. It has been a rough road these past couple of years, hasn't it?"

A late night review? I had been with the Arcane College for roughly half a century, mostly hidden from the world as a glorified librarian. At least until one day, without warning, I was transferred to the TIO as the Arcane College's liaison.

While the Arcane College disdained technology and only used the absolute minimal amount necessary, I always felt drawn to it.

Because of that, the transfer to the TIO was a blessing. Out of old, itchy robes; dark, dank halls; and archaic ways and into the light of the world. I needed to learn to drive, use mobile phones and computers, but I enjoyed the challenges.

I quickly said, "No, sir."

"Good. Your work has been exemplary, and I need you in the field for this one. The team in Ocean's Edge asked for an Arcane Investigator. Lockonis will be pulling double-duty in the lab in the meantime. If you leave her anything that is."

My mind screamed for him to wait. I was just the person in the lab. I had no field experience. I bit my lower lip for a moment before deciding to quietly express my concerns, "Sir, I'm not sure I'm qualified for..."

The look Vince leveled at me clearly stated there was no way I could get out of this despite my reservations. I sank back in my chair and shut my mouth.

Vince hit a button on his desk phone. "Send her in."

The door opened and closed so quickly it barely seemed to move. Retanei, a Dark Elf, appeared and seated herself next to me. Her long silver-white hair was pulled back in its normal, neat ponytail. It was a stark contrast to her ebony skin. Blue-teal eyes were sharp and ready. She nodded at me and leaned forward, her brown leather jacket creaking softly. A pad of paper with notes on her lap - pen poised for more information. This was her time of day.

I felt better seeing my friend. When my sister, Kitteren, was away, which was often, Retanei kept an eye on me. She would joke that us misfits needed to stick together.

"I have an urgent assignment." Vince pointed at the screen behind us. "You two are heading for Ocean's Edge."

The reporters on the screen were giving the latest death toll numbers from the bombing. Many of the casualties were members of the Terran Navy - no names were being released. When they did flash images I could get a sense of the force involved to take down much of the building.

It had been a decent-sized restaurant named the Waking Dawn. One of the outside walls was completely gone with two more missing large chunks. The roof was also gone over most of the building. The blast had been concentrated toward the dining area and left the bar and an inside wall mostly standing. Fires still burned inside and I could see sparks of electricity from where screens and lights once hung. Smoke billowed from the back of the building.

Civilians rushed about injured and crying - some trying to return inside. Emergency response teams were working to contain the fires and get whoever might be alive out.

My nervousness edged toward panic. I had no idea how to deal with a situation like this. I bit my lower lip and looked to Retanei for guidance. She had a lot of experience in the field.

"What's the current situation?" Retanei asked. She must have seen the news already as the pad of paper in her hands already had notes from their report. She always seemed to be prepared for anything.

Vince's voice was all business as he spoke, "Right now, we know about as much as what is being reported. Savanas will be lead since she's the head of the Ocean's Edge branch. She put in a high priority request for a Tracker who specializes in rural areas and an Arcane Investigator. There is a possible connection to a group they've been keeping tabs on for the past six months which has been hiding in the forest outside the city. One of her agents insists it was an arcane-based explosion, but he's not able to pin down a point of origin or get any details."

Nervously, I pulled my lab coat even tighter, hoping I could disappear in the over-sized white garment. Arcane-based explosion - and my level of ability to see the arcane was rare.

Glancing back at the news, I wished I could tell them what they needed through the video feed.

"This crosses racial territories so it falls under our jurisdiction. Given the size of her team, I'm allowing Savanas to call in outside assistance. Whoever this bastard is, he targeted Navy personnel." I heard anger in Vince's usually gruff voice.

He turned to look directly at me before he finished. "The *Traverse* is being held in port while this is being investigated. There is an Arcane College Magister aboard. I trust this won't be an issue."

A Magister far outranked a Researcher, and while I was not directly under the Arcane College's thumb, I was still technically a part of them. "Not from me, sir." A direct "no" would have been a lie. I could not speak for the Magister.

Vince grimaced for a moment. "That's about as much as I can ask for. You two will be taking a Shrike over there as soon as it is prepped."

I knew Retanei well enough to hear her mental groan at the thought of having to pilot. She was more than capable, but preferred other methods of transportation. "Ted?" Retanei asked. He was her normal partner for assignments.

Vince shook his head. "Too delicate to send him. It's up to you if you want to take Artemis - she could prove an asset."

Artemis, Retanei's other partner, was a gray wolf. Rarely were they seen apart, but something about Vince seemed to frighten the animal companions people kept.

"I know you keep a bag at the ready so help Ketayl pack. Ketayl, you need to bring the prototypes you've been working on."

Perhaps he forgot, so I reminded him, "Sir, they haven't been cleared for..."

Vince barked, "I don't care if they haven't been field tested - you're doing it now. I want as much evidence as possible to take this bastard down." He made sure to look directly at each of us in turn as he spoke, but focused on Retanei when he said, "Your primary objective is to get information. Now go."

HURRYING to match Retanei's long strides, I started to wish I had not skipped physical training as often as I did. It was also late and my stomach demanded attention.

Part of me really wanted to go clean up the lab and go to bed, but the images from the news broadcast were still fresh in my mind. How many dead? How many injured? Was it an accident? Deliberate? I had not given the severity of the situation on the newscast much thought until I was being sent to investigate.

Perhaps this would better help connect me with my work - to see the personal side of it rather than just numbers and puzzles.

It could have been an accident by an untrained Arcanist. Thinking further on it, even if I lost control at my current level of ability, I could not cause nearly as much damage as I saw on the news report.

That brought me back to it being a deliberate attack. If it was arcane-based, how much power would be required and what would the caster have used? I was going to have to get there fast to find out before the arcane remnants were consumed by the mites.

"You need to eat." The sound jarred me from my mental evaluation. Retanei was always hyper-observant. "Go to the dining hall and I'll meet you there after I get Artemis."

"You're going to bring her?" I found myself questioning the air and sighed. I could not talk to someone who was not there, and I was, admittedly, hungry. Cadwr usually kept leftovers from the day's meals in the front refrigerator for those of us who wandered in late.

WITHIN TWO HOURS after the initial phone call, I was fed, packed, and leaving instructions with a tired Lockonis, who merely waved me out the door with a gear pack of the field equipment we had been developing.

A male Human mechanic, whose name escaped me at the moment, stood by the control station for the lift, yawning. He said, "I got the flight plan logged and programmed into the auto-pilot. She's fueled and the Chained Lakes office has been notified. They will be sending some of their mechanics to meet you to help refuel and whatever else you might need. Zenmin is doing a final check."

A small form crawled out from under the Shrike and tossed a thumbs up in our direction.

Zenmin, the Halfing mechanic in question, ran a grease-covered hand through his curly hair. I never was sure what color his hair was actually supposed to be.

The smell of the oils and other fluids used in the machine were fresh and overpowering. I swallowed, trying to keep my hastily eaten meal down. Even Artemis covered her nose with her paws. From the random piles of rags tossed around the platform, I could see they were in a hurry to get us in the air.

I looked at the flying machine I was about to board. The Shrikes were used on a regular basis, but as much as I enjoyed watching them take off and land, I still found the twin tilt-rotors intimidating and had not been in one since I arrived at the TIO.

Getting settled into the co-pilot's seat, I focused on the control panel in front of me as the platform the Shrike sat on started to rise. I felt the propellers come to life, vibrating the aircraft. At least the smells drifted away quickly. I was not sure I would survive the four hours to Chained Lakes otherwise.

I turned my attention to Retanei once the control station was out of sight. She was busy getting ready for takeoff, but never seemed to miss a beat and said, "Nothing I say or do will make you stop being nervous. Comes with the territory. I never know what I'm going to find when I go out - especially on such a high-profile case."

I rolled my eyes as Artemis nudged my arm. Running my hand through the soft fur on her head was calming. "Should I mention you're not helping?" I was still working on my sarcasm and was never sure if it came out right.

I was pretty sure Artemis was unhappy about the flight as well, but there was not a mage in the world who could teleport us as far as we needed. Trying to set up chained teleports was both expensive and time consuming, and not necessarily in as straight of a line as we were flying.

My free hand gripped the seat tightly when the platform locked into place, jarring the Shrike. The snow had not stopped, but I did not think the weather would get me out of this.

Retanei grinned mischievously as we ascended from the platform. I started to think she enjoyed flying more than she let on. "At least you know you're not alone."

I took a deep breath and reminded myself on why we were in a rush: I needed to get there as fast as possible to observe the arcane remnants before they had degraded too much. The mites would have begun showing up by now and started breaking it down. I hoped there would be enough left to work with.

2

A couple of local Ocean's Edge TIO members waited in a car by the landing pad. They got out once we settled enough to approach. It was already early afternoon here.

A short, dark-haired Human woman, dressed in a mechanic's orange jumpsuit ran in our direction. She headed straight for Retanei's door.

While they talked, I got out, grabbing my bags in the process. I approached the car and could make out a black-haired male Elf wearing an agent's coat and hat - the same as Retanei and I wore. He stood several inches taller than me - his short, black ponytail whipped in the wind. Even from only a few feet away, he had to shout to be heard over the wind and the engines powering down, "My name is Rathal Dawnseeker and that is our mechanic Sasha Larsen. She'll see to the Shrike. Savanas wanted me to get you two down there hours ago."

I looked back for Retanei, but saw only legs from under the Shrike. I wanted to get back in there because it was warm - I certainly did not want to fly anywhere for a while. I had been too anxious about both the flight and what we would encounter here to get much rest.

"I'm Ketayl, an Arcane Investigator. Retanei is a Rural Tracker." Introductions were not something I did and I bit my lower lip, feeling nervous. Feeling a bump against my legs, I freed up a hand to quickly pet the wolf next to me and added, "This is Artemis, Retanei's animal companion." It sounded more awkward aloud than in my head. I hoped he chalked it up to having to shout to be heard.

Retanei finally joined us, offering Rathal a formal Elven greeting. He made a face at her and half-heartedly returned it. She slid into the backseat with Artemis while Rathal held the front passenger's door open for me. Nodding my thanks, I got into the blissfully warm car. I tried to not melt into the heated seat with relief - I had not realize exactly how cold I was.

Tapping my shoulder, Retanei said, "I'm going to catch a few before we get there." I turned to watch her get settled. *How can she be comfortable half-stretched out on the back seat with Artemis across her lap like that?*

Rathal slid into the driver's seat and made a phone call, pointedly ignoring us. It was short, but I could make an educated guess he spoke with Savanas.

About 10 minutes passed after the call ended and we finally made our way off the airport grounds. I could not decide if I was nervous or excited. I loved puzzles and I always enjoyed the challenges sent to me in the lab, but this was the field and it was a very different set of variables to deal with. There was no controlled environment here.

"Why'd they have to send a damn Drow?" I barely heard Rathal mutter over the heater blowing. His hazel eyes remained focused on the road ahead.

Not sure if I should say something, I looked back at Retanei, but she had her hat pulled down over her face and looked every bit like she was asleep.

It was not fair of him to judge her, but I was unsure where my boundaries were at this point.

I bit my lower lip for a moment before finding a neutral comment, "She's a Dark Elf, not Drow."

The surprise on his face told me he had not expected a response. "They look the same," Rathal shot back. Well, I could not argue his point. They were essentially two factions. The tension in the air was nearly tangible. "Next you'll tell me there are actually Arcane College mages without a superiority complex or that dragons exist."

His words hit a bit closer to home. Sinking into my seat, I pulled my coat tighter around my neck - my Arcane College pin sat below the zipper on my scarf. How was I supposed to handle his attitude? I knew of the disdain for the Arcane College in general, but at the main office I never encountered such hostility. I could not recall any instance Retanei received it either.

The silence stretched out. As we crested a hill, I took brief note of how the snow-covered canopy of trees got thicker the further inland I looked. I was sure it was the last peaceful moment I would have for a while.

Something arcane caught my attention and it was close. I barely caught it. I closed my eyes to focus better. It was too faint to make out any details.

"Okay, I'm sorry. We've been going pretty much nonstop since it happened. I guess I'm a bit edgy," Rathal said and the anger in his voice lightened, but did not disappear completely. "Is this your first time in Ocean's Edge? I could show you around. There are some great restaurants near my apartment."

I was so focused on what bore the faintest arcane scent to it that I needed to replay his words in my head before answering. I was at a loss. He apologized, but I still felt uneasy about him.

Looking out the window, I could see we were coming up on the crime scene. We were quickly waved through the roped off area. "Waking Dawn" was on the side of the blown-out building. There was an Elven woman with dark hair waiting for us - her arms crossed over her chest. Her ears were shorter - perhaps half-Elven?

Reaching back, I tapped Retanei's leg, though I was pretty sure Artemis' stirring would wake her.

As soon as we stopped, I got out. I did not want to answer Rathal. I was still upset about the comments he made toward Retanei. He came around to my door and leaned against the car with a smirk on his face. "So, what do you say, little lady?"

His reference to my lack of height grated on my nerves. The woman was approaching us and Retanei was already out of the car.

Unzipping my coat to show my Arcane College pin, I found my response, "You don't like my type either." Closing it quickly, I went to stand next to Retanei.

I never spoke out. It was never my place to question or judge. At least not openly. It felt like my emotional control was slipping. It must be because I was tired and hungry.

I closed my eyes for a moment, pinching the bridge of my nose to pull myself back together, but I was distracted by the sensations around me. The heaviness to the air. The sense of the arcane, but tainted somehow. I did not know dark had a feeling, but it was the best I could describe it at the moment. It all felt incredibly wrong.

I knew my being here was part of it, but it also felt like voices were raised in pain and anger. At least it sounded something like voices - they were distorted.

Staring at the side of the building still standing, I wondered what awaited me around the corner. Rubbing my arms, I could not get rid of the sensation of wanting to have said more against Rathal's blind judgment. I could not. I would only draw the wrong kind of attention to myself.

And now I was getting distracted. Normally I would jump from one thing to the next and then back, but I needed to focus.

"What's going on?" The woman stopped next to Rathal, holding out her hand to which he relinquished the keys. "Is your mouth getting you in trouble again?" She glared at him. Without waiting for a response, she rolled her eyes. "We'll talk about this later." I thought I heard her make a off-hand comment about womanizer, but I could not be certain. Her face was still hard as she approached us.

I moved behind Retanei. This person was not happy and I just told off one of her agents. Why could I not have kept my mouth shut? I mentally prepared myself for a lecture. Hopefully it was the worst I would have to deal with.

Looking again at Rathal, I saw a correlation between the odd phenomenon I had puzzled over in the car and what little was emanating out of this part of the building. It was not something I had encountered before.

"I'm terribly sorry about whatever that was. I sent Rathal because he needed a break. Retanei, it's good to have a chance to work with you again, though I wish it were under better circumstances." The Half-Elven woman greeted Retanei informally, and I wondered why my friend had not mentioned she knew her. "And this is?"

Then I remembered I was supposed to be part of this conversation. Retanei spoke for me before I could open my mouth. "This is Ketayl. She's the Arcane Investigator you requested. She's quiet and this is her first time in the field."

Giving me a more formal Elven greeting, she said, "Savanas Farstrider. It is a pleasure to make your acquaintance. Rathal is the one who gave the initial report about arcane usage. He's the only arcane sensitive one amongst the lot of us and the closest thing to an Arcane Investigator we've got. My other two field agents are in the back finishing up. The last of the bodies were cleared out a couple of hours ago, though there might still be a finger or two floating around." She signaled for us to follow.

"How much damage?" Retanei asked, all business.

Savanas hesitated a moment before continuing, "I'd watch your step. The floor is structurally sound, but I'd rather not take chances. Trevyn Lavabasher owns the place and he keeps his stock in the cellar under the restaurant so it was built quite thick. The brewery behind this place wasn't touched. We're evacuating a one block radius for now and have a media blackout. The emergency response team leader will let me know when they've cleared the area for safety."

I was grateful I was not going to have to deal with dead bodies right now. Pictures were one thing, but I was not sure I was ready for an actual body.

A wave of pain and anger hit me and just as quickly receded. The voices becoming a blur once again in the background. Where were those voices coming from? As far as I knew, arcane energy, the stuff I could see and feel which simply existed, did not have sound. Perhaps it was from something else.

"What do you have so far?" Retanei continued and I fumbled to dig out my gloves and camera behind them.

Rathal spoke, which I had not expected since he had been silently glaring at me. "Whatever it was, it was big. I can't pinpoint a location of origin. There's a lot going on in there arcane-wise and I can't make heads or tails of any of it."

Savanas took over, "23 Naval crewmen, 24 civilians dead. I haven't gotten an update on injuries. All but one witness report puts it at one explosion. Trevyn swears he saw two or three, but after that, I wouldn't be sure if I wasn't seeing double or triple either. I know of one mage who could cause this much damage, but even she wouldn't have been able to do it in one cast."

I shifted uncomfortably as we got closer to the hole near the front of the building. Something did not feel right. I knew arcane explosions. I knew how they felt even before I could see the arcane remnants. There was a common core - a common feel to them despite whether the base was fire, ice, or what have you. This was... twisted. It did not feel like true arcane. Dark came to mind again and I shoved the thought back. It made no sense.

"Is something wrong, Ketayl?" Savanas stared at me. I had not thought anyone was paying attention to me.

Biting my lower lip, I thought about saying it was probably nothing, but I knew I was not wrong. "Whatever it was, it wasn't a normal arcane explosion, but I can't tell what it is without seeing the arcane remnants." I could feel Rathal glaring at me. What did he want me to do? Lie?

As we rounded the corner, I turned away for a moment. All the images of crime scenes I had gone over had not prepared me for the real thing.

Taking a deep breath, I looked back inside. I ignored the arcane for a moment to look at the large interior. Blown out large screens hung crookedly on the remaining walls. Blood splattered everywhere as if done by an abstract painter. The stench of death, alcohol, and expiring food was overpowering.

Then I focused on the arcane remnants and liked less what I saw. Colors swirled like angry balls of fire. Gold-white light shot out of the center of the arcane remnants at regular intervals. Bands of green arcane text spun wildly about the outside making it a blur. Reading them was going to be next to impossible. I was going to have to observe the remnants for information.

"There are three points of origin," I said softly, unsure if I should voice my observations without a full analysis.

However that was all I would say without a closer inspection. I had a fairly good idea of what was used from here, but I needed details. Being able to see the arcane was both a gift and a curse, and right now I was thinking the latter. I needed to turn it to an advantage. Now I understood why Vince insisted I take the prototypes with me - explaining this to people who could not see would be beyond difficult.

There was silence while I dug out a small circular case. Shaking its contents out into the palm of my hand, I held up a camera filter, looking through it for a moment to make sure it was not dirty.

"A purple filter?" Savanas looked at me skeptically and then at Retanei, who shrugged.

Attaching it to my camera, I used the change of topic to distract myself from the scene before me. "The Director ordered me to bring it. I've been helping Lockonis develop the filters. It's, well, I suppose you should see for yourself." Handing the camera to Savanas, I continued, "We've managed to get this set of prototypes to the point of being about equal with my ability to see the arcane."

Savanas whistled and then handed the camera to Rathal. He cursed under his breath before commenting, "Well, now I feel less stupid for not being able to pinpoint the origin. This is really what you see?"

I nodded, my shyness kicking in, and took the camera back when offered. His face was still hard and judging, but also curious.

"Come on, let's get to work so we can get out of here. Dinner at my place once we've wrapped up. Local law enforcement is keeping a detail on the area to keep people out," Savanas said, all business, striding forward into the wreckage. "Rathal, go see how the other two are doing in the back."

I picked my way through the chaos on the floor with care and knelt at the closest arcane remnant. I was right - I did not like it any better up close. I felt like I was getting buffeted by the arcane remnants. It was uncommon, but not unheard of. It was going to make the headache starting behind my eyes worse.

"Ket, you need to talk. I know it isn't your favorite thing to do," Retanei teased me lightly, but I could tell by her face she was concerned. She waited patiently with a notepad and pen in hand. Artemis was close to her side, ears flat against her head.

Savanas hovered nearby, arms crossed over her chest expectantly. It was time to earn my title.

Taking a deep breath, I said, "The base spell was a fireball, which was combined with additional concussive force and a timing spell. I can tell you better as soon as I look at the others, but I think they were all set to go off at the same time to make it seem like only one."

Lifting the camera to my face, I collected the images I thought I would need. I zoomed in on the signature, capturing it clearly. I was not sure how useful this would be to those who did not have a background in arcane theory. It was more like a fingerprint than a signature and was always a part of the spell regardless.

"Wait, did you just say someone made arcane bombs?" Savanas knelt next to me. "Who in the Hells would be capable of making something like that?"

Biting on my lower lip for a moment, I mentally ran through the ability requirements for each rank. I said, "A High Mage level caster could, though they would be hard pressed to make one. An Archmage would struggle for three identical ones like this, but they could do it. It's a rather complex weave of spells."

I pinched the bridge of my nose to relieve some of the headache. I could not afford to lose focus at this stage. Standing up, I further contemplated the arcane remnant I stood next to. What on Terra fed it energy? And why was it emitting an emotional response? Arcane energy was neutral - it was the caster who decided what to use it for.

"Ket?" Retanei asked, coming up next to me.

Then it clicked and I looked around for Rathal. Not seeing him, I asked, "You said Rathal was arcane sensitive?" I looked to Savanas for confirmation.

"Yeah, I am. Do you have a problem with that?" I had not heard him return. There were two Human men with him as they exited a back room.

"Geez, man, chill." The shorter of the two commented. He had exotic features for a Human and was about my height. His dark hair mostly hidden by his hat.

"The arcane remnants are emitting an emotional response. Predominantly negative. It's only giving me a headache, but I don't know what longer exposure would cause. I sensed a faint arcane scent on you during the ride here. It was similar to this."

"What?!" Rathal looked thoroughly confused and angry.

"I'm sorry! I didn't know what it was and..." I took a step back, afraid of what was going to come at me.

"Enough." It was Savanas. "Let's move this conversation out of the immediate area."

Following her lead, I kept my mouth shut. We paused by the TIO van sitting near the entrance.

Savanas asked once we stopped, "Are you guys done in the back?"

"Yeah, wrapped everything up," the man who spoke before confirmed. "I'm Darius Hensen," he said. "This is Bradley Rios." Darius thumbed up at the tall, dark-skinned man next to him. "I'd shake your hands, but I'm filthy."

"Retanei, and this is Ketayl," my friend said.

Bradley gave a smooth, formal Elven greeting. "You said something about exposure for those who are arcane sensitive."

Savanas ordered, "Not now. You three take the van and head back.

We'll follow once we're done here." As they piled into the van, she grabbed Bradley's arm. "And keep an eye on Rathal. I thought he was just overtired, but if what she's saying is right, I don't want to take chances."

I looked at Retanei, not sure what to do at this point. Artemis seemed to be less agitated now that she was past the edges of the remnants. "Are you arcane sensitive?"

Retanei shook her head. "No. I can sense a bit of divine, but nothing that would be useful to anyone. There's some in there, but it's probably from the emergency responders."

Once they pulled away, Savanas waved us back in. "Let's go. I don't want to expose you any longer than necessary either."

Slowly I made my way through documenting the other two arcane remnants, all the while verbally rattling off observations. They were identical and all the same signature, which meant the same caster. What I could not figure out was why there was no degradation in the arcane remnants. There should have been arcane mites showing up well before now. There was also no power source I could see, but that would be the only explanation for why there was no degradation.

Rubbing my temple, I stood up from documenting the details of the third one. Now to get some overall images for placement...

Feeling the hairs on the back of my neck stand up, I whipped my head around, looking for the source. It was gone the moment it knew I could sense it. Too far gone for me to have tried to follow it back.

"Ket?" It was Savanas this time. Her tone was filled with worry.

I stayed on guard for a moment longer. Using my power, I reached out, looking for intruders. "I'm sorry, it felt like I was being watched. I need a couple more images for placement and I'll be done." I was already heading out of the remains of the building. I had not wanted to admit I made myself dizzy with the sudden movement.

Neither woman said anything as I finished. Lowering the camera to around my neck, I took half a step sideways and tripped over something. I was starting to become lightheaded. At least I had been able to hold on until I was done. There was something to be said about all those years practicing my focus and discipline.

"We need to get you out of here." Retanei tugged on my arm, pulling me along toward Savanas' car.

"Not yet. Something is powering the arcane remnants and I can't see what it is. This doesn't make any sense." I rubbed my temple with my hand again, trying to ease the building headache. It felt like something had been hitting me harder the longer I remained in there.

"No, now." Savanas opened the passenger door to her car and pointed at the seat. I dared not refuse her.

3

Compared to the main office outside of Great Tree, the office in Ocean's Edge was built closer to Human architecture than Elven. To an extent it was expected - most coastal cities were melting pots of the various races.

The brick and mortar building had a few floors to it with massive mirrored windows. It stood out sharply - bare, snow-covered trees dotted around the outside. Elven architecture blended in with nature, becoming an extension of the surroundings. The buildings on the way here shifted between the two, often adapting elements of both.

At least this building was not designed like the medieval castle which comprised of the Arcane College. While I supposed a castle was considered majestic and a show of strength, I doubted many had lived in one without the more current creature comforts.

It was early evening and I dragged behind. It felt like no matter how fast I moved to keep up with Savanas and Retanei's quick pace, they kept getting farther away. I cursed my preference for being in the lab. I was what my sister liked to call scrawny - thin, but no muscle.

As they bounded up the stairs, I stopped to hold onto the railing for a moment to catch my breath. They were out of sight by the time I could continue.

I knew this was pressing, but the elevator had been a lot closer. I did not know this place and I was going to have to find my way back to the woman at the front desk to get directions. I think I could retrace the turns we had taken. This building was large for just the team members I had met.

Rubbing my face with my hand, I pulled myself back together. I was just tired, that was all. I managed to catch about an hour of rest on the flight to Chained Lakes, but that was giving in to exhaustion, not resting.

Looking up the stairs, the room spun. Taking a seat was about the most I could manage. Leaning my face against the cool metal railing, I closed my eyes.

"Ketayl?" Startled, I rubbed my eyes before looking up to find the dark-skinned man I met earlier. He leaned over the railing with a worried expression. I had not heard a door open above. Did I doze off?

I mentally dug up a name for him. Hensen? No, I think it was Rios. They were going to have to wear name badges for me to remember at this point. "Sorry, I just got really dizzy."

He was tall, though most people were tall to me. It did not take him long to bound down the flight of stairs.

"Here, let's get your coat off. I think sometimes Savanas forgets others aren't as athletic as she is. Even I have a hard time keeping up with her."

He wore a gray long-sleeve shirt and black jeans - very neatly dressed despite his casual attire. It looked like he tried to clean the day's efforts off his boots. His dark hair closely cropped. I was not sure why his appearance was important to me right now.

The thick, black, winter TIO coat I wore was stifling. I did not mind being warm, but it had gotten to be too much. Shedding my coat and the soft purple scarf underneath, I felt like I could breathe again. Both were gone from my hands before I could protest. The sweater I wore hung loosely on me and I pushed the sleeves up only to have them slide back down almost immediately.

"You're all skin and bones." Looking at my scarf, he paused at the pin. "I suppose you'll want this." His tone flattened.

My Arcane College insignia pin. My mouth forgot it needed to filter the next thought before speaking it, "I mostly wear it out of habit to tell you the truth." A shiver ran up my spine as the coolness of the stairwell cut through the remaining heat quickly. "I'd rather have my coat back."

It was a hearty laugh that followed. "Alright, let's get going before they send out another search party. Savanas and your friend are setting up a secure conference call with the Director to give him an update."

Blowing a breath through the hair falling in my face, I admitted, "I'm not sure I have the energy to secure us from potential scryers." Taking the offered hand, he helped me up with no effort. I had a moment of dizziness that quickly dissipated.

He handed me my coat and scarf back and asked, "You've heard of the Elven Arcana Consortium, right?" For someone who wanted to get going, he was not moving. He held my wrist awkwardly and I tried not to give into the reflex to pull away.

"I studied with Magus Engelil in Great Tree after I was transferred to the TIO," I replied, not sure what his point was. He was looking at his watch and it took me a moment to realize he was taking my pulse.

I began to wonder what his role here was. I was not sure how the various branches were set up. It seemed like every time I thought I understood from the case files that came through the lab, I found I was wrong.

"We have a good-sized branch here in Ocean's Edge. Darius already called them to send someone over. They should be here soon. I'm going to have Doc take a look at you also. I'm sure he'll be happy to check on someone living," he said.

Well then, I guess the task of securing the upcoming conversation was taken care of. "Sorry if I sound rude, but I've forgotten your name."

"Bradley Rios, but Brad is fine," he smiled and walked back the way I had come.

"Ketayl. It's good to make your acquaintance again. Sorry you needed to come get me." I would find the time to be embarrassed about the whole situation later, but right now I was too tired to care.

"Not a problem. I've always wanted to rescue a damsel in distress," he smirked.

WHEN WE GOT to the third floor, the others had gathered around a large screen mounted on a short wall next to someone's desk. Retanei excused herself from the group to come over to us. "Thanks, Brad. I need to keep a better eye on her apparently," she said.

"Don't worry about it." Brad smiled broadly before speaking to me, "Why don't you sit down and I'll go call Doc."

I was shown to an empty desk - there was a computer and a phone, but nothing personal. There was another empty desk across from me and behind it, short walls sectioning off this part of the office that held Savanas' team. The wall holding the screen was taller, putting it at a comfortable height for the others to view while standing.

Out of the corner of my eye, I caught Brad motioning with his head to Retanei to speak with her aside. I sat back in the chair, observing the others in the office.

Savanas, Rathal, and Darius were at the screen. Savanas stood with her arms crossed while the other two argued over something. Occasionally her gaze would sweep the rest of the room - I could tell she was impatient.

Brad and Retanei moved to a desk next to the one across from me. After a few short exchanges, Brad made a call with the desk phone. I presumed he spoke with Doc, but quickly gave up trying to follow the one-sided trail of medical jargon.

A cup appeared on the desk. "Drink," Retanei ordered before returning to the rest of the group.

I glanced at the contents - water. My body felt heavier than I remembered, but I did as I was told. I started to feel a little better.

I took a few minutes to look around the room and simply observe. Six desks were in this sectioned-off part of the room. This one and the one across from me, the furthest from the large screen, were devoid of anything personal. A wall of windows was on the side near me, and the other was a door I thought was labeled conference room, but I was too far away to read the sign clearly.

Above me there was a walkway which went around above my head and the wall where I thought the conference room was. The skylights making up much of the ceiling were covered with snow.

Savanas gave Retanei a run down on the group they were tracking. Ebony fingers turned the pages of a document she had been handed. Retanei nodded every so often and occasionally asked a question.

Darius continued to argue with Rathal about something, but they were too far away for me to pick out pieces of their conversation. As long as they did not point in my direction, I figured I was safe. Brad got off the phone and watched me. I wondered where Artemis had tucked herself away.

Brad came back over and asked, "Confused by our small team and this big place?"

I nodded, looking around. There should have been far more people here for the size of the building.

He explained, "I don't know how long ago it was, but the main offices were here at one point. We haven't needed anywhere near the number of personnel for our branch, but I guess the Director didn't want to let this place go to waste. It's been kept up and upgraded over the years to continue to support us. It also becomes a training facility in the spring and fall. That's when it gets chaotic and rather crowded."

The elevator dinged and an older Elf with fluffy, graying, sand-colored hair stepped off. He wore a white lab coat - I could not make out the dark blue embroidery over his left breast pocket. He looked around as if he was searching for something. Perhaps he did not come up to this floor often. Or maybe he was from the EAC, but they did not usually wear white lab coats.

Brad turned around to see who I was looking at and waved him over.

The cup reappeared in front of me full again. Retanei stood over me, file in hand. I sighed, picking it up again.

The man who entered came up and introduced himself as Doctor Taron Uirebon, though he said most of the others simply called him Doc. His gentle smile and voice were a stark contrast to the nauseating scent of blood and death which hung around him. Brad and Retanei returned to the rest of the group, leaving me alone with the doctor.

Doctors made me nervous, so I forced a smile and answered his questions. Most of my attention was on the screen waiting to connect for the conference call. It kept me from focusing too much on what Doc was doing.

"When was the last time you ate?" Doc asked.

It was an odd question after the ones more specific to my medical records, which I figured he was cross referencing on the tablet he carried.

I paused, thinking about the question before responding, "When we stopped in Chained Lakes to refuel." I had grabbed something quick which probably did not qualify as a meal. "I'm sorry to have made you to come up here."

"It's not a problem, young lady. You are a breath of fresh air." He stood up with some effort. "Sounds to me like you're just running low." Doc dug something out of his pocket and placed it in my hand. "Here, this should help for the moment, but you need a good meal and a full night's sleep - not just a few hours of rest."

I frowned - I disliked sleep. It meant I was too deep under to wake up quickly if my dreams caused arcane manifestations. It also meant I was not working. Eight hours was simply too long. Although my body demanded extra rest every so often, I stuck to the normal four for Elves.

"I'll see she gets it," Retanei chimed in quickly. I did not notice her come up behind me.

It was really starting to bother me that I had not seen Artemis since coming upstairs.

I looked down at what was placed in my hand. "Chocolate?"

"It'll help, trust me," Doc said, patting me on the shoulder and went to go talk to the others.

Brad came back over as Doc spoke with Savanas. "I hope this case doesn't break him. It's hard enough on all of us, but even with his intern, he must be overwhelmed in autopsy," he said. "Doc's a gentle guy. He's also our doctor on staff so if you need him, his office is on the first floor."

The low murmur between people continued for a few more minutes.

"Melody called," Rathal announced even before he finished hanging up the phone at his desk, "The mage is here and will have the shield up in a couple of minutes."

I got up and joined the others who were organizing their information. I noticed my camera connected to the computer Savanas sat at. At least someone thought to start downloading the images.

"Ket, glad to see you're back on your feet. Tell me when the shield is up," Savanas said, looking up at me briefly before returning to typing on her computer.

"Savanas?" Rathal asked with hurt on his face. He threw a glare in my direction.

"Not now. I need someone who can actually see it. Take your stubborn pride and stuff it." This was the side of Savanas I did not want to be on.

I turned my attention to the shield which was supposed to be going up, but saw nothing.

Perhaps I did not realize how large the shield was supposed to be and wandered toward the large windows. "How big is the shield usually?"

I was surprised it was Rathal who answered. "It'll cover this building. Why? They usually stay in the lobby to cast."

The sense of strong arcane energy being used hit me hard, but I knew it was not the shield. It was wrong, dark, twisted. It felt too much like the arcane remnants at the crime scene.

At that moment, Rathal and I both looked at each other and ran for the elevator. The stairs were too far away and I did not trust myself to not fall down them.

The arcane energy came from below. The sensation of it crawled up my arms and I forced myself not to shudder. We had been too far away to sense its initial creation and I hoped we were not too late to stop it.

I wished I knew where the energy boost came from, but I was running toward the arcane source the moment the elevator let us off. I had already gathered arcane energy in my hands in preparation for what I would need to change it into. Hopefully Lockonis' training sessions would pay off.

I followed Rathal since he knew the layout of the building and frankly, he was faster. My attention was on him rather than my surroundings and I slid on the tiled floor making the sharp turn into the lobby. Recovering my footing quickly, I tried to logically parse the scene before me.

A mage was blocking attacks from a shadowed figure. He protected both himself and the woman who worked at the front desk. She held a firearm confidently, barking out commands at the shadow.

Artemis had put herself between the woman and their attacker as well, growling at the figure, but unsure of the magical wall between them.

My anger surged and all other thoughts ceased. A level of anger I never felt before shot past the carefully crafted and controlled barriers I kept on my emotions. I reacted on instinct, sliding to a crouch next to the defending mage. I slammed my hastily conjured ball of electricity along the ground, directing the individual bolts toward the figure.

Everything hung for a moment, and I heard a deep male voice, "Consider this a warning, fairy girl."

He was gone - like he had never been there. Even the mage standing next to me seemed confused. I looked back at Rathal, who had been getting the woman out of harm's way. I collapsed to a seated position and put my head in my hands. The dizziness was back with a vengeance.

THAT VOICE… it had sounded familiar, but it was not one I dealt with recently or often. No matter how hard I tried, I could not place it.

Although shaken, the mage was able to cast the shield. The others took over the conference call and I sat off to the side and watched them give their reports to both the Director and his second, Lockonis. Doc was hovering at my elbow, sneaking me a piece of chocolate every so often.

It helped, but I was not used to eating sweets. At least not this much.

"Where's Ketayl?" Vince asked, his tone too even to gauge his temperament.

Savanas signaled to me to come over. I had sat in a spot to stay off screen. "She's a bit worn out given the day's events, but she's here."

Pushing myself up, I slowly walked into view of the screen's camera and nervously asked, "Yes, sir?"

Vince pointed up to Lockonis who stood by his shoulder. The fiery redhead shook her head before she said, "Damn, kid, you haven't even been there a day and you're making me look bad."

I was not sure what she was referring to. I wanted to ask, but sensing the people around me, I held my tongue. They were waiting patiently for me to finish my conversation so they could move onto other things.

"Getting back on topic, your preliminary report is the arcane remnants aren't degrading at all?" Lockonis was serious now. She was normally very emotional when she interacted with people and it scared me the few times I had seen her switch to what she called business mode.

I nodded. "Arcane mites should have appeared by the time we arrived - likely entering their second phase, but there were none. There is a supply of power at the central axis of each arcane remnant which may be feeding other information, causing a strong, mostly negative, emotional responses for anyone near them who is arcane sensitive."

"Wait, what?" Lockonis seemed lost and then I realized I also lost everyone else involved in the call. "What could be supplying that kind of power?"

"Better break it down a little more for the rest of us, Ketayl," Vince said.

How could I word it and still get the relevant information across? "Normally, an arcane source of power would be quickly used up since it's all burst energy. A mage could directly maintain something like that for an hour or two at most before it exhausted the mage's reserves. Whatever is acting as the power source is beyond my ability to see."

Vince looked up at Lockonis, who translated, "There was no mage nearby to maintain it so the power source is currently unknown. And that is a very disturbing statement, kid. You see a lot more than anyone else I know."

I ducked my head a little at Lockonis' statement about my ability to see the arcane. I often thought she overrated my ability.

Lockonis continued, "What she's saying about a connection at the central axis, I can point out in the images they sent over later. The emotional part?" She looked at me expectantly.

I bit my lower lip for a brief moment, quickly pouring through whatever information I could remember. I explained, "I don't fully remember what I have read about the phenomenon, but it's extremely rare. The chances of it naturally occurring in three reactions at the same time created by the same mage are slim to none regardless of skill."

The others around me made it hard to concentrate - I did not do well with an audience. I focused on Retanei briefly. She made a small hand gesture for me to keep going.

Taking a breath, I added, "I'll have to research more to find out if there is a method which can purposefully create them, but I have a feeling it's coming from whatever the power source is. It's too evenly distributed through the arcane remnants to be from much else." A very long way to tell them that I did not know.

Vince's gaze pinned me in place as I started to consider my escape route. "You said something about a negative emotional response."

Forcing myself to not back away from the screen, I answered, "Anyone who is arcane sensitive is going to react more strongly the longer they are exposed to it. I can see it and understand what is going on, but..."

Lockonis rubbed the bridge of her nose. "Yeah, I'm going to need a VERY large cup of coffee after this. Your level of arcane theory is usually beyond me. I'll scour the net and see if I can dig up something that can help you."

I wondered whether to tell them about the brief interaction with the shadowed figure and about the feeling of someone watching me at the crime scene. I was not sure if it was just me and I was overtired and my mind was making it up.

Vince asked, "Something else bothering you, Ketayl?" Despite being on a video feed, he looked directly at me, which made me want to squirm under the scrutiny.

I bit my lower lip to give myself a moment longer before replying, "The attack downstairs... I'm not sure. I think it might have been to deliver a message. He told me to consider this a warning. I don't really have anything else other than it felt like someone was watching me at the crime scene."

Lockonis' sapphire eyes went wide and she was off the screen the moment Vince signaled her. He said, "We'll handle it from here. What are the chances of this happening again?"

I looked from Retanei to Savanas who both were waiting for an answer. The others were behind me out of view. "I..." I knew this. I could calculate the amount of arcane energy used and the average capacity any particular rank would have. "If they were to try it again, it would not be anytime soon. It should have drained the mage significantly. They would need a couple of days to recover. Not to mention whatever else they may have been casting recently."

"Is it possible there's more than one?"

I shook my head. It was something instinctual I had trouble describing. "No, it felt like the same person." But even then, I was having trouble getting the numbers to match up in my head. It was possible I was underestimating this mage's arcane capacity, but even at a person's potential maximum capacity the numbers did not add up.

Vince moved his hand over a button on his computer. "Conduct operations as normal, but put yourselves on alert. I'll have more detailed instructions shortly."

The connection was cut and I became unsure of myself again. I hoped I was not wrong in my assessment.

4

Savanas explained en route to her house about the customary event for the Ocean's Edge crew: they often gathered at her house for a meal - especially for large cases where they were going full force. She told us she found it would help the others step back and see things they otherwise might not have if they got too caught up on one aspect or another.

The smell of pastries greeting us at the door. My stomach tried to loudly proclaim its desire for food, but thankfully my thick coat suppressed the sound. I was not sure I could take more sweets after all of the small chocolates Doc kept handing me.

Doc, Sasha, and Melody would not be here tonight as they all had work or other plans.

Hanging back behind Retanei, I looked around her with caution. I avoided social gatherings when I could. Darius was right behind me so I could not linger outside the door.

Savanas hung up her coat and then took mine and Retanei's. She said, "Sorry, I forgot I told Da he could crash here until he could go back to his apartment. He lives above the bakery next door to the Waking Dawn. Granted, he practically lives *in* the bakery with how often he's either working on an order or concocting something new. Just a heads up he's a little eccentric."

She left the others to their own devices.

Kneeling down, Savanas pet Artemis and told the wolf, "Your dad's friend is probably in the common room if you want to meet him."

Artemis trotted off - the wolf's sense of smell likely providing her directions.

I got caught in the flow of people trailing into the kitchen. A Human man with dark gray hair sat peeling apples at the center island. He smiled at all of us. "Ah, wonderful, you brought home guests, Savvy."

I tried to keep to the back of the group. Retanei seemed to have the same idea.

Savanas went to the refrigerator and started digging. "Have you been baking all day?"

The crinkles around his green eyes spoke of mischief. "Of course. When I'm upset, I bake."

"Da..." Savanas' tone was of resigned annoyance. "And then you keep baking. You bake for any reason, not just when you're upset."

"Part of running a successful bakery I'm afraid. It could be worse - I could drink instead." He glanced at the crew gathering in the room before focusing on myself and Retanei. He smiled as he commented, "Oh, you have new guests also."

Savanas placed stuff on the already cluttered island. She introduced us, "Ladies, this is my father, Lou Maponus. Da, this is Retanei and Ketayl. They're here from the main office so please behave. They don't know you as well as everyone else."

"Lou, if you would please. It has been many a year since I have been graced by such fine ladies. Perhaps I should clean up and see if these old fingers can pick out a few pieces to play." Getting up, he came and bowed before each one of us, greeting us individually and kissing our hands.

Eccentric, right. I rubbed my hand to get rid of the feeling as soon as his attention was elsewhere.

"I'll take care of things here." Savanas ushered him out of the kitchen. Once she came back, she apologized, "In his youth he fancied himself a bard. You know, like the ones in the old tales. I don't think it ever left him even after he settled down and discovered a talent for baking."

"Can we help with anything?" Retanei asked. She also seemed at a loss of what to do.

Savanas waved us off. "Go relax. I cook, everyone eats. We're all less edgy and can get back to work refreshed. Brad, can you handle setting up the room arrangements for them? I haven't had a chance to contact the hotel we usually contract with."

"No problem." Brad pulled out his phone and left the room.

"We only use them for visiting agents. It helps they have some impressive security, but they also often host military and media because of it," Savanas said as she pulled out a cutting board and a rather large knife. "Darius is probably in the common room playing a video game if you want to join him. Rathal, can you show our guests?"

Rathal stared at us for a moment, his face neutral. Letting out a breath I did not realize he held, he said, "Come on, I'll show you where the common room is. It's the least I can do after acting like an ass earlier."

As he passed by me, I whispered, "I'm sorry. I shouldn't have snapped at you - it was unprofessional."

Rathal's hazel eyes caught mine before he said, "No, I'm the one who should be apologizing. Not sure what I was going to do running down into the lobby like that. Just because I can sense it doesn't mean I can do a damn thing about it. Not to mention both of you have impressed the boss lady. She's the better judge of character."

***

THE FRESH VENISON and vegetables were simple. I stayed quiet during the meal, choosing instead to watch the interactions between the others. They acted like a family, or what I came to understand of one in the last couple of years.

Even Big Black, aptly named for the very large black dog, curled up by Savanas after having eaten his own meal. The fur on his wrinkled face had turned white in places, indicating he was an older dog. She had said what breed he was, but I could not remember. What I remembered was being greeted by a low growl when I first entered the common room. I was grateful for Artemis' presence calming the old dog, showing him I was not a threat.

Artemis decided at that moment to put her head on my leg, looking longingly at the food on my fork. Retanei tapped her shoulder and gave her a piece of meat. I glanced over and saw the wolf's plate was clean.

We sat comfortably around the large table in Savanas' dining room. A simple black and silver chandelier hung over the table, but was easily ignored for the large glass doors and surrounding large windows looking out into the snow-covered backyard. I could make out an equally large table sitting on the darkened patio. Savanas must entertain frequently.

When Savanas was not busy trying to get her father to tone it down, she would chat lightly with whoever drew her into conversation. Rathal and Darius continued to argue over a video game, which was apparently the argument they were having earlier. Rathal still pointedly ignored Retanei. Brad spoke with Retanei and Savanas primarily, but would throw an occasional jab at the two arguing. Lou finished his gallant tales and was content to observe the table.

Darius grinned at me between bites and I had a feeling my quiet time had passed. "So what does an Arcane College mage do for fun?"

Fun? "Um... technically, Arcane College mages aren't supposed to have hobbies. It takes away from the focus." My wording was deliberate. The Elven Arcana Consortium pushed their students to take up other interests. It was something I had whole-heartedly adopted.

"I sense something more to your story here," Lou said and smirked, "What was your rank, out of mild curiosity?"

With the exception of "Researcher" that the Arcane College used, the ranking system was the same throughout all schools and territories. It was something put into place shortly after the Racial War about 50 years ago. Asking for rank was common enough, though I had not expected the question from Lou.

It surprised me when Rathal spoke up next. "With what happened in the lobby, I'm thinking at least High Mage, though you've got some serious speed. I didn't even hear the incantation."

I was not sure if I should admit I had not used an incantation. Or gestures. I kept my mouth shut for the moment and focused on my food.

Brad weighed in, "Well, the Arcane College won't send out anyone lower than a Magister to be a liaison." His statement was true, though I had not realized it was noted by anyone outside of the Arcane College.

It was Darius' turn to join in, "I don't know. I've never seen anyone from the Arcane College cast that fast. Granted, they rarely cast in the presence of others. Even the guys assigned to the battleships demand privacy when they're maintaining the defense systems. Unless they're wanting to impress someone. Or the captain got fed up with their laziness again."

Looking up, I did not realize how much they studied the Arcane College's typical behaviors. However, this was a port city where many naval ships docked, and with the number of mages the Arcane College sent out to be liasons... Well, it was not hard to see where they came into contact with enough of them.

"Researcher, actually," I got in before the speculation could continue. "Only Humans are allowed to hold rank in the Arcane College."

It was a fact and not something I could find myself to be bitter about. As for my casting speed, I wanted to avoid the topic if I could. I should have controlled it better so it would not have been so obvious. It had been a long time since I reacted instinctively. Normally, I thought through my actions, though now I understood what Lock-onis had been telling me.

"Now that's new." Savanas sat back in her chair and looked over to Retanei sitting next to her. "So I'm thinking it's going to be easier to get you to tell us than her. She seems rather shy."

I could feel the heat rise in my face and returned my attention to the meal before me, hoping the conversation would go elsewhere.

"Well, if you want a hobby, she's a rather talented musician." I caught that Retanei also avoided the topic of my arcane abilities. It was not something to broadcast outside of the organization. I was sure Savanas' father was harmless, but I did not want to take the chance.

I glanced around, sure the others were curious about a few things now. Retanei had to go and say that. I sank down in my chair.

I had forgotten Retanei caught me practicing on the few occa-sions when I ventured into the woods surrounding the main office. I thought to escape my sister, who would let herself into my quarters, but had walked into Retanei's domain.

I heard a groan from Savanas before her father turned his atten-tion back to me. "Really? This I must know more about."

Putting down my fork, I held up my hands hoping to stop the

potential barrage of questions. "I just help my mother with her projects on occasion, that's all. I fear I have no talent of my own."

"Your mother?" Lou's curiosity seemed to only be more piqued. This time I apparently chose my words poorly.

"Lindale Erulastiel - she adopted me and my sister when we were little." I hoped the questions would end there. The circumstances surrounding our adoption was not for idle conversation.

All conversations ended and the others stayed silent, focusing their attention my way. I sank farther down in my chair. Rathal raised an eyebrow and smirked. I wished I could hide on the floor with Artemis and Big Black.

Lou's eyes went distant as he sat back and smiled. His voice shifted to something more melodic when he commented, "Ah, one of the Great Elven Songstresses. Many a story about that one. I've not had the pleasure of meeting her myself."

I had no idea what to say. Her music was popular, that much was true, but his description put her on a pedestal she would not wish to be on. She primarily spent her time teaching, but Mother still continued to produce new music to keep up her business.

Retanei grinned at me, and I could tell she was up to no good right before she said, "I made sure she packed her violin."

———

It was late by the time we were able to check into the room reserved for us. Brad managed to get a suite with a couple of bedrooms attached to a common area with a small kitchen in it. Lou insisted on sending a large bag of pastries for breakfast with us.

"Go get some rest," Retanei said softly.

I nodded and dragged myself off toward the closest bedroom. I wanted a hot shower and bed - in that order. Opening my suitcase, I dug out what I needed for the first part and made my way to the shared bathroom. "I just want to clean up."

"Take your time." Retanei's voice had an edge to it.

The room was dark except for the light coming from the bedroom and she was nowhere near it. "What's wrong?"

I knew she could see in complete darkness, but I grew uneasy talking to yet another shadow, even if it was one I knew.

"I'm concerned if he could get to us at the office, we're exposed here. I doubt their security has taken a psychotic mage into account."

Retanei had a valid point, but... "As I said, I don't think it was really him - just an arcane projection. It was overly elaborate to deliver a message and regardless of level that spell alone would have drained the caster for a while. He's going to need time to recover." There was always stored spells, but it would be hard for someone to predict all of our movements ahead of time. I had a feeling the arcane projection was not planned.

There was a long pause before she spoke again, "You mean it was an illusion?"

I corrected, "More like a puppet than an illusion. The more I think about it, the more foolish I feel about reacting the way I did."

Of everyone there, I should have seen through it immediately, but...

I paced and said, "Rathal and I reacted the same. We had both been exposed to the emotional energy at the crime scene. Whoever it is knew that and that's why..."

If he had been watching for a while, and I cannot imagine it was for too long - it would have seriously drained him also. I got stuck attempting to reconcile the amount of energy required for both. Just the puppet would have required most of his reserves.

"Continue."

I shook my head, realizing my mouth stopped giving information. "When I saw the figure, I became extremely angry and reacted. I don't know if it was to leave a message or possibly to evaluate us."

"That's a disturbing thought. Well, until everyone is rested, there's not much we can do. Do you mind keeping Artemis with you? I'm going to head downstairs and make sure they tell housekeeping this room is off limits," Retanei said as her dark figure moved into the light where I could see her.

She had exchanged her winter TIO coat for the brown leather coat she had been wearing in Vince's office. Why would she be wearing such a heavy coat if she was simply going down to the front desk?

Retanei left before I could ask. I looked at the wolf and tilted my head toward the bathroom. She followed on my heels, settling at the door once I closed it. Retanei often moved in ways I could not understand, but I learned to trust her judgment.

I dropped my bundle on the counter next to the sink and hung my head for a moment. I was still unsure of myself and the team could not afford my self-doubt. I was selected to come here for a reason.

I knew the arcane as well as I knew myself. The problem was I still feared my own power to a certain extent.

Taking a deep breath, I thought again about the attack, but this time on my own reaction. Strong emotional responses were bad. It may have worked out this time, but what about the next? I would have to be exposed to those arcane remnants again in order to force them to dissipate. If I could even figure out how.

I gripped the edge of the gray sink - I was not looking forward to the headache they would likely give me again. I normally did not get headaches, which made me worry I missed something. I needed rest and then I could come back fresh and this would surely all make sense.

I looked up - the reflection in the mirror appeared worn down and older than I remembered. It had been a long day. Just sitting in the big plush chair in Savanas' common room listening to the conversations had taken its toll.

Savanas was not kidding when she said her father baked for the sake of baking. I had to turn down his offers after a while as I was certain I would explode if I ate another bite. At the very least, I was not going to be able to move.

I sighed and rubbed my face. I needed to get cleaned up so I could get some rest.

Reaching behind my head, I started to take my hair out of its confinement. It never took me long to get my hair up, but always seemed to take a while to find the last few hair pins nestled in my bun. Normally, it was a meditative time, though there were days, like today where I wondered why I kept my hair so long since all I ever did was put it up.

My mind kept returning to what I witnessed at the Waking Dawn. It bothered me I could not figure out what the power source was. The effect it was having on Rathal also bothered me. I worried some of the victims and emergency responders would also be affected. I was certain the others thought of that also.

Finally locating the last hair pin, I let my hair cascade down and shook out the last of the twists keeping it confined and freed it from my worn hair elastic. Emptying out my pockets, I placed my phone on the counter and then paused to look at it.

I had downloaded some music recently in hopes I might remember to keep it on me more often. It still did not work, but...

I fiddled with it until I heard music playing from the tiny speakers. I still was not sure how to work some parts of the phone, but at least the music part seemed straight forward enough.

While the soft music filled the room, I set about my previously defined task and quickly cleaned up. Artemis did not seem to care much about what I was doing and could have been asleep for all I knew. It might pose a problem when I was ready for bed.

I paused to look at the large bathtub. It was sorely tempting, but I knew I would fall asleep. Elven tradition was to first shower to clean up and then soak in the bath to relax. It was a tradition I indulged in rarely - I had grown up around Humans. It also felt like I wasted precious time which could be spent on something else.

I had left Mother too soon after she adopted my sister and I, but I was too dangerous to be left untrained. And because we were in Neutral Territory at the time, in a predominately Human area, I was discovered by the Arcane College first. Perhaps if I had grown up more with Elven traditions, I would appreciate them better, but now was not the time to be debating past choices.

After cleaning up and then using my power to dry my hair, I crouched down to rub Artemis' head. "May I get by?"

She nuzzled my hand before she got up.

Retanei had not returned. I was concerned she was not back, but I knew better than to contact her. Sometimes I would find her walking the halls near the lab just thinking and interrupting her only made her walk longer.

Artemis climbed up into the bed and curled against me. She was warm - it only served to lull me to sleep.

5

WHEN I GOT up the next morning, Artemis was still beside me. I was certain she would have left when Retanei returned.

Then I began to worry if Retanei *had* returned. Normally she worked at night and had not been up nearly as long as I had at the time of our departure, but surely even she would have taken the momentary pause.

Glancing at the time, I had been asleep for longer than I wanted. While I felt rested, I was too concerned about Retanei. Maybe she came, rested, and left again? I did not know, but I did not think she would have left Artemis in that case either.

Quickly getting out of bed to satisfy my curiosity, I set about my normal morning routine, not wanting to disturb her if she happened to still be resting. But then why was Artemis still in here?

I was putting the last couple of hair pins in when I heard the door open. Artemis left my side.

A set of keys hit the counter in the common area. "Oh good, you're up," Retanei said, "Savanas will want you in the office as soon as you're ready."

I was not prepared for the image that greeted me when I left the bathroom. I had never seen Retanei so worn down. "What happened?" She had already slid her coat off and was in the process of taking her hair out of its ponytail. Her whole body spoke of exhaustion.

She yawned, holding the bag of pastries from Lou toward me. "I was working."

That was it and I dared not push for more, not wishing to be seen as an annoyance. As soon as I took the bag, she took a quick bite from the one in her hand and headed for the other bedroom.

Retanei said, "I'm going to crash. The fleet vehicle Melody loaned me is yours. It's in the underground garage - level C, section 1. Can't miss it. And don't worry, I have access to transportation."

There was no point in continuing the conversation. I looked warily at the bag in my hands. I think I had more than my fill last night.

Picking up the keys, I was grateful there was a tag describing the vehicle. I was not fond of driving and even less in the winter. I could only hope I did not end up with a little rolling ball of death. Especially with as much snow as there was on the ground.

RETANEI WAS nice enough to have programmed the directions into the truck's navigation system for me. I had not noticed it last night, but the roads near the TIO office were outfitted with the new solar panels, keeping them clear and dry.

I stopped in the office lobby to talk to the woman there. The black name plaque on her desk said "Melody Braddock."

"Oh, hi there. You're one of the visiting agents who came in yesterday. Melody." The brown-haired woman put her hand out. Her chocolate-colored eyes did not speak of the event the previous evening, which I found odd.

Taking her hand, as not to be rude, I said, "Ketayl. I'm sorry about yesterday."

Melody smiled gently and said, "Don't worry about that. It's hard to surprise me much anymore. I'm just glad you were here - I'm afraid the poor mage was fairly shaken after that. Is the dog with you?" She looked around the side of her desk to see if I was hiding someone.

"Artemis?" Come to think of it, she had been down here during the attack. "No, I'm afraid the wolf belongs to Retanei, the other agent I arrived with." I had previously gotten a lecture about the difference between dogs and wolves. While interesting, I doubted Melody would much care, but the least I could do was warn her.

The receptionist came close to pouting. It was odd to see on an older woman. "Too bad. I keep a stash of treats for Big Black, but Savanas doesn't bring him in much anymore. He's getting old. It was nice to have a companion in the lobby again. She's such a sweet thing."

"I'm sure she'll be by again soon." It appeared I was going to have a lot more to learn about how the Ocean's Edge branch operated.

Looking at the rest of the area, I realized I was unsure where I was going. "Where is Savanas' office? I'm afraid with all the commotion last night I'm lost." I mentally kicked myself. Usually I was detail-oriented and only needed directions once.

After getting directions, I made my way upstairs to the big open office. I had no idea what to expect this time. I did not see Darius or Brad. Rathal was on the phone having an animated conversation.

Savanas looked up from her computer to see who arrived, waving me over. She waited until I got close so she did not have to speak loudly across the room, "Please tell me Retanei is getting some rest."

I nodded and asked, "What's going on? She said she was going to talk to the hotel staff last night." I took a step back - I should not have been so forward. Especially when talking to someone obviously much higher up the chain of command. My curiosity was getting the better of me, which could be dangerous.

Savanas blew out a breath and leaned back in her chair. "I had a couple of local law enforcement officers help out last night keeping the curious away. Retanei caught wind of something from their communications and went hunting. No idea if she came up with anything. When she stopped by the office, she didn't say anything to Melody. Don't suppose she passed any information on to you?"

I shook my head. "She left Artemis with me. I didn't think she would go without her."

The look on Savanas' face was of aggravation. "Damn stupid move. I'll talk with Retanei later. Lockonis said she sent over the information she was able to dig up - you should have gotten an update to your library. But before you get started, we need to talk." She hit a few buttons on her computer and pointed at the large screen.

It was the video feed from last night's attack in the lobby playing on loop from the moment Rathal and I arrived to when the shadow disappeared.

"Given how both you and Retanei avoided that particular topic of conversation, I decided to review the footage. Care to explain? I've seen some fast casters in my time, but this exceeds them." Savanas paused a moment, but I was stuck watching myself over and over.

It felt surreal. I had not seen myself on video before and even I refused to believe it was me who was performing those actions, but the evidence was right there.

This was what Lockonis had been trying to get me to do during our last training session. It had come naturally without forcing my way through the manipulation. In a sense, I felt a bit of freedom and pride at finally having completed the objective, but that it took so little effort worried me and more because I reacted on instinct.

Savanas continued, "Thanks to them putting a damn mage on just about every ship passing through our port, I know Arcane College mages have long, drawn out, overly elaborate casting. This is not indicative of that by any means." I could not tell if Savanas was angry about the images before her.

I jumped as Rathal slammed the phone down behind me.

"I just reacted. I thought it was in my file, ma'am, I'm sorry. I trained with..."

Savanas cut me off, "I read your file. You also trained at the EAC after coming to the TIO and Lockonis has been working with you. What you may not realize is since I used to be partnered with Lockonis, I know how fast a highly-trained Warmage can cast in the heat of the moment. This exceeds even her speed." She leaned forward, looking me directly in the eye. "Ketayl, I need to understand the people I work with."

Apparently not everything was in my file. I looked over at Rathal who patiently waited for an answer. Well, it was bound to come out sooner or later. "I'm an Arcanist."

"Arcanist?" Savanas looked to Rathal who turned to watch the screen.

Rathal looked back at me for a moment, pursing his lips. "It makes sense now. I heard of Arcanists from Maewon thanks to a case we had a few years ago. The simplest explanation is they are so tightly connected to the arcane it takes only thought to use it. Genetic

I believe. It would explain why I don't remember hearing an incantation or seeing gestures."

Raising an eyebrow, Savanas cut the feed on the screen. "Damn good reaction then. What I can't figure out is how this guy got in and out."

"I've been thinking about that." Her surprised look told me she had not expected me to say anything. "I think he sent what amounts to a puppet. I'm not sure how far away he would have been."

Should I tell them I had not been able to reconcile the amount of energy required for everything we had seen thus far? It did not seem like a good idea without a different theory to give reason for the discrepancy.

Savanas did not seem eager to accept my theory and even in the position I was in, I was not sure I could accept it either. "Fine. Work what angles you can. You can work over there." She pointed at the desk I sat at yesterday.

I was back to not being sure where I stood with people. Though I found it curious Rathal knew so much. When I had time, I would have to look into the case he referenced.

TIME WAS LOST to me as I dug through the new information Lockonis found.

We had decided to add to the copy of the Arcane College's library I brought with me when I was transferred to the TIO. It seemed counterintuitive to have multiple databases.

The new information was mostly news reports and what little I could cross-reference with the Arcane College's library gave me little information. Though it was worded differently, from what I could tell it all repeated itself.

I wondered if I should stop looking at the descriptions and look at the events surrounding them instead. There always seemed to be at least one dead body tied to it.

I rubbed my eyes with the heels of my hands - I had been staring at the screen for a while. I knew better than to sit in front of a screen for any length of time without a visual break, but I had to come up with something.

It felt like I was going in circles. All I kept finding was it was a random occurrence with no known origin. There must be a way to nullify the effect so it was not so dangerous to those of us investigating, but I needed a point of reference to begin figuring it out.

"Take a break." Retanei stood in front of me.

When did she get here? I glanced around the office. When did Savanas and Rathal leave?

Blowing a stray lock of hair out of my face, I knew my exasperation showed. "I don't understand why I can't find any specific information on this. I don't know where to start figuring out what kind of mage we're dealing with." Finding out the mage's specialty would at least narrow the field.

"A demented one. That's all I need."

I rolled my eyes before I said, "It's too dangerous not to have more information. I wish I hadn't been so tired when we got to the crime scene yesterday."

"We can go back over to the Waking Dawn after lunch," Retanei said, leaning against the filing cabinet next to the desk I was working at.

Darius' voice came from above me. He said, "Have you checked with the EAC branch here? They aren't as big as the main campus in Great Tree, but they have a decent-sized library."

Looking up, Darius rested his arms on the railing above my desk, looking down. I had not known he was here. Or what was up there, but it mattered little.

I felt like an idiot. "No, I hadn't even thought about trying them."

Darius made his way down the stairs. "Sorry, didn't mean to interrupt, but I needed a break from reviewing the security footage we were able to recover. It's worth a shot - they've been helpful in the past when we needed to research something."

Retanei reached over and pushed the button on the computer screen. "You need to have lunch."

I turned it back on and swatted her hand away. "At least let me save what I'm working on."

"Tell me again how you're an Arcane College mage?" Savanas said and her sudden reappearance made me jump. She strolled by with Rathal, looking to be at the end of her patience. "I really don't see it. Not compared to that pompous ass we just tried talking to."

I already knew the attitude she referenced: the person who is always looking down at you, truly believing they are far superior to you. Telling you that you are wasting their precious time with things which do not concern them. That you should have been able to produce their requested information far faster than you did.

It was the problem I generally faced. People expected that behavior. "Try having hundreds of them around," I muttered.

"No, thank you, my blood pressure is high enough as it is," Savanas said and collapsed in her chair. "I probably should have brought you with me. Rathal had to keep me from ringing his neck, which is rare. Usually I'm reigning in his leash."

"Hey!" Rathal's face flushed for a second.

Darius laughed at the exchange. He said, "I should get back to the footage. I've almost got the three nailed down who carried the arcane bombs in." He did not wait for a response and went back upstairs.

The thought of facing the Magister was not one I wanted. Anyone higher ranked always liked to push around those lower - it was how the Arcane College was. Being on the bottom of the ladder, I was often a target. I would be set with the mundane or difficult tasks they could not be bothered with. Constantly reminded I was so bad at handling the arcane that I was just a Researcher. Harassed without end for being Elven.

A few times they had dangled a possible promotion in front of me, but it was hard not to see the pattern of only Humans holding rank.

But here I seemed to actually be able to contribute so I asked, "Who is he?" My fingers were already dancing across the keyboard, bringing up the Arcane College's administrative records.

Savanas held up a notepad. "Magister Bernard Browne. Browne with an 'E' at the end. He seemed rather concerned our misspelling his name in our reports would cause him grief. Why? Do you know him?" It seemed to perk her up a bit.

I shook my head and replied, "Not off-hand. I'm trying to find any information I have on him. Too bad it's such a common last name." Even as busy as I was, I did not miss Retanei's glare at Savanas. "This won't take long. Lockonis built a good search algorithm into the library."

"Wait, you have access to Arcane College records?" That had both Savanas and Rathal coming around the desk to look at my screen.

It was not going to do them much good at this stage so I told them, "We haven't built in a translator yet." Everything was in arcane text. The runes usually meant nothing to people outside of arcane casters. "This copy is a couple of years old. I haven't been back to the Arcane College to update it."

This was quickly becoming frustrating as I hit one dead end after another.

"And you, what was so damn important you went hunting last night?" Savanas was now speaking to Retanei and I really wished they would pick somewhere other than directly behind me to have their conversation. Rathal hung by my shoulder.

"I needed to get on the trail while it was still relatively fresh. A report came in from a farmer outside the city with signs of an encampment. It was already a couple days old. Their tracks disappeared with the fresh snowfall."

"Is this it?" Rathal asked and pointed at a name on the screen. That he could read it made me pause to look at him. "I studied for a bit at the EAC," he explained, "I'm afraid I have no talent for it though."

Reading what he pointed at, I said, "I'm grateful for the second set of eyes. That's close, but..."

"But?" Rathal waited for me to explain why I wanted to dismiss the record.

Retanei and Savanas moved their conversation elsewhere.

I caught myself chewing on my lower lip as I sometimes did when I had a confusing puzzle before me. "He specified the E at the end of his last name. It would change the last letter to this one." I pointed at the rune elsewhere on the screen. "As for the different first name, I've seen others prefer their middle name, though more often, they will use their full name or at least give their initial. Not to mention this person was awarded the rank of Magister well over a decade ago and is currently an Archmage. People don't stay at the lower ranks for that long and remain in the Arcane College."

"Weren't you a Researcher?"

Rathal seemed to have a better understanding of the Arcane College and the world of arcana in general than I realized, but I could see where he was confused.

I clarified, "Researchers are tolerated for the labor provided to the ranked mages. Human Researchers rarely make it to being a ranked mage, but it has happened. Most leave the Arcane College after a few years."

"Do you still consider yourself a part of the Arcane College?" Rathal's question caught me off-guard.

It was a fine line to walk to explain where I landed in the grand scheme of things. "I'm supposed to be their liaison, but I'm not sure anymore. I was transferred without warning and I haven't had any contact since. The TIO has become my home... my family." I paused, replaying what I said in my mind, cringing. "That sounded sappy, didn't it?"

"It did, but I think I could use a little sappy right now." Rathal stood up to his full height, stretching. "But this Magister could still order you around?"

I rubbed the bridge of my nose. It was not a conversation I wanted to have, but I understood the need for it. "Technically, yes. It's a gray area. There were never any boundaries set, and previously, there was never a need for them. This is a TIO investigation. If I get in trouble for it later, I guess I'll have to deal with it then."

Savanas yelled at him from across the room, "Rathal, quit interrogating her. Vince wouldn't have sent Ketayl if she was going to pose a problem. We'll handle the Magister if he decides to make one of himself."

I had a feeling Savanas hoped Browne would. It was a feeling I could relate to - I wanted to vent my frustration on a number of them over the years.

Shrugging, Rathal leaned back down with a mischievous smirk on his face, his eyes still on the screen as he asked me, "So, want to go get dinner with me sometime?"

Savanas' voice rang out with a sharp warning, "Rathal!"

6

I PULLED my TIO coat closer around me, my hat and hood did little to protect me from the cold. I stared at the remains of the Waking Dawn from what Retanei deemed a "safe distance." I had more questions than answers.

There remained the three arcane remnants, stronger than when we arrived yesterday afternoon. Even where the outer wall of the building once stood, I was getting buffeted by the emotional energy. It was not too bad out here, but I could only imagine how much more intense it was closer to each point of origin.

Retanei stood alongside me, staring in the same direction, and said, "I don't like that look on your face."

I briefly wondered what my face looked like to get that kind of comment. I said, "It's getting worse. No degradation - the emotional responses are getting stronger. I don't know what to do. I don't know if it will even stop growing. If it doesn't, it'll eventually spread far beyond this building." And in a city of primarily Elves, it spoke of further chaos. So many would naturally be arcane sensitive.

She rubbed Artemis' head. The wolf seemed confused by the scene before us. I wondered if she could also sense the emotions in the arcane remnants. "So you think the whole package was deliberate?"

"There's no way for it to have occurred naturally. I still want to see if the EAC branch here has anything in their library that might be of help. I'd hate to be wrong." It was a long shot, I knew, but one I had to explore. "I just wish I could figure out what was powering this."

Retanei was silent for a moment. She looked around the wreckage as if she could see something I could not. I knew she had limited divine abilities. I came to realize while many casters have developed some kind of sixth sense, the ability to actually see was limited.

"Can the magics mix?" she asked.

It was a question I had not been prepared for. Chewing on my lower lip for a moment, I considered the possibility. I knew of a Researcher who had been trying, but I had been away for a couple of years. I then questioned if our mystery mage could be him and quickly dismissed it. He had a difficult time casting even the simplest of arcane spells. To progress that far in only a couple of years would be impossible.

"Theoretically it would be possible to combine the arcane and the divine. There was another Researcher at the Arcane College who dabbled in the divine and trying to merge spells, but he hadn't gotten anywhere with it. Why?" I said.

"I'm wondering if the power source might be divine, given your ability to see the arcane. Divine energy would provide a longer supply of power than what you've described of arcane energy. Granted, my knowledge in the field is limited," Retanei said.

Her statement made it seem so simple. But would it work outside of theory? The types of energy were so vastly different, but I suppose there had to be some common trait between them which could be exploited.

I made my way back to the truck. I had stood in the cold long enough. "What do you have in mind?"

Retanei looked back at the blown-out building. "I'm going to run it by Savanas and see if I can get someone over here who is more in tune with the divine than I am. It'll give you some time to see if you can find more information."

THERE WAS a bustle of activity at the EAC branch similar to the one at the main campus. Students milled about the hallways with a few here and there entering a classroom. While most of the students were

Elven, there were a few of the other races as well, predominantly Human.

The tone was solemn overall. There was the occasional student trying to liven people up, but given recent events it was easily understood.

I wished I wore my other coat. The long, black leather duster my sister insisted on buying for me was soft and covered more, but had less padding to help keep me warm. With the large white TIO letters on the back of this coat, I felt like a target.

The person who greeted me at the entrance said the library was in the center of the school. The directions I got were for someone familiar with the layout. I stopped at a directory along the wall to get my bearings.

"You're the mage from last night." Those words cut through the murmur of the crowd moving around me.

The Elf who spoke looked familiar. He was the mage who had been sent over to put up the shield.

I had not paid much attention to him then, which I felt slightly guilty about. He had shoulder-length blond hair which hung with a life of its own and dressed like many of the students did, which was not much different from my casual shirt and jeans.

"Ketayl," I said and offered a more traditional Elven greeting. I really was not sure what kind of etiquette was required in situations like this, but it seemed logical.

"Angolon. My apologies I haven't thanked you sooner," he returned the greeting, which was a mental sigh of relief for me. I was still rather far behind on social norms.

"It isn't necessary. I'm still unsure what exactly happened to be honest with you," I said. How the figure appeared and disappeared and why, I was pretty certain. How I reacted was what I did not understand. I was not effectively trained for combat, despite Locko-nis' attempts otherwise, and strong emotional responses strained my control. I had not acted on instinct since I was a small child - it could produce disastrous results.

"So, what brings you to our humble school?" Angolon asked and adjusted the books under his arm.

The actual reason seemed so silly all of a sudden - at least from where I stood. "I'm looking for the library. I need to research something pertaining to a case."

"Is that all? I would be more than happy to escort you. The next class I'm teaching is in the same direction." Angolon smiled at me and signaled with his free hand for me to follow.

He piqued my curiosity so I asked, "What are you teaching?"

Angolon laughed lightly for a moment. "I'm teaching first year classes. I have a bit of a passion for them. Having a solid understanding of basic arcane theory will become a good foundation for my students."

"Actually, going back to basic arcane theory has helped me solve many puzzles." While I usually worked with much more advanced arcane theory, it was nice to return to the basics.

Angolon laughed and joked, "A woman after my own heart." He reached for the door. "Well, here you are. I'm sorry we can't speak further right now."

"I understand. And thank you for the escort." Letting him hold the door open for me, I bowed and headed in. It did not hit me until the door closed that I had spoken with a higher ranked mage with such informality. I was not sure what to make of it since he seemed not to mind.

Biting my lower lip in worry, I slowly moved away from the door to take in my new surroundings. The room was so large, and bright. The sun shone in through the ceiling windows and it was warm. A bit too warm to be wearing a coat. I shed it and took off my scarf, shoving it down a sleeve. I knew my Arcane College pin was still on the scarf, but the pin felt as stifling to wear as my coat.

The multiple levels in the library caught my attention as I wandered away from the door. I could easily spend years in here reading everything. The plush chairs and couches tucked into nooks and crannies made the thought tantalizing.

My sister would make fun of me if she heard those thoughts. While she enjoyed reading, she preferred fiction. She certainly would not want to be stuck inside a library either.

I noticed a group of students gathered at one of the tables in the center of this section, pouring over books and sharing notes with each other. Part of me longed for that kind of ease with others, but perhaps I had too many years of solo study drilled into me.

Not wanting to disturb them, I found a terminal nearby attached to the EAC's library catalog.

My hands hovered over the keyboard as I debated where to start.

Emotional responses in arcane remnants which would not dissipate was such a rare thing there was barely a mention of it in the Arcane College's library. I ran through a few keywords and jotted down the numbers for the books, hoping I would find some sort of answer.

Once I got a list I was comfortable to start with, I realized I had no idea where in this vast room to begin. I needed to stop calling it a room. It could have been a building by itself which just happened to be attached to the school.

Each section had a different color for a theme. Green was up a floor to my left and blue was to the right of it. The section of the floor I was in was tan. Looking at the list of numbers again, I realized there was no reference to the section colors.

Taking a deep breath, I headed toward the blue room where I thought I spotted someone shelving books.

Poking my head down a couple of aisles, I eventually found an older Elf. He had long white hair hanging down his back like a sheet and he dressed a little more formally than Angolon. He seemed content in his work and I hesitated disturbing him.

"Come, child, you have a question?" Soft, gold-colored eyes turned to me.

Child - I was still considered a child by Elven standards, but because of the great toll in the war half a century ago, Elven traditions had changed to accommodate the nearly missing generations.

"I'm so sorry to disturb you, sir. I'm a bit lost." The paper remained tightly clutched in my hand.

He waved me over to give him my slip. "I'm a librarian - you are not disturbing me." He pulled his glasses from where they sat atop his head. "Ah, many of these are in our restricted section. Why would you be interested in this subject?"

"My name is Ketayl, I'm an Arcane Investigator with the Terran Intelligence Organization. I need the information for a case. I'm dealing with arcane remnants which are emitting an emotional response." How much was I allowed to tell him? I should have spoken with Savanas first about it.

He bowed to me, "Maewon." I recognized the name from Rathal. He handed me back my slip of paper. "This is dark magic. Very dark. I am willing to help you, but I must first know if you are looking to learn this yourself."

"I need to know how to disperse it. I don't understand. I thought it was a natural occurrence." I felt strangely satisfied that I predicted it was not, as many sources claimed, a natural occurrence. However, the discovery was quickly overridden by my concern over his words.

"Come with me, we should speak where we will not be over-heard," he said. I had a feeling Maewon was going to be a better source of information than the books I had listed.

Something else told me I was not going to like what I heard.

THE WORD "ARCHMAGE" was on the door as we passed through and his relative comfort in the large office had me bowing and apologizing. "I'm so sorry for my rudeness, Archmage."

"Please sit. That title suits me as much as it does a fresh student. I'm little more than an administrator," Maewon said, putting some books down on the cluttered desk, "I fear I spend more time in the library than here."

The office was sparse. There were windows for walls with a view out over the port. The Naval battleship dwarfed the other boats in the harbor.

Inside the office, large seating pillows were lain out around the floor. I settled onto one as requested and watched him pull another pillow from behind the cluttered desk.

Once settled, Maewon eyed me for a moment before he said, "Your response to my title is not one of a typical Elven mage."

I sighed; habits were hard to break. Being privately instructed by the Magus because I was an Arcanist had not given me much to base a whole school off of. I had little chance to interact with the rest of the school during that time.

Digging into the sleeve of my coat, I pulled out my scarf and the Arcane College pin attached there. "I studied for a bit with Magus Engelil after transferring to the TIO, but I was a Researcher at the Arcane College."

Maewon smiled; it was gentle and sad. "Engelil is a good friend of mine. I had heard whispers of one of our kind being freed. Though I am glad you decided not to show that around here - it is not a welcome insignia. I take it you are not fond of it yourself?"

Being questioned on my loyalty had gotten irritating. I could understand though - even I questioned where I stood anymore.

Looking down at the pin - the gold, diamond-shaped insignia only had a couple of differences from the student version. Being almost the size of my palm and the gems inlaid to create the background being the quickest to identify. It was only a Researcher's pin and not nearly as large or elaborate as the ones the higher ranked mages would wear. I had no emotional attachment to it.

When I first received my student pin, I was filled with hope and wonder. When I received this one, I knew very well what life I would lead at the time and felt no reason to celebrate the accomplishment.

"I fear it only brings me more trouble than I care to have," I said. I shoved the scarf back down my coat's sleeve.

His voice was gentle as he said, "Do not fret, child. I heard what you did for Angolon yesterday. Getting back on topic, what do you know about the art of necromancy?"

How was that back on topic? "Very basic information. Mostly that it exists and a few historical references."

"As I told you before, it is a very dark subject. I personally witnessed the madness which will drive someone to study it. The intentions may even be noble in the beginning. I have seen these emotional responses in arcane remnants... Perhaps I should go back to the beginning a bit and explain," Maewon said.

Beginning? Shifting in my seat, I got more comfortable as I sensed a long story ahead.

"Necromancy is a forbidden art which is either discovered on the caster's own or taught directly by another necromancer. There is a key involved though - the caster has to be highly proficient in both the arcane and the divine, for it takes the darkest sides of both and twists them, merging them into something of pure evil."

He described it like something out of a fairytale. Though all stories have some sort of base in reality - it was simply a matter of how deep you had to dig to find it.

"During the war, someone I was close to, like a brother, lost himself to the madness. The Human contingent that had engaged my unit had a necromancer in their group. If I had known..." Maewon trailed off.

His attention was torn between his memories and the present - his eyes would lose focus and then he would look back to me.

"My friend was a healer. The death and destruction day in and day out took its toll on all of us, but even more so on the ones who watched friends die under their care," Maewon paused and folded his hands in his lap. I parsed the information he gave me. I knew I could quickly jump from one train of thought to another, but it was something else to follow another's.

Even being as young as I was in comparison to Maewon, I was old enough to have seen part of the war from a civilian standpoint. I watched it tear friends and families apart. The fighting remained outside of the area my sister and I lived, but the aftermath of the bodies returning home from the war...

To this day I remained uncertain what happened to our village - all I remembered was being told to take Kitteren and run. Mother had participated in the war, though she refused to speak of it.

Getting up, I moved to a closer pillow and reached over to touch his arm. Maewon looked up at me and smiled, but could not hide the haunted look in his eyes. While I did not like to be touched under normal circumstances, I normally would not have reached out for him, but something told me I needed to help keep him grounded.

Maewon took a deep breath and continued, "Even though I was part of the Arcane Division, my friend and I had grown up together. As much as my unit tried, we were losing ground and it was only a matter of time before we would have to evacuate our base camp. Before that could happen, he begged me to teach him about the arcane. He wanted to be able to protect his charges."

It gave me some insight into divine casters. At least those specialized in healing. They may have spells for defense, but a well-timed fireball in a fight was an equally good deterrent.

He said, "I thought nothing of it, knowing little about necromancy and aware of certain casters in the unit who were able to cast both, but they were in support roles as their knowledge of either was limited. I quickly discovered though my friend had as much of a gift for the arcane as he did for the divine."

Being proficient in either was something I knew the Researcher at the Arcane College who was dabbling in mixing arcane and divine was not. Perhaps it was why he had been unsuccessful.

"It wasn't long after his lifemate fell in battle the experiments started. He was driven mad by the loss - he wanted to find a way to bring back the dead. He needed her. She kept his balance and sanity. My words were lost to him." Maewon's eyes turned to the windows this time and I feared losing him to his memories.

I started to understand what he meant by the process could start with noble intentions. The loss of a lifemate was detrimental to an Elf - the bond so strong it was like losing a part of yourself. I did not have a lifemate or anyone I was even remotely close to in that regard, so I was unable to fully relate.

"Eventually we managed to capture the necromancer. I'm still not sure how he did it, but he convinced the guards to let him speak with the woman. After that... well, he killed her and then drove forward into the fight himself. Being untrained in arcane combat, he didn't stand a chance. It was the best possible ending at that stage."

Taking a deep breath, Maewon returned his attention to me. "I apologize, you came here for answers to a current situation and here I am telling you about things past. However, there is something within this story to share. My friend managed to recreate the emotional responses you are curious about. I couldn't see or understand where they were coming from. He was able to successfully create them each time. The strongest healers in our unit would not speak of what they saw, but through much effort, they were able to cleanse it. I spent a long time searching for answers in books, like you are, but to this day, I still do not know."

That meant... "You think I'm dealing with a necromancer?"

"I'm fairly certain given your list of books and brief description of the problem you face. I fear, however, you won't find what I told you in any book." Maewon got up, straightening his clothes. "I wish I had more to offer you than old stories. I do not wish to see another, especially one so young and full of potential, go down this road. If you really require the books, however, I will not interfere with your investigation."

I stood with him and said, "It is the past which will help guide us in both the present and the future."

Raising an eyebrow, Maewon smiled, "It has been many a year since I have heard such wise words." He held his hand out, palm up to me.

I hesitated before taking it in a familiar Elven greeting. "I am only repeating the lesson you taught. I think you've given me more than the books could, thank you."

"Of course you will be welcome if there is more information you require. Especially since you managed to sit through one of my lectures without falling asleep in the first couple of minutes," Maewon said and smiled. He escorted me to the front of the building.

It was not the same bustle as before, but many students once again wandered the halls. I supposed it would be about the time of year classes would be wrapping up. The Winter Solstice was coming up soon and they would be taking a break for the holiday.

I again thanked Maewon as we parted at the entrance. Digging my scarf out, I took the pin off and stuffed it in one of my coat pockets. I was done with the thing.

7

IT WAS late afternoon by the time I got back to the office. Artemis was in the reception area again. I wondered if it was because Melody kept spoiling her or after the attack yesterday evening. At least her presence told me Retanei might be in the building. Big Black picked his head up to glance at me as I came up on the side of the desk and then put his head back down. He was curled up on a large pad behind Melody's desk.

I paused to take my coat and scarf off and pet Artemis when she trotted over to me. I was tired even though I had not physically done much this afternoon. I knew we would be working late into the evening so I was going to have to find more energy somehow.

My mind had been running nonstop since I left the EAC. I should get upstairs and start directing my search for more information about necromancy. If I could get even a historical point of reference, it may give me a better idea of how to dissipate the arcane remnants at least. Well, once I figured out how to disconnect whatever the power source was.

It sounded like I was going to need the advice of someone specialized in the divine. I wondered how Retanei faired in getting someone.

Savanas would not like the information I was coming back with. I was still working out how to tell her.

I was also trying to remember where I had found the basic information from when I was copying books at the Arcane College. I had access to their restricted section since I was one of the few Researchers who actually put effort into finding information.

Fear of punishment for failure was usually a good motivator.

"Oh my..." I looked up at Melody when she spoke. I followed her line of sight, hoping it was not another puppet. Although not a puppet, I was unprepared for the sight before me.

"Pardon me, ladies, but by chance would either one of you be Savanas Farstrider?"

I wondered if maybe I had fallen asleep during Maewon's short lecture. In the real world, there would not have been not a male Elf with long, braided silver hair wearing full plate armor. On one arm, he carried a large shield with a golden sun decorating its face and a long sword sheathed at his hip. Instead of a helmet, he wore a circlet. His blue eyes completely serious.

A paladin would be someone specialized in the divine. Perhaps he was here for another reason. Melody did not seem to have expected him and certainly this office would have more than just this investigation going on.

I looked to Melody who hid her face behind the tall counter of her desk. She managed to sound calmer than she looked when she replied, "No."

It was one of the few times I easily understood another's amusement. Artemis sniffed at him from a distance, uncertain about the metal man. Big Black had not even lifted his head. Why had he growled at me when we first met?

Standing, I felt incredibly short - I only came up to his shoulder. Giving him a formal Elven greeting, I said, "My name is Ketayl. Can I help you with something?" I noticed a large canvas bag by his feet stuffed to capacity and a bound packet of papers in his shield hand.

He tried to mimic my greeting, but could not manage the flowing movement in his armor. "Paladin Silver Blaise of the Holy Church of the Sun. I was dispatched here by my mentor who was contacted by your Director..." he trailed off, stroking the small patch of hair on his chin.

Melody and I looked at each other while he tried to come up with a name. I knew the Arcane College was behind the times, but this was right out of one of those medieval fantasy novels my sister liked to read.

"I apologize, I am unable to recall his name. I was told to report to Savanas Farstrider." This paladin must have felt as out of place as he appeared. Kneeling before me, he took my hand and kissed the back of it. "Lady Ketayl, is it both an honor and a pleasure to meet you."

"Uh..." That was less than eloquent. I caught Melody's amusement out of the corner of my eye before she busied herself at her desk. "I can bring you upstairs to talk to Savanas. Does he need to sign in or anything?"

A clip board and a visitor's badge appeared on the counter. I took that as a yes.

———

THROUGH SOME EFFORT I managed to get the paladin signed in and upstairs. He wore fingerless leather gloves instead of the metal gauntlets I had seen in historical texts, which made the process a bit smoother. His sword and shield had disappeared, but I had not been paying attention when it happened.

Melody entered the information into the computer almost as soon as he wrote it down. Having him follow me, I escorted the Elven man upstairs. As the elevator dinged, I stepped off first, hoping to catch Savanas' attention.

"Ket! I was wondering when you were going to get back, Vince called..." Savanas paused, her eyes moved to the paladin behind me. She coughed and hid her mouth with her hand. "I see you've met our new consultant."

Brad's head popped up from over his computer screen. "Silver?" He quickly got up and came over to us, offering his hand in a familiar greeting to our consultant. "I heard we were getting a paladin. It's good to have you here. I was worried we would get Paladin Marsh."

The paladin smiled, taking the offered hand like he was greeting a friend. He said, "If it wasn't his week to lead prayers, you might have. I'm afraid I haven't yet had a chance to read the book you lent me."

I was lost and confused at this point. Quietly excusing myself, I headed for my desk.

"Take your time reading it," Brad said and signaled him to follow. "This is Savanas Farstrider, the head of the Ocean's Edge TIO branch."

As I sat down, my desk somewhat faced toward Savanas' and the other desks in this area, which allowed me to see Silver simply bow to her. For some reason it bothered me, but I also did not like to be touched and I figured it was simply annoyance.

Our consultant said, "Lady Savanas Farstrider, I am Paladin Silver Blaise of the Holy Church of the Sun. I have been sent here to assist you with what matters you would need." He handed her the bound packet of papers he carried.

"You're certainly silver, I'll give you that. And you can drop the formality," Savanas said, probably unsure herself on how to react to him. "It's good to have you on board. I'm glad to see you already have a friend here." She opened up the packet to read the information provided.

I looked up at Retanei who quietly exited the bathroom and took the long way around to my desk. She knelt down next to me, keeping a wary eye on our newcomer. It was odd to see her act like this.

"What did he do when you told him you were a mage?" Retanei whispered the question.

"Hm?" I had pulled up the Arcane College library again. I said, "I haven't mentioned it. Why?"

Retanei made a face and said, "That explains why he wasn't up in arms. You do know that most devout divine casters don't like arcane casters, right?"

Oh, right. I forgot about that and I was not wearing my Arcane College pin. On the positive side, it felt like a weight had been lifted now that I had taken it off.

Savanas was still talking to the paladin, going over information in the packet. They had stepped to the side and despite her height, Savanas still stood visibly shorter.

Retanei stood up. "When Savanas and I called Vince earlier, he said something about calling in an old favor. I'm not sure we have anyone in the TIO *that* specialized in the divine."

I chewed on the bit of information. The TIO employed a vast diversity of backgrounds and specialties. There were other arcane casters besides myself, but none as deep in the theory side of it as I was. It gave me a unique position, but not one I took for granted.

Glancing quickly at our new consultant for a moment to see where he was, I returned to the library in front of me. There must be something useful on necromancy in here. Or at least I hoped there was. I might be visiting other libraries otherwise to gather more historical information. Especially since they had taken part in the war.

Retanei leaned back against the filing cabinet and stayed quiet. She would not be able to help me with my search and I wondered what she was doing. There was too much to do to satisfy my curiosity at the moment.

My search was turning up nothing useful. Archmage Maewon gave me more in his story than the Arcane College had on the subject.

Pinching the bridge of my nose, I stopped to rethink my current search. A direct search was not working. How would I look for it indirectly? It would make sense if the information existed it would be spread out so no mage could easily access it. It would not be the first time I stumbled upon information spread out like that.

My fingers flew across the keyboard trying a different starting point. The combining of spells might be a good place and I could cross-reference my notes from previous projects at the Arcane College.

Savanas finished her conversation and introduced the others in the office. She then headed our way with the paladin. "These two are from our main office outside of Great Tree. I believe you already met Ketayl, our Arcane Investigator, and this is our Rural Tracker, Retanei."

The paladin eyed Retanei cautiously for a moment before turning his attention back to me. "You're an Arcane Investigator?" He seemed confused by the statement.

How was I supposed to respond to a question that had already been answered? I nodded.

"So, Ket, did you get anywhere at the library?" Savanas asked and either had not noticed the awkwardness of the situation or was doing her best to ignore it. I was uncertain at this point. "Oh, hey, where'd your pin go?" She seemed genuinely surprised it was missing.

"It's in my coat pocket," I said. It was the easiest answer and she seemed to approve. "I spoke with Archmage Maewon. The books are in the restricted section and he'll let me look at them if it's needed. He thinks we're dealing with a necromancer. I'm trying to pull up what is in my library to get a better idea of what we're up against."

Savanas made a face telling me she did not like my answer. I knew she would not. "At least we have a better picture of what we're dealing with. Maewon is a good source, I should have thought to tell you to feel free to pick his brain."

The paladin's face twisted for a moment, but it was enough.

I asked, "What's wrong?" before I filtered I should not speak out of turn.

Silver said, "I've only heard rumors about necromancers in the historical texts. It is an evil beyond that of normal mortals." The flowery words only said the same thing Archmage Maewon had earlier.

I said as I typed, "From what I've been told, they are casters of both arcane and divine magic. So there's a chance whatever is keeping the arcane remnants powered is of divine origin. It would explain why I can't see it. I can tell you whatever the power source is, it is charging straight at the central axis and the emotional responses have slowly grown since yesterday."

Wait, was I supposed to say so much with our consultant in front of me? I took a moment to glance at Savanas whose face told me she was more concerned with what I said instead who I said it in front of. I rationalized he would have to find out at some point if he was here to help with the investigation.

"I don't know if most other arcane sensitive people can get inside the building anymore without being severely affected," I added, continuing my previous thought. I paused in my remaining thoughts to look at the three around me who simply stared. I pointed to Retanei. "It was her idea."

Someday I would figure out how to translate for people. I understood the arcane on a different level and it often made it hard to explain to others. Not to mention I tended to get a bit overzealous about arcane mysteries.

"Ugh, Ket, don't do that," Savanas said and rubbed the bridge of her nose. "Look, Paladin Silver Blaise has been temporarily transferred to my command. Don't ask details. For now, can I put him up with you two until I can make other arrangements? I'd put him up with Brad, but I have a feeling he'll need to stick fairly close to Ket."

I looked at Retanei and shrugged. I did not have a problem with it. If what we were dealing with was a combination of arcane and divine magic, we would not get far in solving this without the other. I just hoped what Retanei said about the most devote of divine casters did not apply to this paladin.

Rathal made a displeased face from his desk, but said nothing.

Retanei voiced her consent, "I guess it's a good thing I like hunting at night. Ket and I can share." Though I could tell my friend was less than pleased. The tightness in her voice betrayed her unease. It was something I picked up in the short time I had known her.

"Good, why don't you take him over there and get him settled. Afterward, you can head back to the Waking Dawn to see what else you can figure out," Savanas said and left the paladin in our hands.

Silence hung like a crooked picture. I asked, "Sir, what would you prefer to be called?" Not much better, but it was something.

"It would please me if you simply called me Silver, m'lady."

Rathal was glaring at him and I wondered what they could have already said to each other to be causing such animosity.

———

AFTER BRAD HELPED Silver take his armor off before getting into the vehicle, Retanei and I split up. She needed to run an errand so I took Silver to the hotel. He sat beside me uncomfortably in the passenger's seat while I navigated the slick roads. There had been patches of the city which had been outfitted with the solar panels keeping the roads dry and clear, but they had not made it to the area of the hotel yet.

"We aren't far," I tried to comfort. I eyed the shiny metal bracers on his forearms. He told me his sword and shield were tied to those and his belt. He kept the circlet on as well. I wondered about the magic behind all of it, but now was not the time to get distracted.

Silver wore the padded garments he had on under his armor and while I blasted the heat, he still had to be cold. I was glad I packed my personal coat - he might be able to wear my TIO coat for now.

"I'm sorry, m'lady. I'm not used to riding around in these." He waved at the vehicle and turned his attention from out the window toward me.

I could not help but smile a bit. Realizing the uneasy silence, I said, "Oh, I don't mean to make fun of you. I was just thinking I'm still kind of the same way. I've gotten used to driving, but when I had to fly in the Shrike... needless to say I didn't get much rest on the flight here. How did you get to the office?"

Silver said, "One of my order specializes in transportation spells." He kept his eyes on me and I gripped the wheel tighter. I could not afford to take my eyes off the road to see what his expression was.

A few minutes passed and the hairs on the back of my neck were standing up with the scrutiny I was under. I started to think maybe we had something in common - both being out of place in the modern world. It did not change the fact he made me nervous and it was not recommended while I drove.

"You... are not like the others," Silver said after a few moments. I guessed my confusion was apparent because he continued, "I'm not sure how to explain it. Like in the entry hall, the other woman found much amusement to my presence, but you greeted me like a person."

Oh, that. I did not want to tell him my disbelief upon his arrival, and honestly, I had been in his position. I just had people around me to support me when I made my transition. I kept my reply neutral. "I was in a similar position a couple of years ago when I transferred to the TIO." So I was right in my earlier thought about his unease.

"How is that?"

Being an Arcane Investigator and outright admitting I was a mage were vastly different things - being born with the ability to sense the arcane was a far cry from channeling the energy to my will. I was not sure I wanted to be in tight quarters when the information came to light. Granted, it probably was a fairly educated assumption at this point. Hesitantly, I admitted, "The place I transferred from - they're rather archaic."

"Lady Ketayl, you seem to avoid saying much about yourself. I would most like to hear more about you. Especially given that we will be working together."

I could feel those blue eyes on me and wished he could find someone else to be fascinated by.

Silver kind of backed me into a corner. Keeping my eyes straight ahead, I gripped the wheel tightly and said, "Well, I guess it really depends on how you feel about mages."

Silence hung for a moment and I wished I had perused the radio stations in the area to fill the void. It might have given him something else to focus on.

Then Silver laughed. It threw my concentration for a moment and I could feel the truck's four-wheel drive kick in.

"My apologies - I understand your hesitation. If it were my

mentor or many of the older paladins at the Central Seat, I would also give pause. However, I have discovered in my own personal study of the scriptures that everything must have a balance and therefore has a place in the world. Besides, the world would be boring if everything was the same."

I caught the change in his speech and wondered if the rest was an act. "Good to know."

The sight of the hotel was a relief. Silver was not bad to deal with, I just was unused to the attention. I started to think I should have asked to switch with Retanei.

"I'm sorry, I pry too much. It is a failing of mine. I am usually more curious about people than is necessarily healthy." The conversation hung there as I pulled into the underground parking garage for the hotel.

Once the vehicle was parked and off, Silver moved to the back to get his stuff.

I said, "Actually, why don't we get one of the hotel's carts to bring that up?" Mostly because I really did not want to have to carry his armor.

He took a moment to think before accepting the idea.

I made sure to keep a straight face when Silver jumped as I locked the vehicle with the remote.

BY THE TIME we got everything upstairs, it had started to snow. I let him get settled in the common area of the suite until at least Retanei and I could figure out which room we were going to put him in.

As he set about putting his armor out of the way, I moved toward the window and watched the fat flakes fall, covering the area in white. I heard this storm was supposed to last for a while.

I imagined it was going to make the investigation more difficult. Especially for Retanei who would be combing the woods. If she could find at least one of them, then we could try to get some answers.

It frustrated me the big picture was still elusive. I could only hope returning to the Waking Dawn would shed some more information now that we had someone who specialized in the divine.

I barely heard the bathroom door close and kept watching the snow. It fell harder and I was not overly looking forward to driving to the crime scene later. It was also starting to get dark. What if we were able to piece together the full spell used? Or set of spells. I was not even sure how to classify what I did know.

Fire-based, what was more often referred to as a fireball because of what the original spell looked like when cast. Added concussive force and a delay spell to act as a timer. Both of those were smaller parts of other spells. The amount of energy the caster would have needed to create each one would be...

"M'lady?"

This time it was my turn to jump. I had not heard him come out of the bathroom while I watched the snow fall.

Silver had changed clothes. The short-sleeve, high-collared white dress shirt and pants he wore now were only broken up by a deep blue and gold trim. The shirt was loose on him while the pants appeared to be fashioned after common dress pants. He still wore the fingerless leather gloves, metal bracers, and circlet. Even his boots were white.

"I hope you don't mind I took the time to change into something more appropriate since it has become apparent my armor is not suitable for this task," Silver said.

It was the first time I truly noticed how long his hair was with the silver braided tail hanging over his right shoulder to his waist. It had blended in too well with his armor before.

Shaking my head, I smiled to put both of us at ease and said, "No, it's actually a good idea. But you don't have a coat, do you?"

Silver shook his head and informed, "The grounds are kept warm by the grace of the God of the Sun. It is like an eternal spring. I rarely have need to leave the grounds."

Digging my Arcane College pin out of the pocket, I shed my coat and handed it to him. "I have another. This might still not be big enough for you, but at least it's something." The coat was over-sized on me, but he was so much taller. Only coming up to his shoulder, it was a little intimidating and I mentally cursed my lack of height.

Silver began to turn it down, but suddenly took interest in what was in my hand. "Is that a brooch, m'lady? You should wear it."

"Um..." Well, this was awkward. I said, "It's more of an insignia pin. I wore it out of habit." Why was I saying so much? I avoided talking about myself at all if I could help it. Mostly because I found myself to be uninteresting compared to others.

"May I?" Silver asked and held out his hand. Reluctantly I gave it up. "The Arcane College? But you are Elven. I don't understand."

There went the hope he did not know about the Arcane College. Something caught my attention with the pin as he held it. It almost looked like a thread was leading back to me. I could not recall seeing something like it before. I knew the secret it contained, but that was because I put it there. Was it connected to that somehow?

I said, "It's not a Human-only organization. I am the first non-Human to be sent as a liaison to another organization though. I was a Researcher there for a few decades. Aren't you a bit of an oddity yourself? I didn't know that there were any Elven paladins." The last part sounded rude, but I had grown increasingly tired of people asking me.

"I'm likely the only one," Silver said. I could not tell what his thoughts were. "Others who have shown interest have not had the dedication to the training required."

Silence hung awkwardly again while I filed the information away.

Needing to do something, I decided to change the subject, "You have an interesting name." And if I could turn the conversation around back to him, I would.

Silver handed my pin back and said, "It was given to me by my mentor's father. He had an odd sense of humor. My first name is because of the color of my hair. My last name is his first name. I cherish it. And you?"

Putting my pin in a pocket on my pants, I backed away a step and said, "I didn't mean to offend you. I'm afraid mine is boring. It was whatever I could remember like many others who were orphaned during the war. That's why it isn't a traditional Elven name."

"You have a sister?"

I turned away, rubbing my arms. That, I should have not mentioned, but it was already out so I said, "Kitteren. Half-sister actually - she's a couple of years younger than me. She's also a Tracker in the TIO, but not specialized like Retanei."

Silver seemed to be digesting the information. Before he could ask further, I heard the lock on the door unlatch and Retanei struggled to get in with bags and drinks in hand.

I rushed over to help alleviate the load. "You should have called and I would have come down to meet you."

"I tried - you must have left your phone on silent again," Retanei chided. "It's no big deal. Artemis, come here."

She was right - I had left the ringer on silent after my visit to the EAC branch. Turning it back on, I also missed a message from Brad stating he was unable to get Silver another room. I showed it to Retanei who nodded. There was one more missed call from my sister. She must have gotten back from her assignment. With people in the room, I figured she could wait a little longer.

Artemis padded in with a bag in her mouth. She obeyed the call immediately and relinquished her parcel.

"Sorry I took so long. I was running low on food for her and figured I better stop for more while the stores were open. I don't keep much around since she usually hunts with her pack. She made good friends with the butcher," Retanei said and held the bag up in front of the wolf who promptly sat and waited for her to dump the contents into a bowl.

I pulled things out of bags, flipping the smaller wrapped packages over so the labels could be easily read. My phone dinged with a new message. Glancing at who it was from, I put my phone back in my pocket. Kitteren could be impatient.

Retanei said, "Feel free to dig in. I got some sandwiches. Find something you like and take it. I got extras, not knowing appetites, not to mention I'll want something while I'm out hunting tonight."

I reminded her, "I just had lunch not that long ago."

Retanei rolled her eyes and shot back, "You barely ate. And you skipped breakfast." Then she pointed at the sandwiches in front of me. I picked one and slid it closer to me, cursing her powers of observation. She would have noticed I had not taken any of the pastries.

Silver had not moved from his spot by the window.

I said, "Come eat. They won't bite."

My phone dinged again and I did not bother looking as I knew Kitteren's patterns. Retanei looked at me expectantly, and said, "You better respond to her soon. It'll only get worse and then she'll start calling me."

Reluctantly Silver came over and browsed the labels on the sandwiches before picking one and making his way to the table, keeping a wary eye on Retanei.

I rolled my eyes and sighed, looking at Retanei. Silver did not have a problem with mages, but he did with Dark Elves. I felt bad for my friend.

She shrugged and commented, "It's not his fault he can't tell the difference between a Dark Elf and a Drow. We look the same."

"Dark Elf?" Silver was watching us.

Retanei stepped around the counter, rubbing Artemis' head as she passed. "We're not like our underground cousins. Most of Dark Elven society are either farmers or are deeply connected to nature in some way. We have no quarrel with our lighter-colored cousins."

Silver seemed to let it sink in for a moment before he said, "My apologies, Lady Retanei."

Crossing her arms over her chest, the look Retanei gave me was an odd mix of annoyance and relief. She said, "It's a start. Just do me a favor and drop the formality."

Excusing myself, I took my food to the couch in front of the windows and called my sister.

"Dammit, Ket. Learn to pay attention to your phone," my sister said and I had to hold the phone away from my head at her volume.

"Kitteren..." I warned. "I'm sorry, my ringer was off and I was busy." If I did not give a little, we would be butting heads instead of having a conversation. Both of us could be stubborn to a fault. It drove Mother mad on more than one occasion.

"Couldn't even leave me a note - I'm crushed. You know I went scouring over this whole place looking for you? Finally Wade said you and Retanei took a Shrike out to Ocean's Edge," Kitteren's tone was playful despite the hurt she was trying to put into it.

It told me she was not actually upset I had not left a note. It was easier to let her get it out. She was the far more vocal and animated of the two of us, but she also was not an Arcanist either.

Glancing up, Retanei spoke quietly with Silver, but I could not focus on more than one conversation at a time. Especially not at Kitteren's current volume.

She dropped back to a normal level. "First field assignment - must be exciting. How's it going so far?" Kitteren would want to talk for quite a while if she could.

Shifting my phone to see if I could balance it between my ear and shoulder, the sandwich on my lap called to me, but I could not get the phone to stay securely. I was hungrier than I thought. All I wanted to do was eat and get back to work. Shifting uncomfortably, I told her, "Going, I guess. Hopefully we'll have more answers soon."

"What's wrong?" Trackers and their powers of observation. Kitteren had also been training with Retanei in between assignments, which meant I would never get away with anything. She changed to the common dialect we spoke when we were little, *"You're doubting yourself, aren't you?"* It was something few people could understand even though it was based off of the common language. We continued to use it with each other when we wanted to make sure our conversation was private.

Taking a deep breath that wavered slightly, I said, *"Yes. Kit..."*

"Don't. You know you wouldn't be there if you weren't ready," Kitteren cut me off. *"Ketayl, you'll be fine as long as you keep your head and don't do something stupid."*

I rolled my eyes and leaned back against the couch, stretching and looking up out the window. Kitteren was right. I started to get emotional and doubt myself.

I sat back up and glanced over at the two in the room with me. I managed to get this far and now I had more help to piece this puzzle together. Silver looked at me with a surprised expression. I could not figure out why and turned my attention to trying to open the wrapped sandwich with one hand.

I said, *"Thanks, Kitteren. I should get going - there's still a lot of work to do and I need to eat."*

"You better eat - you're too damn scrawny. And take care of yourself. I don't want to hear you're working yourself to death," Kitteren chided. *"Love you, sis. Talk to you when you get back."* Then she hung up before I could say anything further.

Dropping the phone onto the couch next to me, I ignored the questioning faces of the other two. Retanei knew about our habit, but did not understand it. Hopefully Silver would forget about it.

8

It was completely dark by the time we got to the Waking Dawn. Retanei and I caught Silver up en route to give him an idea of what he was walking into. The snow continued to fall heavily, making visibility difficult. I was glad Retanei offered to drive.

Sitting in the backseat with Artemis curled up next to me, I pulled out my camera and prepared it for easy access. I checked the lens to make sure the arcane filter was still attached. Seeing the translucent purple, I put the lens cap back on.

As soon as I opened the door to get out, the cold took a bite at me. I pulled my hood up, trying to get as much of it to cover my head, but my bun made it difficult. I should have remembered my hat.

The TIO coat barely fit Silver, but it was better than nothing. My black leather duster was not as thick, but with more of the wind blocked due to it being ankle-length and a hood, I felt a little warmer than in the TIO coat. We approached from the side of the building again, where most of one of the remaining walls still stood.

As soon as we rounded the corner, however, Silver stopped. Retanei and I had gotten a few feet away before she realized it. Turning back, as I got closer to him, I could more clearly see the horror on his face and hear the prayers he muttered under his breath. Or at least I assumed they were prayers by the tone of his voice.

"What is it?" I asked. Even from here I could feel the emotional reactions. The remnants were still getting stronger and expanding. I could not remain this close for too long - it taxed my control.

"I..." Silver started, visibly ill. He turned his gaze to me, looking for all the world like he had seen a ghost. "The dead - their souls. They're trapped here. They're screaming in so much pain and anger."

I had gotten the same impression when I first arrived, but it should have been impossible for me. Unless what Silver spoke of was bleeding through the connection into the arcane remnants. It was a theory I had previously, but souls being trapped pushed the limit of what I could readily accept. "What do you mean?"

I needed the rest of the puzzle filled in, but Silver said nothing. His eyes kept scanning the interior for things I could not see. I looked to Retanei, unsure of what to do.

"Silver!" Retanei yelled.

He snapped out of it, shaking his head, "My apologies. Perhaps it would be best if I showed you."

I had no idea how Silver would show me, but I already had my camera out and dangling around my neck. With gloves on, it took a minute to get the lens cap off, but when I looked up, Silver had gone into the building.

Now I had the answer to what the power source was. I could see the connection between the two, but I could not get past the souls of the dead chained in place, screaming and crying.

"What? How can I see this?" I barely heard the words escape my lips. My hands on the camera shook, though not from the cold. Ghostly figures of people, transparent blue-white, were anchored to the ground with black tendrils. They screamed in pain and anger, as Silver said. Children cried, trying to grasp the adults near them, but were either out of reach or simply fell through. Had this been here from the start?

"Breathe. Focus on me for a moment," Retanei said calmly and stood between me and the scene of death.

I stared at a spot on her coat. Focusing on the tightly woven fibers helped me regain my balance.

As soon as I calmed, Retanei explained, "His aura is making everything visible to us - though I thought it was a myth. I'm not sure how to explain a paladin's aura. Listen, you don't have to do this. I can take pictures instead. Just tell me what I should be looking for."

Artemis plastered herself against my legs and I took half a step not to get knocked over.

My head was clearer now that Retanei grabbed my attention. Locking my mental barriers in place, I forced myself to put my emotions away. "No, I've got it. Thank you," I said.

Professional pride pushed me to work through the harm the arcane remnants were caused and the pain and suffering shown before me.

"If I hadn't already seen things which rivaled this, I'd probably be in the same boat." Retanei moved away and wrote things down on her notepad.

Taking a deep breath, I raised the camera to my face before I focused on the scene before me again. There was a chance that with or without the filter, the camera would not pick up what Silver's aura revealed. At least I would be able to review the images to see if it was worth the effort.

As Silver walked among the dead, he would gently touch the head of a soul as he passed, calming it for a moment.

Snapping a couple of images of the whole scene, I checked to see what the camera picked up. I was not sure if I was surprised or not that the bright, colorful flows of the arcane remnants were mixed with the ghostly images of the trapped souls.

The black tendrils anchoring the souls in place also wound their way up into the arcane remnants, feeding power. That was where the gold-white light pulses originated from and the thought made me ill.

Silver walked back to us, his expression still grim. "I wish to release them so they can move on. I can only comfort them for so long being tied to this place."

Retanei stood between us. "Ket, what do you think?"

"I..." I wanted this nightmare to end, but said, "I need to go and take a few more detailed pictures now that we can see the whole set of spells." I really did not want to go back in there, but we needed more evidence. I needed to show what kind of twisted magic was being used.

"That's not a good idea, Ket. You're barely standing as it is," Retanei pointed out. I had been ignoring the abuse from the remnants. "Tell me what you need and I'll go get it."

Immediately I shook my head, and shot back, "No, I need to do this. Not much of an Arcane Investigator if I stay on the sidelines.

Besides, I'm the only one who can dissipate the arcane remnants once the power source is removed." Power source, not souls. I needed to distance myself as cold as it made me sound.

"M'lady..." Silver started in as well.

"No, I'm doing this," I snapped. I could deal with their concerns later.

Without waiting for another response, I stepped forward toward the closest arcane remnant and immediately regretted my stubbornness, but I was not about to back down now.

Silver grabbed my free hand. I could feel his warmth through my glove. "At least stay close to me. I don't know if it will help, but it couldn't hurt. I do not wish to see the pain about you worsen."

At that I had to pause and look at Silver. "What do you mean?"

Silver would not look at me and moved ahead, releasing my hand. "This place hurts you, right? We should get moving."

Retanei stood on my other side and said nothing. Artemis remained where she was. I wanted to push for more information, but Silver was right - we needed to hurry.

I took the images I needed. Retanei followed closely. She took pictures of each of the dead with her phone. Possibly for identification purposes. I briefly wondered how closely they would resemble their living selves.

Chaos was what this was. I could not think of a better way to describe it.

Focus on the job at hand. Ignore the incessant pounding in my head continued to build. Lifting the camera up as soon as I reached the closest arcane remnant, I fiddled with the zoom, having a hard time seeing the connection of the black tendrils amongst the bright colors. The bands of runes were still spinning at a dizzying rate. Colors swirled and collided angrily. The sea of reds and oranges overpowered the other colors. I had to believe it was just the effect it had on me, but adjusted my shutter speed in case I was wrong.

I lost track of time as I mentally fought against the onslaught. I felt like I had been working for days by the time I was satisfied enough to say, "I'm done." My head felt like I had a drummer inside of my skull.

We stood in the center of it all and it was taking every last shred of willpower I had to remain standing. It also took longer than expected because I needed to check every image to make sure it was not blurry.

I knew the shutter speed was quite high to capture the arcane movements clearly, but I still did not blindly trust it. I also did not trust it with how badly my hands were shaking by the end.

I could admit to myself I needed downtime after this, but I would not tell the others. I was already the weakest link in terms of the field agents with this being my first time out. I refused to appear even weaker than I already did.

"If you could take Lady Ketayl out of here, I would like to get started. It will take a while to release them all," Silver said and escorted us to where the furthest victims lay. He handed my TIO coat to Retanei so he could call his sword and shield and waited until we were back next to Artemis.

Before Silver returned to the interior of the chaos, I reminded him, "I'll still need to dissipate the arcane remnants."

He nodded, looking at me longer than I was comfortable with. I still shook, but reigned in as much as I could. Silver said, "I know. Take the time to recover while I handle this. You need not be in there longer than necessary."

I watched silently as he made his way back in, rubbing my arms, I tried to get the feeling of death off me. I would have to push him for information later.

Though there was so much information to process. I was not sure how I was going to write up a report. The first thing would be to sit down with Silver so I could get his expertise. There was so much in front of me I did not understand.

I pulled out my phone and quickly glanced at the time. I had been in there maybe 15 minutes. Certainly not what it had felt like. Taking a deep breath, I rubbed the bridge of my nose, feeling some relief.

Silver knelt down next to the closest soul and spoke too softly for me to hear. For some reason, I felt the need to take pictures of the event and lifted my camera back up, steadier in the short time out of there. My lens had a good enough zoom I could get in tight to watch him. The tip of his sword came down on the black tendril anchoring the soul in place. Quickly it dissolved, freeing the little girl. She went from crying to peaceful, her form rising and disappearing in a mist.

I felt something break inside and stamped it down. This was not the time to get emotional. Artemis whined next to me.

I also noticed as each remnant lost its power source, arcane mites started to appear. The wild swirling of colors slowed. I stood too far away to make out the bands of runes.

The snow continued to fall silently as the souls of the dead were released one by one, and I made sure to document each. Perhaps knowing their friends and family had moved on would help those remaining heal.

Did I need to dissipate the arcane remnants? They looked like they would naturally do so on their own. But they already caused enough problems and I should collect a sample of the arcane mites. I did not know how the arcane remnants would react after being attached to a divine power source - especially for a length of time.

I put my camera back in my bag and dug out a small container, using my power to line it with arcane energy. The arcane mites would need something to eat. Protocol said I should coat it with energy from the arcane remnant, but it was so tainted. I did not want to be walking around with a miniature version of this spell, remnant or not.

I waited for neither of my companions as I waded back into the chaos. The last of the souls had been freed, the black tendrils gone, and all that was left were the arcane remnants. What was left was a mere echo of its former power. I could handle this. My head still pounded, but I could work through it.

Kneeling down next to an arcane remnant, I gently scooped up a few arcane mites. Putting the cover back on, I looked at the little worm-like things a moment before putting it into my pocket. My backpack was too large and I did not want to risk it getting damaged.

Silver stood over me with his arms crossed - his sword and shield away. Retanei handed him the coat as I stood up. I turned away - standing stubbornly before him and daring him to say something would be ridiculous given the height difference.

Putting my bag on the ground, I opened my arms to the remnant, mentally preparing myself for what I had to do.

"Ket, do you have to do this? Don't these things dissipate on their own?" The sound of worry was distinct in Retanei's voice.

I paused, my arms drooped slightly - the shaking I was trying to hide showed itself. I already considered the option, but Retanei questioning my choice made me rethink my course of action for the moment.

"Lady Ketayl, you're still shaking. This can wait," Silver said, his hand on my left arm, gently pushing it down.

Out of reflex, I jerked my arm away. "I don't know if the arcane remnants will dissipate normally and I don't want to chance it. They have already caused enough damage." I stopped and took a deep breath, centering myself. "This doesn't require much." My words sounded more sure than I was. It did not help I was chilled through either.

Retanei moved, digging into my bag. "You can get so stubborn about things. I never thought I would find someone worse than your sister. The least we can do is document the arcane remnants are being destroyed." She pulled out my camera, the arcane filter still on it.

Destroyed. That was the word I needed to firm up my resolve for this. Opening my arms back up fully, I closed my eyes, feeling for the arcane remnant before me with my power, slowly breaking it apart. First was to pull the blended spells apart, then break down the power woven into each individual spell.

I felt sorry for the arcane mites which handled this naturally, but I could not risk anyone else being hurt by this twisted magic.

Anger again pushed at my control and I focused it, using the power it provided to destroy the arcane remnants faster. Perhaps not the wisest option, but an effective one.

It still took me the better part of an hour to finish. Silver casted something under his breath and stood close to my back. I was not sure if it was him or if I had simply gone numb, but I did not feel the bite of the cold as much.

As the last arcane remnant was shredded and disappeared into nothing, my body gave up the pretense of being strong and I collapsed. I had nothing left. It should not have required much of my energy to do this task, but I was exhausted. Silver managed to catch me before my knees hit the floor. It took a moment to realize it was not my arcane reserves which were drained. This was something different.

The cold came back in a rush as did my headache.

IT WAS late by the time we left the Waking Dawn. Silver insisted on carrying me back to the truck and I fought him the whole way. He wanted to head directly back to the hotel so I could rest, I needed to head back to the office to download the pictures to add them to the case file for the others.

Retanei settled the argument by calling Savanas. She in turn ordered us back to the office for a report on what we found. From what little I caught of the conversation, Retanei had not given any details.

I was not sure why I fought so hard against Silver. We had to figure out how to work together. Thinking about it a bit more, I pushed against Kitteren when she gave me unwanted attention. I hated being treated as if I were glass. But even Kitteren did not know what I was able to take.

It did not change the feeling of being weak in the eyes of the others.

Retanei drove as I huddled in the backseat with all the heat vents pointed toward me. Despite Silver's protest that I should take the front, I was smaller and it made more sense to let him with his long legs have it. I also found it meditative to rub Artemis' head - the action took the edge off my headache.

I was thoroughly frozen through. Both physically and mentally. How could one person do this? What would drive someone to do something like this? I should have inquired more with Archmage Maewon. I would have to get Savanas' permission to discuss further details of the case with him.

"M'lady? Are you well?" Silver asked and tried to turn to look at me, but I had huddled in the seat behind him out of his line of sight. It was an odd question given that he knew what I just put myself through. Or maybe I was better at hiding how bad I hurt than I thought.

And how could I be well with what we just witnessed? Thinking about it made me sick again. Taking a slow, deep breath, I replied, "Yeah." It was the most I trusted myself to say. A lie for certain, but they did not need to know the truth.

"You're not, but you will be. It takes a while to get past something like that." Retanei's words of wisdom yet again and it did not surprise me she saw through my front.

It was odd she was several years younger than me and yet was the one keeping a level head. I did not want to think about what horrors she had witnessed. Even though I had become close friends with her, I was finding I truly knew little about her.

Silence was our companion the remainder of the way to the office. Artemis rubbed her head against my cheek and I curled into her, finding warmth and solace.

GETTING OUT, Retanei tossed me the keys. "Sorry, Ket, but you're going to have to get the two of you back to the hotel. We're going hunting. Tell Savanas she'll have my report by morning."

"Sure thing," I replied. If I did not have Silver with me, I would probably have simply decided to stay at the office and rest at my temporary desk. Rest would help alleviate the pounding in my head.

"Move my stuff to your room so Silver can have the other bed," Retanei said, waving and headed for a different vehicle with Artemis at her heels.

Hefting my bag up on my shoulder, I signaled for Silver to follow. I was not exactly in the mood for conversation. Thankfully, he seemed to understand and remained silent.

Brad greeted us as we got off the elevator. The smile quickly left his face. "Hey, you two don't look so good."

At this stage, I did not care. The most I mustered was a half-hearted wave. I collapsed at my temporary desk, digging out the camera and cable to get the download started.

I should be more careful about my appearance in front of others, but I was too tired to care. I was also too busy fighting to keep myself centered, which was not helping the headache. Pleasantries were not high on my priority list at the moment.

I normally worried about appearances as to not draw attention to myself. To look normal, blend in, what have you. I knew how different I was and I long learned the importance of hiding everything. Even how I felt.

I could not look up when Savanas commented, "You two look like you've seen a ghost. Why do I have a feeling I should have gone with you?"

I had... I had seen many ghosts. I merely pointed to the computer to which she promptly came over.

Savanas said in a breath, "Gods preserve us..."

Before the others could wander over into the already too tight space, Savanas quickly typed on my keyboard and put up one of the first images I took this evening on the large screen. My own gaze was drawn to the blown-up image.

It was one of the entire scene: wildly swirling colors of the arcane remnants contrasted by the agony of the souls trapped by black tendrils. The blown-out walls, the broken bar, the thrown about tables and chairs, the blasted bottles and screens, the blood splattered everywhere - none of it had anything on the magic used to cause the destruction.

"Can one of you explain to me how this was possible?" Savanas asked, looking at both of us. The rest of her crew were busy in different stages of shock and repulsion. Brad covered his mouth while Darius stared with his wide open. Rathal clenched his fists and looked away, muttering something under his breath.

Silver found his voice first, "My aura - I am a Paladin of the Holy Church of the Sun. It illuminates the darkness. Apparently the camera was able to pick it up. I didn't see all of this though." He moved toward the screen and pointed at the arcane remnants.

I jumped into the conversation, "That's essentially my ability to see the arcane. The camera has a filter on it to be able to capture it." This was something I could focus on. "These images will show the full spell used. I was unable to see the divine side before."

The change to business helped regain the level of control I needed - I could push my emotions back and focus down on the pure facts. Like I did back in my lab.

Savanas had gone back to her desk and typed quickly. She asked, "What else happened?"

"I released the souls so they could move on and find peace," Silver said.

I quickly added as I dug the small container with the arcane mites out of my coat pocket, "I took pictures of everything."

Rathal asked, "Did it look like the arcane remnants were starting to degrade at all?"

"Yes, I collected a sample of the arcane mites that appeared once the power source was disconnected. I also destroyed the arcane remnants - I wasn't sure how well they would dissipate normally given that they were attached to a divine power source for an extended length of time," I said.

That was it: cold, hard facts. I did not need to think about the horror of souls being used as a power source. Though it did not give me much respite from the building headache.

"Leave your gear here and go get some rest. I'll review the files and plan our next course of action. I take it Retanei already left?" Savanas asked. She never seemed to skip a beat.

"Yes, she said she would have her report to you by morning."

Savanas cursed under her breath.

Hesitantly I requested, "I would like to speak in more detail with Archmage Maewon on this case. See if he can't give us something more substantial to go on," I had nearly forgotten about asking to speak with him again.

Savanas chewed on her bottom lip for a moment. "Fine, but I may call you in depending on if we get authorization to speak with Magister Browne again. Silver, do you mind accompanying her?"

Speaking with the Magister was another headache I was not looking forward to.

Silver bowed and said, "It would be my honor."

Again, Rathal glared at Silver and the paladin returned the look. My headache was getting worse and I did not want to be between them right now. Pinching the bridge of my nose, I tried to think of what I needed to do next.

"Ket, why don't you head down to Doc's office and get yourself looked at?" Savanas suggested, "You really don't look good and I don't think you're safe to drive right now."

Her look told me that while her words and tone sounded like a suggestion, it was an order.

Rathal and Silver both offered to go with me at the same time. It only made my head hurt more. What was with the two of them. I could understand if Rathal had not been able to burn off the effects of his exposure. I did not understand Silver.

"Rathal, escort her down and then get back up here quickly. We have work to do," Savanas said.

While Savanas ordered Rathal, I switched to rubbing my temples. Neither spot worked to relieve the headache. The fact my normal means of soothing the pain were not working was only frustrating me and made the headache worse.

Rathal basically pulled me from my chair. "Definitely time to go see Doc."

Before he could get an arm around me, I moved away. "I can walk." I could not afford to appear weak at this stage. I made it through the chaotic hell in the Waking Dawn, I could get down a couple of floors.

9

As soon as the elevator doors closed, Rathal stood directly in front of me and pulled me against him. Until I felt his warmth, I had not realize I was still chilled. My headache had taken priority. "What are you doing?" I asked as evenly as I could. I was scared - I did not understand this behavior.

"Trying to help."

I rolled my eyes and regretted doing so as a sharp pain shot through my head. Rest would help more than this awkward hug.

Trying to back away, I found I could not break his hold. I simply did not have the energy for it. It bothered me I could not figure out why I was so tired. It felt like physical exhaustion, but that made no sense.

"When this is all over and you don't have your shadow, we should get dinner. There's a really nice seafood place near my apartment. Best seafood in Ocean's Edge."

Black hair dangled into my vision as he rested his head on mine. One of his hands rubbed my back.

I refused to admit the action made me feel slightly better. I tried to squirm out - my discomfort overrode Rathal's attempt at soothing. As soon as the elevator dinged, I managed to break out of his loosened hold.

"Um, thanks. Maybe. I can find my way from here." I hit the

button for the third floor and stepped out of the elevator quickly before Rathal could respond.

Once the elevator started making its way back up, I leaned back against the wall and rubbed my arms. I dislike being touched.

After finding out Doc was not in his office, Melody directed me down to autopsy with a packet to deliver. The elevator dinged again and I cringed, the sound making my headache worse. At least I did not have an escort anymore.

The doors to autopsy were within view of the elevator. There was no getting lost this time. I peeked in through the glass doors, not wanting to walk in and disturb him.

The lights were off on this side of the room. Doc was at the other end of the large room, almost out of view, next to a large bank of small doors. I could not see what he was doing so I gently knocked on the door in front of me, jumping when it made a louder sound than I intended.

Looking up, Doc smiled and waved me in. As soon as I was inside, he asked softly, "Ketayl, what brings you down here?"

Walking slowly, I took in the room around me. I had never been in an autopsy lab before. It was cold; I ran my free hand over my arm, huddling at the temperature change.

"Savanas wanted me to come see you. Melody also sent me down with this," I said, holding out the packet.

Doc adjusted the height of the wheeled table he was next to and pushed the platform a small form laid upon onto the shelf at an open door. The sound felt sharp and final. "Thank you. That is probably the paperwork so I can release a few more of my charges back to their families."

He had a Human adolescent laying before him. The boy was clean and for all the world looked like he slept - the white sheet only showing his head and the tops of his shoulders. I had to back up a few steps and cover my mouth, knowing he was one of the victims.

Doc quickly covered him with a sheet and pushed the shelf back into the wall. The sound of the door slamming shut echoed loudly through my already hurting head. I felt like I could not breathe.

Suddenly Doc stood before me, asking something, but I could not hear over the pounding. I fought for control as I felt the wave of arcane energy surge in me. Then the world went black.

THE FIRST THING I noticed is it was not as cold. Opening my eyes, I could not get my bearings as to where I was. It looked a lot like the examination rooms at the main office.

"Hey, girl," said a female voice I did not recognize.

Turning to look, I felt like I should know her. The orange suit reminded me I had only seen her in passing when Retanei and I arrived. Her name escaped me.

"I'll be right back. Need to let Doc know you're back in the land of the living," she said.

The one thing I remembered was having one of the worst headaches. My head hurt significantly less. I managed to sit up and was immediately hit with a wave of dizziness. A small, strong pair of hands steadied me.

"Easy there, girl. You gave Doc quite a scare." The woman was back - I had not heard her return. She continued, "He'll be here in a few minutes. He's still talking with the boss lady."

Her dark cropped hair was tucked up under a hat. Grease smeared her cheek.

It took me a minute to follow what she said. I finally asked, "Where am I?"

"This is one of Doc's patient rooms. After you passed out, he called me to help bring you up here. I was in the garage behind autopsy servicing the van so sorry if I got you a little dirty," she said, sounding a little too cheerful. "My name's Sasha by the way. We crossed paths briefly when you landed."

"Ketayl," I replied. What else could I say? I have never had this problem before. Blacking out only made me look weak and incompetent. I was not sure how I was going to explain myself to Savanas and the others. Retanei certainly would lecture me later.

Doc entered, his tablet in front of him, humming softly. He tucked it into one of the large pockets on his lab coat before sitting down on a stool next to me. A smile was on his face, but I was not sure why his eyes did not match that expression.

"How are you feeling?" Doc asked.

"Better," I said, "I'm sorry."

"No need to apologize. Thank you for keeping an eye on her, Sasha. Sorry to have kept you."

Sasha quickly got to her feet and smiled as she said, "No worries. I was waiting for the recycler to finish running anyway." She waved as she left.

Once the door closed, Doc turned back to me, pulling up a stool. His face turned to concern. "Ketayl, I need you to tell me how you were feeling before you passed out."

"I had a bad headache, then I saw the boy and..." I had a hard time breathing again. Closing my eyes, I pulled myself back to center and blocked everything else out. I had seen some gruesome images sent my way. Surely I could deal with seeing a body in person.

I knew I was in my meditative state for at least a few minutes. I had no idea why I struggled to maintain control. Normally it was not this hard, even when something caught me off-guard.

Taking a deep breath once I found my balance again, Doc's face was far too close to mine and I jerked back. Savanas was also in the room. She occupied a seat along the wall - her expression neutral.

"Well, that was something else," Savanas commented. I had no idea what she was talking about.

I looked away, and said, "I'm sorry. I needed to regain control." I had no idea what she spoke of, but I could at least apologize for not responding.

"I'll say you did," said Savanas cryptically again. Now I was confused.

Doc made me open my mouth to take my temperature. He chided, "Savanas, take it easy on the poor girl. I didn't think anything of her entering autopsy with how often you folks upstairs just pop in. I'm sorry about that, Ketayl."

I nodded, unable to say anything with the thermometer in my mouth. I heard it beep and was grateful to be free of it a moment later.

Noises came from the phone in Savanas' hand. It was too low to make out what was going on. For all I knew, she was playing a game.

"Do you still have a headache?" Doc asked me, jotting something down on a clipboard.

"A little. Not like before."

Sitting back on his chair after a few more tests, Doc looked at

Savanas and said, "Her vitals look good. Physically speaking, I have no problem with releasing her. This new problem, I'm not comfortable with." Then he turned back to me, "I have something I can give you for the headache." He patted my leg and left.

New problem? By his statement it was not physical. I would have to ask when he returned.

Savanas was staring me down. She said, "Just so you know, I had to contact Retanei and nearly interrogate Silver to find out what happened earlier. Both seemed reluctant to talk about the risks you took at the Waking Dawn. That's saying little of the protocols I needed to remind Rathal of."

I could not remember swearing them to secrecy. I also had not thought much time had passed. I sat quietly and waited for the rest of what she had to say.

"That was when you passed out," Savanas specified. "This," she turned her phone toward me so I could watch the video, "has so far stayed between myself and Doc."

The video showed me sitting perfectly still, but the occasional wave or spark of pure arcane energy wove itself up my arms. It was more of a reaction than I ever had before. I tilted my head, not understanding what I was seeing before me.

"By the look on your face, I'm going to guess this is new," Savanas said as she turned her phone back.

Doc returned with the medication and a cup of water. I did not like medication - especially if I did not know how it would affect me. Sometimes it made it harder to maintain my balance.

I took it without putting up a fuss. He was just looking out for my well-being and right now, there was a better chance of it helping me regain my balance than not. And I trusted he consulted my records. There were a couple of medications I reported not having an issue with.

"Ket seemed surprised. You want to keep this between us for now, Doc?" Savanas asked.

"Confidentiality is a specialty of mine," Doc said and smiled. "Though I'm not happy about not understanding what that was."

Savanas pursed her lips before she said, "I don't either, but I've got two hotheads upstairs. It would be adding fuel to the fire. On the other side, I don't want Vince or Lockonis here if I can help it - I've already got Naval Command breathing down my neck. I'll bring

Retanei in on this since she knows Ket better and I'll make some discreet inquiries with the EAC."

I ducked my head, now I was a liability. I wanted so much not to show weakness I ended up with the exact opposite. I worried I would not be taken seriously.

I also wish I understood what Savanas was talking about half the time. What was going on upstairs? I opened my mouth to ask and then closed it. The exasperated expression on her face had made me reconsider.

She blew a sharp breath of air through her bangs. Crossing her arms over her chest, Savanas said, "Ket, let's get your stuff so you can get some rest. We're going to need to figure out what caused this so it doesn't happen again. Consider it a side project and report directly to me. Also, anymore of whatever that was, I need you to report also. Understood?"

"Yes, ma'am," I said quietly. I hoped there was not a next time on a reaction of that magnitude.

10

Once I parked at the hotel, I rested my head on the steering wheel. I was not sure I could continue this investigation, not with what was happening to me. I thought about calling Lockonis and discussing the idea, but Savanas had not wanted to alert them to the problems I had. I questioned how good of an idea it was.

"M'lady?"

I sat up straight, gripping the steering wheel tightly enough to make my leather gloves creak. "Ketayl. It's Ketayl and I could really use some normalcy right about now." Him calling me that made me snap and it came out sounding more whiny than aggravated.

Calm - I needed to calm down and find my balance. My headache still had not gone away, but medication took time, right? Rest would be the best cure.

Silver left the vehicle and I thought perhaps I drove him off. I was not sure how I felt about that, but then my door opened and he held his hand out. "Ketayl, let's go get some rest - at least some place more comfortable than here," he said.

I could not help but give him a small smile. I said, "Sure." Logic was usually the best way to get through to me. I ignored his hand and got out, but he grabbed it anyway.

I reclaimed my hand under the pretense of taking off my gloves and putting the keys away. Silence fell between us as we made our way to the suite.

When we arrived, I went into the room Retanei had claimed and moved her belongings to my room. Silver said nothing and moved his own stuff.

Once the task was done, I stood there in my now shared room, unsure of what I should do next. The instrument case sitting next to my suitcase caught my attention.

Mother let me try a number of different instruments to see what I might take to. I handled a fair number in the short time from the major races, but the violin was my favorite. She and my sister were the only ones who understood why, though I never spoke of it.

The Magus pushed me to explore things outside of the arcane. Many students took to music and Mother happily taught anyone interested. She said it helped to keep her grounded. I never quite understood her statement as well as I did right now.

A knock on the bedroom door made me jump. "I'm sorry, Ketayl. I saw a restaurant downstairs and thought we should go get... Who owns that?" Silver was pointing at the violin case.

For a moment, I considered lying, but realized it was pointless. It was too late to hide it. "It's mine. Retanei made me bring it for some reason."

It had fit inside of my suitcase so it was not a burden to bring. I did not have many clothes. Thinking about it, I would have to take the time to use my magic to clean them soon.

"Did you want to play?"

I turned away from it. "Maybe later. I can go downstairs with you."

A fourth, smaller meal was common amongst Elves, while I had no appetite, I remembered I skipped breakfast. I knew the sandwich earlier would not be enough to last until morning. I should be able to get down a small snack. I was not even certain the restaurant would still be open, but it was likely as we were in Elven Territory.

<hr>

THE RESTAURANT WAS STILL OPERATING and busy, but not so busy we waited to be seated. I could hear the murmurs from other tables talking about the bombing.

Savanas was not kidding about the range of people here, though most looked to be military or media. I pulled out my phone to send a quick message to Savanas.

"What's wrong?" Silver asked, looking worried.

I signaled him to wait a moment so I could finish and send it. Then I said, "I want to double-check and see what the policy is about dealing with the media. We're the ones investigating, so to them, we'll be the ones with the answers."

I found amusement in Savanas' response. Silver looked at me expectantly, so I read it aloud: "I'm not answering questions - send them to Vince." It was the rare occasion of watching something get passed up the chain of command. For us to take the time to stop and answer questions would only slow us down in finding them.

He pointed at the menu and said, "Please, choose something. I have enough to cover both of us."

I raised my eyebrow at his offer. "You're under the TIO for the moment..."

Silver quickly countered, "I may be, but we're not working. Besides, I have never had the pleasure of treating a lady to a meal. At least not outside of church business."

Those blue eyes locked with mine and I figured arguing would only give me a headache on top of the one I was still getting rid of. Silver said he rarely left his church's grounds. It really was not far-fetched as I had only gone out to eat when Kitteren and Mother visited me at the Arcane College. Otherwise I stayed within the confines of the school.

Begrudgingly, I put my phone away and looked at the menu. Pushing recent images aside, I settled on a salad.

Silver apparently did not like my selection and commented, "You should eat something more substantial than that."

I rubbed the bridge of my nose. "Sorry, but my appetite is pretty well gone after what we witnessed earlier."

"I understand." Silver let it hang there as a waitress came to take our orders. Once she left however, he was intent on figuring out my motivations. "Why did you do it, Ketayl? I could see how hard you were fighting to remain in there. Retanei offered to take your place for taking pictures."

"She couldn't. I could have tried to describe what I was looking for, but there was a chance she wouldn't understand and I would not have the images I need to do a full analysis."

I knew the reality was Retanei would have taken far more than I needed. I certainly would have had enough to work with, but professional pride was something I could not ignore.

I was also not about to bow down to someone who sent a shadow puppet.

Then I wondered where that last part came from. Perhaps I was picking up on Kitteren's stubborn streak.

Silence settled between us until our food was delivered. Then he asked, "So, you are also a musician?"

"I wouldn't say that. Mother taught me, but I fear I have no real talent for it," I admitted. All I could do was play what was before me. I could not create like she could.

The fork stopped halfway to his mouth. "Mother?"

"Adopted."

"Oh." The remainder of our meal continued by Silver pressing me for more information, and in turn I would turn the questions around without answering if possible.

<hr>

ALL THROUGH OUR MEAL, I could feel the gazes of people linger on us. Neither of us carried any outer markings of being with the TIO. Perhaps we were an oddity between all the military personnel and media. I was dressed more commonly in a sweater, jeans, and boots, but Silver's attire stood out. The large amount of white would draw anyone's attention.

I was grateful we decided to go to the room first to leave our coats. I could only imagine the interruptions we would have dealt with my TIO coat out.

There was an older man in a highly decorated military uniform who kept his gaze on us the entire time we were there. It made me nervous and I ate quickly, not even tasting my meal. I wanted to get out of the restaurant and Silver seemed to be of the same mind.

When we got back to the room, I decided to clean up before getting some rest. A normal four hours of rest would be enough even given the day's events.

I left the door to my room cracked so I could hear Silver moving about. He had also decided to wash away the day's grime before trying to get some rest.

As I brushed my hair, I found myself staring at the black violin case. It was something I found myself doing more to maintain my balance rather than to actually practice.

Using a quick spell to dry my hair, I picked up the case and put it on the bed. Being an electric violin, it was quiet so I would not disturb anyone.

My fingers brushed the purple and black finish before picking it up and pulling out the headphones. I had it tuned before I realized what I was doing.

Sitting in the middle of the large bed, I lost myself in the music. Songs I had studied. Pieces Mother had written for me. Anything.

Most of them ended up sounding as sorrowful as I felt. I kept my eyes closed and let the sound coming through the headphones wash away everything. Just as the water washed away the physical filth, my mind felt clearer. The remainder of my headache was gone.

I did not know how much time had passed. My fingers hurt and my arms felt heavy, I knew that much.

Pulling the headphones down to hang around my neck, a sound by my door caught my attention.

Silver stood there. The heat rose in my face in embarrassment. I avoided playing in front of others if I could. Mother I was used to, but I rarely let Kitteren around.

I forgot to fully close my door before I started. While it was quiet, the faint sounds would still have drifted out. "I'm so sorry," the apology came out more like a whisper.

His face was solemn as he said, "No, I'm sorry for disturbing you. You play beautifully. Well, good night."

Silver was gone before I could say anything further.

11

IT WAS STILL DARK when I woke. I got ready quickly and quietly. After last night, I wanted to push off interacting with Silver. Perhaps I should not have so readily agreed to let him stay with us.

Finished, I was not sure what to do next. It was early, but not so early I could not blend in with the morning crowd and find something for breakfast.

Figuring it the best course of action, I put on my personal coat and grabbed my tablet, stuffing it into one of the large pockets as I made my way toward the door. Going for a short walk also granted me the ability to avoid Silver for a while longer and mentally work through what I knew on the case. Perhaps I could also find a quiet corner to curl up in and do some research.

Thinking it would be rude to leave Silver with nothing, I scribbled a note on the hotel stationary, leaving it on the counter with my phone number. At least he would be able to use the hotel phone if needed. I also left a promise of returning with food.

I headed out, wondering if I would pass Retanei en route. I was not sure how long she planned on hunting for, but as long as it was dark, she would probably be out there. I worried for her safety, but I understood her task. With her skills, she stood the best chance of tracking down the group and her vision in the darkness granted her an advantage.

As soon as I left the warmth of the hotel, I pulled my coat closer around me. It stopped snowing, but it was still frigid out. I quickly made my way to a cafe I drove past a few times now - it looked like a cozy place to study.

By the time I got there it was so busy I had no chance of finding a corner to huddle into. Students of both the EAC and the local University had taken over the place. I guess I would have to get something to take back for myself, Retanei, and Silver. Looking around, I made a mental note to get here earlier next time.

Since the line was nearly out the door, there was time to figure out what I wanted at least. Then I realized I had no idea what Silver's tastes were. Retanei, at least, I knew well enough to guess.

Having ample time to browse the menu high above the back of the counter, I still spent too much time making a decision on what to get Silver. Then I was at the front of the line with no solid plan. Taking a chance, I ordered lavender tea with honey for both of us and a selection of different pastries, hoping he would find something he liked. Retanei did not seem overly picky, but any hot drink I got would likely be cold by the time she got to it.

Cold lavender tea was good, but not in the middle of winter so I hustled back to the hotel with my purchases.

The hotel lobby was busier and I bumped into the same portly gentleman in uniform from last night. He was an older man, dark gray hair starting to lighten further at his temples. An impressive set of ribbons adorned his dark blue uniform.

"My apologies, sir. Please excuse me."

"Ah, the girl I was hoping to run into. Do you have a moment?" He asked and gestured to the side, away from the media gathering. It was still a public venue, but it would afford us a moment to speak quietly.

I nodded and followed him.

Once we were out of earshot he said, "I'm Admiral Jonathan Scott from Terran Naval Command. I was hoping you could give me an update into this investigation."

I could not salute and he probably did not want me to in order to avoid drawing attention. Otherwise he would have approached me last night. I could see a few curious glances our way from people who looked like they belonged with the media.

I shrank back and answered, "Sir, I'm sorry, I was told all questions are to be sent to the Director."

Admiral Scott seemed disappointed, but not surprised. "I had a feeling that would be your answer. Then let me make a suggestion: you need to talk to your Magister and tell him to get the Arcane College off my ass." He walked away.

Arcane College? I hurried to catch up and said, "Wait, sir. Please, tell me what is going on."

Admiral Scott stopped and turned to glare me down. He kept his voice low, "It's simple, the Magister has filed complaints against anyone who has even broached the subject of this investigation and now he refuses to talk. If you're the agent I think you are, you should have some pull."

He left me standing there, wondering how this Admiral even knew who I was. I had been hoping to speak with Archmage Maewon this morning, but it did not look like I would get the chance.

But why would the Arcane College get involved if it was just a Magister? High Mages would barely be given a thought.

Taking a few steps back, I quickly headed for the elevator. There was a phone call I needed to make.

SILVER WAS NOT out in the common area when I got back. I dropped everything on the counter and pulled out my phone. Then I noticed the note was gone. I paused wondering if I should let him know I was back.

I shook my head and called Savanas. I bounced on the balls of my feet.

"Farstrider."

The moment she answered, I spoke rapidly, getting it all out while I still held the train of thought, "Savanas, it's Ketayl. I ran into Admiral Jonathan Scott in the lobby. He wants..."

"Hey! Slow down. Admiral Jonathan Scott of Terran Naval Command? Crap, I was hoping to not have to deal with him. What did you tell him when he wanted answers?" Savanas asked. She seemed to be taking this a lot more calmly.

I could not slow down and my mouth was getting ahead of me. I told her, "Nothing, well, not nothing. I told him to talk to the Director."

"Okay, so what has you so worked up? Did he threaten you?" Savanas' calm started to wear off on me.

I said awkwardly, "I don't think so?" I was not even sure what the encounter was. "He said he wanted me to talk to the Magister since he's been filing complaints with the Arcane College and the Arcane College has been harassing him." Harassing? Was that the proper thing to infer from our conversation? "Admiral Scott thinks I might have some sort of pull with the Magister."

"Not likely, but it's an avenue I have been considering. I'll get in touch with Admiral Scott and get a better idea of what is going on. Cancel your plans for the morning and come in." Then Savanas hung up.

"Ketayl?" Silver asked. He stood at the doorway to his room. "I was finishing my morning prayers when I heard you. Is everything alright?"

"I don't know, but I bought some food if you're hungry. I wasn't sure what you liked," I said and forced a smile, taking one of the cups of lavender tea to hide behind. The scent helped calm me. It was my favorite, but some thought it odd.

Silver took the other cup and took a moment to smell what it was before putting it back down. His face told me it was not something he much cared for. He said, "Ketayl, you can talk to me. I'm here to help where I can. I doubt my part ended with releasing those souls."

I dug in the bag for one of the apple-filled pastries while I was settled enough to eat. "Admiral Scott of Terran Naval Command caught me on the way in. I'm afraid this is my first field assignment and I'm not used to dealing with anyone outside of the TIO - I got a little worked up over nothing." It was a lie - I knew it was not nothing.

Silver took a random pastry and sat down on the couch just before the door opened and a worn out Retanei strolled in with Artemis at her heels.

She shook her hair free of her hat and said, "Someone could have warned me about the media vultures." Her coat was wet. Had it snowed overnight?

"Sorry, it was my fault," I admitted.

"Don't worry about it - I'm good at dodging people. I'm going to clean up and get some rest. You wouldn't happen to have any extras?"

Retanei pointed at the pastry in my hand and it took me a second to follow her train of thought. I pushed the bag over to her - I had gotten plenty. She had a thing for sweets.

Silver offered up his untouched drink.

Retanei snagged food and then hurried off to our shared room. Artemis collapsed on the floor by the couch.

I apologized, "I didn't mean to interrupt your morning prayers. Once you're ready, we should get going. Savanas wants us at the office." I should have thought to ask him about the customs of paladins.

"If I was back at the church, I would have wanted you to. Paladin Marsh is leading prayers this week and he can be a bit of a windbag," Silver said it so calmly I choked on my drink. "Are you okay?"

Waving him down, it took a couple of moments to clear my throat. "Sorry, wasn't expecting that."

Silver's smirk told me a little more about the person behind the paladin's armor.

"We should get going," he said. Silver was right, we had no time to spare.

***

I stood before Savanas' desk, explaining why the whole thing bothered me more than she thought it should.

Savanas summarized, "You're saying it is highly unusual for them to care about one of their own they sent into the field? Maybe because of the circumstances?"

I said, "Not likely. I've read the reports from other incidents the Arcane College has had with liaisons. They often distance themselves from anyone lower than an Archmage to keep up relations."

It was an odd setup, but I understood they would rather let one of their own take the fall so they could keep up appearances. It did not happen very often, but there had been a few instances over the years. Mostly involving incidents of the mage forcing another to join with them.

Savanas sat back in her chair and looked over to Rathal who had been interested in our conversation. She idly tapped the arm of her chair, considering something before she said, "Given what we've been able to find out, I've managed to get a warrant to search the Magister's quarters. You are going with me and Rathal. Silver, I don't know what to do with you, but if this is our guy, we'll need someone who is specialized in the divine as well."

"You think it's the Magister?" I asked. I did not understand - a Magister was below a High Mage. I thought gave them a base level before.

As Savanas got her coat on, she said, "We've put eyes on *all* ranked mages in the area. There aren't as many as you would think. The only one we can't account for at the time of the bombing, as well as the lovely little greeting in our lobby, is the Magister. Since he is the only one who won't cooperate, the judge was more than happy to issue the warrant."

Rathal jumped into the conversation and asked, "What about Brad and Darius?"

Savanas shook her head and said, "They're still conducting interviews - I'd rather they kept priority on making sure we find out who else was affected and how badly. We don't need that large of a team to talk to the Magister."

1 2

IT WAS NOT long before we were loaded into Savanas' car. She had brought Big Black in, but left him with Melody who was intent on spoiling him. There would not have been enough room for all of us.

Once we turned down to the docks, the massive naval vessel came into view. All I could do was stare at the size of it.

I had never been this close to one before and I edged on excited to get on board and explore.

As we got out of the vehicle the salt air and sounds of maintenance greeted me. The mounted guns were the largest I had ever seen. This was a battleship class vessel - its offensive and defensive capabilities were the best of all the vessels currently in service.

Rathal spoke about them during the ride. He called the battleships "the lone wolves of the fleet" as they often sailed without other vessels.

Nowadays, with a mostly centralized government, the navy spent more time tracking down pirates than engaging in inter-territorial disputes. A mage was needed to power the defensive shielding. I wanted to know how it worked. Perhaps if there was a chance I could get a quick look at the system...

"Wonderment later, work now," Savanas scolded gently. "We can ask the captain after the investigation is over if we can have a quick tour before they depart." She winked at me.

I was not sure what to make of Savanas. She knew what happened yesterday and yet she acted like nothing was out of the ordinary. A comment about two hotheads came to mind and I eyed Silver and Rathal who were glaring each other down. When we loaded up, they argued so much over who would should sit in front that Savanas ordered me take it.

What the problem was between the two, I still did not understand. Why I seemed to be in the middle, I understood less.

I followed, pushing those thoughts aside and hefting my bag. I was not sure what the Magister would truly be like. I had a good idea of what his general personality would be, but given the circumstances, it could send it to an extreme in a few undesirable directions.

He would likely focus his attention on me to further avoid questioning. I was unsure if I should expect stark-raving mad or to be verbally torn down in that monotone so many of the higher mages adopted. Either way, if he decided to use his abilities to make an example or punish, I doubted I could defend myself against him.

My Arcane College pin was in my pocket. I thought about putting it on if only to give the Magister one less thing to be mad about. The movement would be obvious and I did not want to draw attention to myself. I also really did not want to put it back on - the thread bothered me.

We met with the captain first. He was an older Human - his cap sat on a bald head. "I wondered how long it was going to take you guys to come for my pain in the ass. I didn't think it possible for him to get worse, but he managed it after your last visit."

Savanas' face remained neutral. "I would like to hear more of your take on him. I had the pleasure of hearing your first officer's opinion the last time," she said.

"If you can get him out of his room it would be a sheer miracle. He hasn't left in over a day and won't even accept the food he insisted be delivered to his quarters," the captain said. Once he stood up, the captain stood taller than me and despite his visible age, he was fit. "Last time you met with him in the conference room, but since we can't get him out, I'll take you to him. I should warn you he's used his magic to alter his room to his liking. Wish I could have thrown him overboard for that."

We followed the captain through the narrow hallways in single file. I ended up at the back of the group. Rathal and Silver had an ongoing rivalry, trying to not appear as if they were shoving each other into the bulkheads. I should have been weary of their actions, but it gave me something to focus on other than the impending meeting with the Magister.

Granted, I was not completely unaware of what was going on - I knew Savanas planned to use me as bait to lure the Magister out. I just hoped she knew what she was getting us into and had some sort of plan.

As we approached, two men stood outside as guards. At some point, Silver managed to push his loaned coat's sleeves up to his elbows and called out his weapons. I could not recall seeing the dagger before on his right hip. He left both blades sheathed for the moment.

The captain knocked hard on the door and called out loudly, "Magister Browne, open up! The TIO needs to speak with you."

Silence was the only reply.

The captain shook his head and admitted, "I wish I could order him around since this is my boat, but he's not one of my sailors and I prefer not to have the Arcane College up my ass."

The corridor was silent except for the sounds of the ship's daily activities. What was maybe half a minute felt so much longer. What if he decided to attack? Being as gathered together as we were made me nervous.

Savanas tried next, "Magister Browne, this is Agent Savanas Farstrider with the TIO. I brought our Arcane College liaison with us to speak with you."

Again, more silence.

Savanas signaled to the men to open it and drew a gun from under her coat.

Rathal followed Savanas' lead and I stood back with Silver who drew his dagger. I sensed no arcane traps at the door, but it did not mean we were free of dangers. Savanas looked back to me and I nodded, conjuring a small ball of arcane energy in my hand. It would be easier to manipulate to my needs in this state.

The captain turned his attention to me. I had given my TIO coat to Silver and left my hat back at the hotel again. And now I was conjuring arcane energy. I made myself his target. At least I decided against wearing my pin.

I shrank back from the captain and dispersed the energy. I had not thought about the crew's reaction to that bit of information.

I heard a "Clear!" from the other side of the now open door.

"Farstrider, care to tell me why you neglected to mention you brought another Arcane College mage?" The captain asked angrily.

"Calm down, Captain. Ketayl is our Arcane Investigator. She previously served at the Arcane College as a Researcher, but she's one of mine now. If it wasn't for her, we might still be chasing our tails at the crime scene. I hoped her presence would lure him out, but he's obviously not here," Savanas said, standing in the doorway. She signaled me to come in.

From where I stood, I could see the changes made to the room. Wood flooring and walls, it was also made to be larger inside than the dimensions of the room would normally allow. Antique-style furniture adorned the room, though the bed was pushed against the wall to allow for more working space.

It was going to take a lot of effort to reverse the changes made by Brown. This was permanent magic in the sense the changes he made did not require any further power to maintain.

Walking in cautiously, I put the gloves on Rathal handed me. My eyes were drawn to a point on the floor in the center of the room. "He teleported. Late last night was the last one." I dug into my gear bag and grabbed a sample of the arcane mites before I pulled out the camera and took pictures.

"Wait, he teleported more than once?" The captain asked, anger still in his voice. I wondered how much was still directed at me, but I needed to focus.

Kneeling down in the spot Browne preferred to perform his teleportations, I prepared to trace the golden lines, grateful they did not disappear as quickly as remnants did. I was familiar with teleportation. I knew what it felt like to ride the wave of magic. How disorienting it was to appear somewhere else. Well, unless you were used to it.

Letting my eyes unfocus, I used my power to ride the golden arc. No need to physically follow it. It was still a bit of a head rush to extend myself like this. I was glad it did not take long to hit the end of each and see where he had been. The level of degradation on the arcs gave me a timeline.

"Every couple of days or so. Some are too far away now for me to follow, but the more recent ones…" I trailed off, memorizing the area of the last teleport. "He went into the forest outside of the city on this last one. Prior, he was near the Waking Dawn, and not far from the TIO office - those are the anomalies in the pattern."

I stood up, rubbing my eyes to get my bearings back to my immediate surroundings. Savanas stood next to me, but made no comment about my actions. She wrote down what I told them. Though it was hard to read her shorthand.

"Well, if that isn't suspicious. Unfortunately, circumstantial," Savanas said.

Silver folded his arms and remained as far outside the door as he could, which caught my attention. I asked, "Do you see something?"

"There has been death, but the power holding it is gone. I don't want to shock anyone if I walk in there," Silver said. He stayed as far as he could given the tight quarters.

"Not much left you can shock us with at this point," Rathal said, sounding bored, as he combed through the Magister's closet.

Silver strode forward slowly. The faded images of animals appeared near the outer walls of the ship - the Magister must have been using them to test his spells. I took pictures as fast as I could.

The captain continued to focus on me and asked, "Is that camera special? Because outside of what your boy here is doing, I can't see these teleports you're talking about."

I looked to Savanas who nodded her consent before I walked over to the captain.

"We've developed a prototype filter to see the arcane. It can't follow a teleport line, but at least it can capture the remnants of the spells used. May I show you?" I said. I turned the screen toward him and explained the images I had taken. If nothing else, I could at least put his mind at ease about me.

Rathal dug in his closet and pulled out an emerald green robe. "Well, I can tell you he has no fashion sense."

If the strap had not been around my neck, I would have dropped the camera.

"Oh no…" it came out as a whisper.

"What? Was it something I said?" Rathal asked and looked confused. His attention was on me, but I barely noticed it next to what he was holding.

Walking closer to the garment he held, I pick up the edge of the sleeve to check the embroidery and length. I ran my gloved thumb over the intricately woven threads to see if the color would change as some mages had attempted. The illusion would disappear with contact. It did not and there was no doubt.

"He was an Archmage, not a Magister. The robes can be any color or design, but the sleeve length and the embroidery colors have to match the rank. This gold and platinum embroidery - that's an Archmage. A Magister would be silver and gold and the sleeve would be significantly shorter," I explained after my examination.

"Bag it," Savanas ordered, "Ket, Silver, come over here and tell me if this means anything to either of you."

It was quick, but again I caught Rathal's glare in Silver's direction. It had to be an arcane versus divine disagreement between them. That was the only logical reason I could come up with. Though Silver had no problem with me. I pushed the thought aside as it was only a distraction.

Papers and books were scattered about. Likely he did not care about hiding them since few would be able to read it.

I spoke first, moving a few pages to see more of the arcane theory, "This describes the arcane side of those bombs at least."

Silver simply nodded and looked paler. I would have to ask him later what was written.

"Looks like we have our man. Now to find our Archmage. Ket, I don't care if you wake Retanei. Get on the phone and describe to her the last location you saw him teleport to," Savanas ordered.

Time passed quickly. I called Retanei as ordered. Initially, she sounded groggy, but it disappeared quickly when I explained why I called. After, I went to read the papers, but Savanas stopped me. She wanted everything collected - we could go through it back at the office.

As we left with evidence bagged, the captain stopped me. "I'm man enough to admit when I was wrong. Sorry, kid. I'm damn glad you are on our side."

I smiled and bowed to him. I was unsure what to say at this point. We had so much work ahead of us I tabled my curiosity about the ship. I had a big enough puzzle to put together in the evidence bags.

ONCE WE GOT BACK to the office, I copied the documents left behind by now Archmage Browne.

Silver watched as I touched each document with one hand while keeping my other hand on the computer, using my power to copy the information. I could tell he had questions, but he held his tongue.

Rathal, however, did not and asked, "When did someone develop spells to use with technology?"

I needed to concentrate and took a moment to signal for him to wait. This would not take long, but unlike the books I copied as full volumes, I did notes individually. Also copying directly to the computer took more effort than my old method of storing information.

Once I finished, I put in a call to Lockonis.

"Heya, Ket. What can I do for you?" Lockonis' usual chipper self greeted me.

Taking a deep breath, I organized my thoughts to give her warning her within requesting the favor. I said, "I've added some new files to the library. They're from Browne - he's the caster."

"Oh, this should be juicy. I'll fix the files so they show up in searches. By the way, thank you so much for the horrors we received this morning. I wasn't that fond of breakfast," Lockonis said.

I forgot the files were being uploaded to the central servers. Though access would have been limited to the team working on it and of course those who had access to everything such as Vince and Lockonis. "I'm sorry. I didn't know anyone else was reviewing the case."

"Vince got me started this morning to see if I couldn't give some help from this end. Warped use of magic," I could clearly hear the revulsion in Lockonis' voice. "Listen, Ket, I don't know if anyone has told you you're doing an amazing job - especially given the circumstances. Just don't put yourself at unnecessary risk. I don't think any of us were prepared for this. Necromancers? That's something we haven't seen since the war. Any clue on where this is coming from? There have been no warning signs at all."

Dark auburn strands fell in my vision. I brushed the stray lock of hair out of my face and looked up at Silver, signaling to him to pull up a chair. I said, "Not really. I saw something in the documents referencing either 'True Gods' or 'Ancient Gods' the wording is weird."

Lockonis noted, "I've read Savanas' interview with the first officer who said something about he overheard the crew members who volunteered to deliver Browne his food talking about them also. He thought it might be in relation to some new video game. They were among the dead."

I had not read those documents. Perhaps I should take the time to read the rest of the case file. It might have a piece of the puzzle I was missing.

The typing in the background got louder from Lockonis. She changed topics, "In those pictures, that Elven guy with the silver hair - he's cute. What's it like to work with a paladin?"

I looked up at Silver who now sat at the side of my desk between me and Rathal. I felt the heat rise in my face. I did not understand my reaction, but I was dealing with Lockonis and she often could get past my barriers and confuse me. I redirected, "Um, I better get back to work."

"Awe, you're no fun. He's right there, isn't he? I bet you're turning a lovely shade of red. Okay, I'll be done in about half an hour. Bye!" Lockonis said and hung up before I could say anything further.

"Are you feeling ill? Your face just became flushed," Silver asked and put the back of his hand to my forehead.

I shifted away, but caught the glare coming from Rathal. It was annoying and I wished they would work out their problem, but it was not my place to interfere.

I said, "I'm fine. Lockonis likes to tease me when she can. She's going to fix the files and make them available for search."

"This library, you said it was from the Arcane College?" Silver asked. Rathal rolled his eyes in the background.

Savanas was busy, but she likely saw everything going on. It was something I noticed in the short time I had been here.

Ah, yes, I could see where this might be viewed as a problem. "It's a copy of the Arcane College's library. They don't have access to this one. Oh, shoot, I wanted to ask her about that."

"Ask her about what?" Savanas asked. Well, I was not wrong about her perception.

"The Arcane College's involvement. They were still referring to him as Magister, but he couldn't have had those robes without direct authority from the Circle of Magi," I said.

Darius passed by my desk, tossing a bottle of juice in the air and catching it as he walked. He stopped to ask, "You think the Arcane College is covering for him?"

"It doesn't make any sense. Have they sent a representative to deal with the situation?" I asked. He might not know, but it was worth a shot.

Darius paused and looked back at Savanas who gave the conversation her full attention. He asked her, "I haven't heard of anyone, have you?"

Savanas shook her head and got on the phone.

While we waited, Silver looked at me and finally asked, pointing at the computer, "There are arcane spells to put information on there?"

Rathal's curiosity overrode his dislike of Silver temporarily. Though I heard a low growl from his direction. I had told him to wait, but I needed to finish my train of thought at the time. Then I had gotten distracted.

"Sort of?" It was a difficult subject to explain to someone not well versed in arcane theory. I tried anyway, "There is a program I can send the information to but you need both the science and the magic to work in tandem. Since silicon is a crystalline substance, it takes information well and the program is able to read and process the information I'm storing. It's a little more complicated than that, but..."

I could tell by Silver's face I lost him. Rathal raised an eyebrow.

"It was a lot of trial and error to get it to work," I admitted. And some sleep-deprived inspiration.

Darius still hung by my desk, shaking his head. "Even I don't know that much about computers."

The phone on my desk rang, causing me to jump. Who would know me here? "Terran Intelligence Organization," I said, not wanting to identify myself.

"Oh good, you're there. Savanas isn't answering her phone." It was Retanei and she sounded as if she had run a race.

"Savanas is on the phone with someone else. Are you okay?" It worried me to have her calling like this. Patience was something Retanei was well known for.

"Yeah, we're fine. I found the clearing you described and wanted to report in. Can you put me on speaker?" It was common for Retanei to refer back to herself and her companion.

There were simply too many buttons on this phone and I looked up to Darius for help. I said, "It's Retanei. She wants me to put her on speaker."

Savanas finished her conversation and made her way over.

Darius took the handset from me and pushed a couple of buttons before hanging it up. He told her, "You're on speaker now."

Even Brad and Rathal came over to listen.

Savanas said, "Alright, you've got the entire team here. What do you have?"

"We found the clearing Ket described. There were nine people here last night. The camp was cold by the time we got here. I've tried tracking their path, but the fresh snowfall erased most of their tracks. I'm about a mile from the road out of the city and couple of miles northwest of the church."

Silver's face paled at the mention of the church. I was guessing it was his church. It was pretty far out of town, but it was not uncommon for non-Elven run sanctuaries to be located away from the cities. They were not the most welcome in Elven territory, even in a mixed racial city like this.

Retanei continued, "We scoured the area heading up to the church and out to the road, but we can't find any other sign of them. It could have been a diversionary tactic."

"Alright, head back and we'll figure out where we're going from here." Savanas picked up the phone's handset and set it back down, ending the call. Then she looked at me and waited.

I almost forgot I was the supposed expert on mages, and specifically Arcane College mages. I said, "An Archmage could teleport a group. His distance would be shortened to a few miles with so many people. It would take a lot out of him unless he stored the cast in something, but he would still need prior knowledge of the area. Maps would only be able to give him so much information - it would almost be a blind teleport if it was all he used."

Now I lost everyone.

Rathal was the one to speak first, "I thought stored casting was a lost art."

"The information still exists in the Arcane College's library. I did some research on it for someone a number of years ago. I use a modified version of the spell to store information." I went to pull up the library on the computer, but forgot it was down while Lockonis worked on it.

Pulling my Arcane College pin out of my pocket, I got up. When I had enough room, I placed it on the floor and pulled my hands up and out from it, expanding a portion of the information stored in there.

I also caught the thread leading back to me again, but ignored it for the moment.

I explained, "In this format the information is more difficult to sort through, but..."

I swiped at the faded versions of the books before me, sending them spinning around the room. I looked at the information somewhat recently when Lockonis and I were working to convert the information to digital.

"Um... here," I said and pulled the book out - its color became opaque. The book hovered before me as I paged through it. "This spell is the one. The spells that can be stored would primarily depend on the caster's ability. It could be stored in any mundane item." I turned it around to show the others. They all looked at me like I had grown another head.

"Are you sure you were just a Researcher?" Brad asked and looked at me skeptically.

Rathal glared at him and came closer to look at the book. He commented, "Wouldn't it make sense for a Researcher to have easier access to a library of information?"

"You have a point there. I haven't seen anything like it outside of the holographic projectors the science division has been toying with," Brad admitted and seemed embarrassed by his previous statement. "Sorry, kid."

I shrugged in response. At this stage, I did not care about the questions anymore.

Rathal paged back and forth for a bit before saying, "This is way beyond me, but I can get the gist of it. So any item?"

I pointed back to my pin sitting innocently on the floor and said, "Pretty much, but at least when it came to storing information, I found crystalline materials to hold the most. Metals being another good one."

Silver was the one who asked next, "You mean gems and the like? Jewelry?"

"Yes, and it is innocuous enough no one would think it out of place," I agreed.

Savanas leaned her hip against her desk. She said, "And when we spoke with him, he wore some of the gaudiest jewelry I had ever seen." Her desk phone chose that moment to ring.

Rathal gave me back the book and I returned everything to the pin.

Silver reached down and picked it up, turning the pin over in his hand for a moment before giving it back to me. He said, "I really didn't see that one coming."

I ignored it before when I was intent on getting to the information, but the thread bothered me. Turning the pin over in my hand, I did not see what could be creating it, but it was another mystery for another time.

"Sorry, the digital library was down while Lockonis was updating it. I rarely use it anymore," I said as I put the pin back in my pocket. "The digital library is easier to search and also contains my more current research."

"The Admiral is on his way up," Savanas called out. I was not sure if it meant I needed to do anything special like salute or be prepared for a barrage of questions.

Before I could decide on a course of action, Admiral Jonathan Scott strode out of the elevator as if in command of this office.

Savanas moved to greet him, "Good of you to come, Admiral. We were hoping you could enlighten us to the Arcane College's involvement."

"Outside of getting a call from one of their Circle of Magi representatives every hour on the hour to either register further complaints or check on the status of resolution? Maybe you can tell me why they thought they could order me to pull the TIO off and especially that one," the Admiral said and pointed at me.

Savanas did not seem overly happy about hearing that piece of information. She said, "Browne was not a Magister, but an Archmage. If Ketayl wasn't here, we wouldn't have known. He's also the caster responsible for the bombing."

The news settled the Admiral. "Good, now I have something I can use. I don't suppose you have him in custody."

Savanas crossed her arms over her chest, keeping her face neutral. "No, my Rural Tracker is on her way back. Ketayl was able to track his last teleport. The camp was cold, but we have a search area now."

"Keep me informed." With that the Admiral left.

There was so much more to the investigation, but he seemed only interested in the end result. The big picture was what I worried about. There must be more to it than bombing a restaurant. The chaos left was bad, but something told me the Archmage had a different end goal.

NOW WHAT? We had the identity of the man we were looking for. Well, I thought we did. For him not to be in the records...

I checked the library again - it was back up. Pulling up the records regarding the specific topic, I followed the trail I created to remember who I did the research for. Brown. William Bernard Brown to be precise. That's why he kept emphasizing the spelling of his last name. Why would he try to deceive us on his name?

Silver had moved to the desk across from me and went over the documents we recovered. I must have made some sort of noise because he asked, "You have something?"

"I have the Archmage's real name. I remembered doing the research for someone years ago on stored spells. I generally ended up with workloads from the Archmages, which is why it hadn't clicked before," I said and wrote down the information, translating it into common.

Retanei had gotten back a short while ago. She was resting and warming up after giving her full report. She asked, "So who is this guy?"

"It was the same name Rathal pointed out before. William Bernard Brown - no E on the end of his last name. He enrolled in the Arcane College roughly 30 years ago at the age of 23. He rose quickly through the ranks and..." I clicked through the information as fast as I could, Rathal came to hover over my shoulder.

He leaned down to whisper, "So, does this mean you owe me?"

I rolled back in my chair to get Rathal to move and ignored him as I continued my report, "He has also been sent out on multiple assignments, but mostly to be a liaison with specific local governments - all in Human Territory. This was likely his first military assignment."

I probably should not have done that to Rathal, but his closeness only made it harder to maintain my control. This investigation needed to end soon as I was not certain how long I could hold. I needed to do more than minor casting to lessen the strain, but I doubted they had the facilities here to let me unleash. I was actually starting to miss Lockonis' arcane combat training sessions.

Savanas stepped in and told me, "Get the information to Darius so he can put out a bulletin. Rathal, stop bothering Ket and go get lunch."

He grumbled something as he moved away, stopping by his desk to grab his coat before storming out. I watched Rathal go as I handed the information to Darius who waited patiently in front of my desk.

Darius gave me a smile and a salute before taking off with it.

I wondered how effective a bulletin was going to be when dealing with an Archmage who was teleporting.

"Retanei, go get something to eat and get some rest. You'll need to be hunting again soon," Savanas ordered her.

It took Retanei more effort than I had seen before to get herself up. "Come on you two, you need to eat. Besides, there's safety in numbers with the media vultures about."

Turning to Savanas to make sure she did not mind, she waved us off.

I quickly saved my work and logged out, hurrying to catch up with the others.

After hitting the button in the elevator, Retanei leaned back against the wall and closed her eyes - her arms folded over her chest. Silver was putting me under intense scrutiny for some reason. It felt like forever to get down to the main floor. I was the first out the door.

Artemis greeted me as I neared the lobby. Speaking for a moment with Melody, I realized I had fallen behind the others and hustled to catch up.

We were in the truck before Retanei broke the silence. "I wanted to talk to the two of you away from the others," she admitted. "I have an odd feeling about it being a diversionary tactic, but I don't know the Arcane College or the order of paladins that well. I need more information to track these bastards - no matter how far-fetched."

Stretching out in the backseat, I leaned against the cold window and contemplated for a moment. "I can tell you it wouldn't be common for an Archmage. But Brown has tried to divert us prior. I don't know what his end goal is." Artemis plopped her head on my lap and my hand automatically went to petting her. The motion soothed my strained control.

"How about you, Silver? Is there anything at the church a necromancer might want?" Retanei asked, glancing at him out of the corner of her eye.

Silver sat quietly for a moment and from my position in the back, I could not see his face. He then said, "Maybe. The texts might contain some information. I can't really think of anything that would be of much interest. Though..."

Retanei was busy driving and I wondered if I should have insisted instead given how exhausted she was. I watched a few buildings go by, patiently waiting for Silver to continue. I could not stand the silence any further and asked, "What is it?"

"My mentor has been acting very strangely recently. He lost his path when his wife passed a couple of years ago, but the last month or so it has been worse. I have been trying to guide him back toward the Light since his abilities as a paladin had waned. I know he has been receiving many missives lately, but has always burned them immediately," Silver added, "I'm not sure if that is helpful at all."

I chewed on my lower lip at this piece of information. The story sounded awfully familiar to what Archmage Maewon told me. I found myself hoping it was only coincidence. Though Silver said nothing about his mentor taking up the arcane arts, and with his divine abilities waning, it did not sound like he would have the prerequisites to take up necromancy.

Retanei pursed her lips before saying, "Good enough to give me something to go on when I go hunting again tonight. What is your mentor's name?"

Silver seemed reluctant to give up the information. I could only imagine how hard it must be for him to think his home might be the next target. He quietly told her, "James Sutton. He hasn't been attending prayers, but you will likely find him at his wife's grave at almost any hour. Maria was his life."

13

____

THE DRIVE back to the office was quiet after we parted ways with Retanei. Even I could tell Silver tried to cover his worry by asking Retanei about herself. His cheerful tone sounded forced.

And now he was silent.

I was certain he was genuinely interested in getting to know Retanei, but his mind was noticeably elsewhere at the time. What I did not understand was why Retanei would not involve Savanas in the conversation. Savanas was lead after all. Unless she already told her and was simply not involving the others. I could not decide which thought made more sense.

I thought about asking my friend, but it did not seem right to question her judgment. If she had not seen fit to fill me in, there had to be some reason.

"Ketayl? Is something wrong?" Silver's quiet voice startled me out of my thoughts.

I said, "I'm not sure yet. Things aren't adding up and I haven't figured out if it's real or if I just haven't been doing the math right."

"Math?"

"Figure of speech. How are you holding up?" I took a moment to figure out where that came from. I generally did not ask questions and worried I was being too forward.

Silver forced smile, but even from the driver's seat I could tell. He said, "Worry not for me, m'lady. I am a Paladin of the Holy Church of the Sun. The Light will soon guide us to our answers."

That was a leap of faith if I had ever heard one. Silver's attitude might be something I needed right now - let the answers come. Waiting for an answer which might not come did not sit well with me though.

"I wish I could have faith like that. I feel like I've been running in circles," I admitted. Sure, we knew who we were searching for now, but the Archmage's actions made no sense. There was no benefit - no reward. For an Archmage, this test of power would not be enough.

"You don't worship any of the Gods?" Silver asked, confused by my statement.

Again, I quickly regretted not checking every statement before I spoke. I found some relief as we pulled into the underground parking garage for the office. I started this awkward conversation, so it was only fair I answer, "I'm not allowed to as an Arcane College mage. I wouldn't know where to start anyway and I'm usually buried in my work so..."

"Well, if you have time after all of this is over, I can give you a basic introduction to the Gods. Books can only tell you so much," Silver offered. He continued to surprise me in his openness toward the fact I was essentially his polar opposite.

"I'd like that." It would be something new to learn and frankly, I could use another friend. I had not called Kitteren again and Retanei had been busy working. Until now, I did not realize how much I came to rely on their presence.

SAVANAS AND DARIUS pulled Silver into the conference room as soon as we got upstairs. I was not sure what was going on, but he *was* our divine consultant on the case. A field I knew nothing about.

My mobile phone rang, ending any further thought on the matter.

I dug it out of my pocket. The caller ID told me it was from the main office, but not who. "Ketayl," I answered. I still thought it odd to answer with my name.

"Heya, Ket. Thanks for having your phone on," Lockonis' cheerful voice greeted me. She also knew my bad habits regarding my phone. "Is that paladin friend of yours around?"

Maybe she needed to speak with him. I told her, "No, Savanas and Darius just pulled him into a private meeting. Why?"

Lockonis's tone changed slightly, "Perfect, what I need to tell you is not for his ears. I've already filled in the others. You're the hardest because he seems to have attached himself to you. Weird - I thought his type didn't like mages. You know, the heathens that we are."

I managed to balance the phone between ear and shoulder, shedding my coat while she went off on her short tangent. It was common and I found it easier to indulge her.

Sitting down, I powered up the computer, waiting to log in. I relayed what he told me, "Silver says he takes a more balanced approach given his study of the scriptures."

Lockonis said, "Hm, interesting. Anywho, I've been digging further into these 'Ancient Gods' Brown was going on about. The group, or rather cult - very fanatical - tends to be nomadic, moving from town to town looking for more followers. Occasionally they might get some idiot to believe their rhetoric, but for the most part, they are fairly quickly driven away."

I absently pulled up my messages while I waited for Lockonis to get to her point. It looked like I was going to have a backlog to catch up on when I returned to the main office.

"About six months ago, a number of them split off and moved from the Human Territories to Elven and have pretty much stayed outside of Ocean's Edge. It's probably the longest they've stayed in the impact area of any city or town. They also don't usually stay near some place as large as Ocean's Edge." Lockonis said a lot and nothing at all. It was one of her quirks I supposed. I knew very little about her even after two years and others seemed to know about as much after decades.

Leaning back in my chair, there was not much I could do about the requests until I got back to the lab. I decided it was probably more prudent to keep an eye on the conference room door. I asked, "Are they connected to the Archmage?"

"Yes, I was just getting to that. You could tell me better how Brown might fall in line with these morons, but the group worshiping these 'Ancient Gods' and claims one day they will return and remove the blight upon our land. Then they will take their place as the rightful rulers of the world. You know, the usual crazy stuff. How familiar are you with the Great Historian?"

Sometimes following Lockonis' train of thought also required a suspension of one's sanity. Eventually you would get the whole picture, but until she brought all of the parts together, you could drive yourself mad.

I admitted, "Not much. Wasn't the Great Historian banished Earth-side at the end of the Racial War roughly 50 years ago?"

I pulled up my own mental records of what I knew about Earth. It was a copy of Terra, only it was predominately inhabited by Humans. There were a few of the races native to Terra who made their living trading back and forth through the portals linking the worlds. For the most part, I thought Earth-side was oblivious to Terra's existence.

Lockonis corrected, "More like a forced retirement. See, Kage - by the way, that's the name those of us who knew her would call her - made a deal to end the war and move there. The war was not as much racial as wanting to control her. Except no one can control her. Seriously, if she wanted to, she could rule both worlds without breaking a sweat and no one would have the power to stop her. It's not like the guards at the portal entrances even matter if she decides to come back."

"How?" I asked. It did not seem possible for one being to have the amount of power Lockonis implied.

"You've never met Kage. She's old. I mean really old. Like she makes Vince look like a baby old. Kage is sometimes called the Keeper of Atlantis, which is what this group wants access to. Actually, they were the main reason for the war, though you will never find any of this in a history book," Lockonis said, "Most people believed it to be racial so it was the easiest way to write it."

Well, now I had even less reason to like them. But Atlantis? I believed the lost city a myth.

Lockonis continued, "That group is splintered now. They never were popular with the general public in the Human Territories where they held power during the war. You can only imagine what happened after they were removed from power."

I had a hard time keeping up with the new information. But one thing did click. "They have information, and information is the most important thing to any Arcane College mage. With him being an Archmage, he would value power as equally."

"Exactly what I was thinking, but I wanted your input," Lockonis said, "I'm guessing they offered Brown access to information on necromancy and a place of power once these Ancient Gods, which, they actually do name, come back and essentially kill Kage and take over the world, granting them access to Atlantis' knowledge and power."

Something in that caught my attention and I quickly found a break in her story to ask, "The Ancient Gods are named?"

Lockonis continued, "Yeah, I'll tell you later, but you know about the whole names have power thing, right? That's why the widely accepted Gods are not named even though there was a push a few decades ago to use the Earth-side equivalents. It's rather interesting diversion, but one I shouldn't get off on a tangent about right now."

Well, that was a first for Lockonis to talk herself out of a tangent.

"The reason this cult hasn't been on our radar for a while is because of how quickly they're driven from gathering more followers. Plus, they've kind of gone off the deep end: claiming responsibility for natural disasters and the like. This is the first real threat they've posed in over half a century," the speed at which Lockonis rattled off information was almost too fast for me to keep up, but now I had the whole picture.

I also had a little more information about the former Warmage.

I found it interesting Lockonis seemed unafraid of this Kage. The Great Historian was known to have untold power, which I also thought a fable. Come to think of it, at no point in time had I heard of her taking control over anyone. But there was one better question: "Why did you not want Silver to hear this?"

"Because his order backed the war at the time," Lockonis said matter-of-fact.

That was like a fireball in my face. Why did I suddenly feel betrayed?

I had no words as I stared at the closed conference room door. Was he hiding something? Is that why he was being so nice to me?

"Ket, I can hear your mind churning. Stop it. It's only speculation at this point. The leaders of his order at the time were held accountable for their transgressions and in more recent years, have actually been a lot easier to deal with as the old guard passes on leadership to the younger generation. Not to mention, he's Elven. Humans aren't exactly trusting of their darkest secrets to us. How old is he anyway?

Savanas never sent over his file, but it should be in your local system."

It was enough to snap me back into action. I fumbled, "Um, give me a minute to find it. The way he talks, he was also an orphan of the war. His mentor's father took him in. Blaise? Blaise Sutton I would guess if I remember how family names work in most Human communities." Genealogy was not on my list of things to study. "Found it, Silver is 60 years old. I can send you the file if you want." He was only a couple of years older than me.

"Do it," she ordered.

I fumbled for a minute to get the file sent.

While she waited, she said conversationally, "So he's a baby like you. Too bad, I like them a little older, but there aren't many left in my generation."

"Lockonis!" I never heard her talk this way before. A confirmation of the file being received popped up on my screen.

"I'm just teasing, Ket. Lighten up. Now, is Blaise spelled the same as Silver's family name?"

Recalling what Silver had told me, I said, "I think so. He said he was first named after the color of his hair and then his mentor's father's first name." That was a mouthful.

"Well, that's one way of naming a nameless kid. It's not surprising given how many orphans there were on all sides. Did Savanas ever tell you how she got her name?" I could hear Lockonis typing in the background so I guessed she was just idly chatting at this point.

I paused, not sure why it was relevant, but said, "No, I can't say she did. I've met her father though. They don't share a family name."

Lockonis said, "Because when he named her and her brother, he wanted to give them what sounded like Elven names, but he had this overly romanticized idea of Elven culture that was clouded by the naming conventions of the orphans at the time. Lou's a sweet man even if he's a little nutty. Ah, here we go." I was not even sure what she might be searching for. "Blaise Sutton, deceased, had only one son, James Sutton. I take it that's Silver's mentor?"

"Yes," I said. Silver still managed to tell very little about himself. "Silver's been worried about him since he lost his wife."

"Awe, how sweet. Got anything else?" Lockonis asked. I was not sure if the first part was sarcastic.

It felt wrong telling Silver's secrets to Lockonis, but I knew what she was doing. I also knew she would badger me endlessly until she was satisfied I had given her as much information as I could.

I said, "Not really. Other than James Sutton has been acting strangely and Silver can't find out why." I was losing time - that door would open any second.

"Well, it's worth looking into. I should let you go…"

"No," I cut her off and then realized I just rudely interrupted the second in command of the TIO. This would have consequences, but I had to know. "Please, I wanted to talk to you about something."

"Sure." I wanted to breathe a sigh of relief she took no offense. Even two years later, I forgot the people I now worked with were far from the easily angered mages of the Arcane College.

Even though I was the only one in the main part of the office, I dropped my head and my voice. "What is the Arcane College's involvement? Why do they want me off the case?"

There was a long pause and I wondered if I finally crossed the line.

I was about to retract my questions when Lockonis said, "Well, I suppose now is as good of a time as any, though I would rather have told you in person."

I did not understand what she was getting at. The TIO had been open with me about things up until now.

After a deep breath, Lockonis continued, "It was my call to intercept all communications from the Arcane College. They didn't want to give you to us in the first place."

Wait, what? I still did not understand how this answered my previous questions. Being over the phone made this conversation difficult so I said, "I don't understand. Archmage Donovan…"

"Archmage Donovan *did* want an Arcane College mage at the TIO - one of his choosing. The Circle of Magi had been trying to send us a liaison for I lost track of how many years," Lockonis' voice had an odd sound to it - almost like she was tired, "He dragged me and Vince in front of the Council to force the issue. I made the arrangement we would only take you. He fought the condition, but was overruled by the Council. I have a copy of the Council proceedings, but I don't think now is a good time."

I stared at the screen on my computer. What made me special? Why would they keep this from me? Why would Archmage Donovan act like it was his idea to send me?

"Ket?"

Why was Lockonis intercepting communications from the Arcane College? Why would the Arcane College care about losing a Researcher?

"Ketayl!"

That made me jump and I squeaked out an apology.

"Ket, I had known about you for years before that," Lockonis admitted, "Curiosity got the better of me and I would follow Kitteren and Lindale when they visited you. You, I knew I could get out of there, and I also knew there was something different about you. It wasn't until Magus Engelil evaluated you that we found out you were an Arcanist and it's probably why the Arcane College was not happy to let you go. If there had been any communication which didn't involve trying to recall you, I would have let you read it. It wasn't my personal grudge against the Arcane College."

I rubbed the bridge of my nose to ease the start of another headache. I said flatly, "You make it sound like I was a prisoner."

Lockonis shot back at me, "Well, am I wrong? They may have paid you for your services, but how much of it did they demand back for a closet-sized room and barely enough food to live on?"

Nearly all of it was the answer. I scraped together as much as I could each month to send to my sister. It usually meant skipping a few meals and making do with fewer supplies and thread-bare clothes.

She continued, "You came to us severely underweight. Why they didn't treat you better, I don't know, but they were adamant about wanting to keep you. Since your sister worked for us, I knew you would have someone you could turn to." Lockonis' voice softened, "All of us care about you, Ket. You've worked hard - harder than everyone else to overcome that label. Savanas and her team have had nothing but glowing things to say about you. Though you did shock them when you pulled out the old copy of the library," she laughed, "I wish I had been there to see their faces. Why did you do it, exactly?"

I got up and left my desk before they came out of the conference room. Standing next to the window, I watched the snow falling again. "You were updating the digital library and I wanted to access the information."

"Oh, right," Lockonis said and was back to typing like a

madwoman on the other end. "In any case, now that I've broken you and probably your trust…"

"No, thank you," I responded quickly before she went off on a tangent again. I was grateful she told me, but I remained unsure how I felt about what was revealed.

Lockonis said, "You deserved to know, Vince and I, well, we wanted to watch and see what you would do. It was about time we told you."

Come to think of it, Vince's talk with me before Retanei joined us in his office seemed like a prelude to this.

"I'll give you a call when I have more information," she said and then hung up after a long pause. I did not know what to say.

I put my phone away and leaned my head against the cold window. After this was all over, I wanted to sit down with her and talk. And I hated sitting down and talking, but I needed to this time.

"Ketayl, what's wrong?" Silver asked from behind me.

Standing up straight, I could not bring myself to turn around. I steadied my voice and said, "It's nothing. We should get back to work."

I kept my head down as I walked past, but a hand caught my shoulder, and I looked up.

Savanas took a moment to study my face before she concluded, "Lockonis told you, didn't she?" It was not accusatory or even demanding of an answer.

It meant Savanas knew also.

She admitted, "It has been eating at her for a while. The only reason I knew was, well, she had been my partner for a long time and I could tell when something was bothering her. It wasn't my place to say anything. You were going to find out sooner or later. Especially when the Admiral told us about the Arcane College's demands. I'm just glad it came from her." She left it at that and went back to her desk.

Strong hands gripped my shoulders gently and I looked up at Silver. He asked, "What's wrong?"

The information about his order's past came back to the forefront in my mind. It did not even process in my mind that he was touching me.

"Silver, drop it," Savanas barked at him. "We have work to do. I want Brown's head on a pike outside of this building."

I quickly rushed over to my desk to get Silver's information off of the screen. Last thing I needed was for him to question us.

I could feel Darius' eyes on me, but he said nothing. I wonder how many others knew.

The more I thought about it and about my time with the TIO, the more I realized while these secrets were kept from me, it was not out of malicious intent. How blind I had been my whole life thus far.

But what do I do with this information? Who do I trust? How did this all fit in together?

14

"KETAYL, Silver, wrap it up and call it a night." Savanas said as she got off the phone.

Looking at the time, it was late. Silver and I had been going over Brown's documents. With each of us only able to read half, it looked like creating a translator was going to be necessary sooner rather than later. It was slow going to correlate useful information. Admittedly, I was at wits end at this point and with the day's revelations, I felt exhausted.

"Yes, ma'am," I said. Getting what I had been working on into some semblance of order, I left Silver to organize his work. He kept scribbling down information on the notepad he was using. "Silver?"

"I will, just a minute," he replied without looking up. Maybe he had something.

For me, I was too tired and I started to get a headache again so I left him to whatever train of thought he had, I got my coat on and my bag ready to head out the door. I was worrying there was something more to these headaches.

They started at roughly the same time I felt the strain on my control. It could just be a side-effect of keeping myself reigned in. I might ask for a day off when this was over. Curling up with a good book in my quarters sounded perfect.

"Ket, can you bring this down to Melody for me while you're waiting?" Savanas asked and held up a large manila envelope. "Tell her there's no rush."

I took the packet and headed for the elevator, barely acknowledging Savanas' thanks.

I mentally went back over what I had read. Most of the pertinent information so far had been in Silver's set of documents - information about these 'Ancient Gods' and notes about the group in general, but nothing specific to this one.

My pile seemed to be all arcane theory so far. There was still more for each of us to sift through, but I was losing hope. There must be something to point me in the direction of the Archmage. A clue to his ultimate goal. Some reason why the Arcane College backed him.

After hitting the button for the main floor, I leaned back against the wall. I wish I knew how the others continuously worked. I knew Savanas had some of the local law enforcement officers helping out, but I had not seen them. I really had no clue about the rest of the investigation. Secrets were being kept and I wondered if it was going to become a problem.

Once the elevator let me off on the main floor, I dragged myself to the lobby. Melody seemed to always be here also. Then again, Fletch was known to pull some lengthy hours. Neither one ever seemed to mind and I thought maybe it was a special type of person who could fill the role.

"Artemis?" I was not expecting Retanei's wolf companion to be curled up in the lobby.

"Oh, hi, Ket. You have something for me?" Melody asked, holding out her hand.

I handed the packet over to her, but never took my eyes off Artemis, whose attention was firmly on me. I was unsure why it felt like she stared directly into my soul, but I figured I was overtired and had spent way too much time going over a necromancer's notes.

I pinched the bridge of my nose and the sensation was gone. It was just Artemis again.

Melody continued, "Retanei dropped her off a few hours ago. Said something about having you take her. I guess whatever she has planned for tonight, Artemis isn't ready for."

Artemis was still fairly new to working in the field with Retanei, but something still did not seem right about it. Kneeling down next to my unexpected four-legged companion, I pet Artemis. She always seemed to have a calming presence. I remember Retanei telling me once it was because she was an Omega, but I did not understand what it meant.

Artemis nuzzled my face and all I wanted to do was curl up around the warm wolf and go to sleep.

"You look like you've seen better days," Melody commented, typing away at the computer hidden below the counter level of her desk.

Sighing, I sat back on my feet and told her, "I feel like I'm getting nowhere in a hurry. Or looking in the wrong place. I'm not even sure anymore."

Melody smiled and said, "It happens. That's probably why Savanas is making you go get some rest. She's pretty intuitive like that. She also knows how to schedule us so we have the most coverage during a difficult investigation without burning out team members. Trust me, when this is all done, she's going to have a big dinner at her house. Savanas cooks to unwind."

They were like a family and I commented, "It's a small office here. You must all be close."

"We are, and we all have our quirks. Darius and Rathal like to play video games and harass each other until they're exhausted. Brad cleans and reads. Doc tells stories. Sasha tinkers. And we all somehow end up at Savanas' house about once a week regardless. What is it like at the main office?" Melody did not stop whatever she was working on.

Artemis decided I was not petting her enough and went to nuzzle me, but only succeeded in knocking me on my butt. It did not matter so I stayed where I landed. My butt would have to deal with the hard-tiled floor.

"I guess with so many people it's harder to connect like that. I keep to myself mostly. I see others interacting, but it's enough for me to watch," I admitted. People found it odd, but it worked for me.

Melody raised an eyebrow at me and commented, "That's so lonely. Do you do anything for fun? Hobbies? You can't possibly work all the time."

I never considered it lonely. I clarified, "I don't keep completely to myself. I have people like my sister and Retanei. I also play the violin. Not well, but I like to practice in my quarters."

"Hm, never pegged you for a musician. Interesting. I try

different crafts. Still haven't found one to can keep my interest for very long. With my kids grown and out on their own, what's a mother to do? Outside of wait for grandchildren that is," Melody said with a wink. She seemed like a nurturing person. The elevator dinged and she smiled. "It sounds like your knight in shining armor is here."

The way Melody said it made me blush.

"It's not like that," I whispered quickly before he could get close enough to hear.

"Right... Just don't forget about the other one." Melody never skipped a beat with what she was working on.

Other one? What was she talking about?

"Ketayl, why are you sitting on the floor?" Silver asked as he stood over me, concern obvious on his face.

Shifting Artemis off me, I went to move, only to have a hand waiting to help me up. Not wanting to be rude, I took it and said, "I fell over. Well, good night, Melody."

"Good night," Melody said winked. I fought down the heat rising to my face. Perhaps I should blame Lockonis for putting the concept in my head.

I did not understand why people made things out like that. Silver acted as he was taught. Perhaps it was their way of poking fun of his being somewhat out of touch with the current world.

I just wish they left me out of it.

ONCE WE GOT BACK to the hotel, Silver and I went straight up to the room to avoid the "media vultures" as Retanei liked to call them. I mostly wanted to avoid the Admiral.

I was also a bit hungry and kicked myself for not stopping en route to pick something up. I vaguely remembered seeing some menus in the suite and I wondered if I could get away without having to go downstairs.

Opening the door, I noticed a note on the floor.

Carefully stepping around the folded piece of paper, I wanted to get my coat off first before dealing with it. I hoped dealing with one thing at a time would help not aggravate the dull pounding in my head. I only got as far as unzipping it.

Silver decided it was more important and picked it up. "It could be from Retanei," he reasoned.

Rubbing the bridge of my nose, I tried to alleviate the headache building and said, "No, she would have left a note on the counter. Or with Artemis." I was not sure, but I knew the floor near the door was not a place she would leave a note.

"It's from the Admiral. He wants us to meet him in a conference room on the second floor," Silver said and looked over the note.

I figured it would not be hard for him to find out what room we were in to slip a note under the door.

"Now?" It came out a bit whiny, but I really did not want to deal with the Admiral.

Silver said, "There's no time on it. We should go down and see if he's still there."

"You mean I should." Taking the note from Silver, I confirmed it was only addressed to me. It was an easy assumption as he singled me out previously.

"No, we. Savanas asked me to keep an eye on you. And also to make sure you got enough rest." Oh, is that why she sent me down as a messenger to Melody? Who knew, and more importantly, did it even matter?

But what about the information about his order? Obviously Savanas trusted him enough and Lockonis said she told the others, right? What did she tell them? Suddenly I was not so sure anymore.

Silver suddenly appeared in front of me and tilted my face to look at him. It was a far more intimate motion than I was prepared for. He said, "And even if she hadn't asked, I would."

I backed away from him quickly as a flash of a face from the past overlaid itself on reality. Then it was back to Silver. He was too close. He could be...

He could be what? The information about his order was decades old. Silver had been but a small child, not yet grown.

He was as deeply buried as I was trying to figure out who did this and why. He had been horrified at the crime scene when he first saw what I could not.

Putting my hand to my temple, I tried to stop the sudden sharp pain that had previously only been a dull throbbing. I shut my eyes tight for a moment, but it did not help. Where were these headaches coming from? I panicked something was very wrong with me.

There he was again, very close, saying something, but I could not hear him over the pounding.

I was losing control fast. I warned him, "Get back!" I stumbled and tripped on my long coat, landing hard on the floor. Now I added a sharp pain in my left hip to everything else. "Stay back - I don't want to hurt you," it came out as a soft plea, but it was the most I could manage.

I felt it before I saw the arcane energy manifesting along my arms, wrapping itself around me and fought as hard as I could to pull it back under control.

Artemis scampered for cover.

Again, he was close. Stupid paladin.

Silver pulled me against his chest and rubbed my back. "Find peace."

I'm not even sure how I heard him. Or that I heard him with my ears. The pain in my head subsided and I stopped fighting him, having no energy to spare. I put everything into regaining control.

"That's it, Ketayl, breathe." That, I knew I heard with my ears. He continued softly, "Just relax and breathe. Focus on my voice."

We sat there awkwardly on the floor for I do not know how long with him gently repeating those words. But I knew there was still work to be done before I could truly relax. There was little I could do to force him away - I was simply too exhausted to fight.

Eventually, I interrupted him, "It's hard to focus on much else. You're kind of squishing my face."

Silver laughed and moved back, apologizing. "Sorry, but you scared me there. We have many mage parishioners at the church. Even in their most distraught, I've never seen that happen before."

Rubbing my face, I realized Silver was never told. It was not exactly something I advertised, but he deserved to know. Especially after putting himself in danger, which I still thought was stupid.

I said, "I'm an Arcanist. I have to keep my emotions in check or it makes for embarrassing moments like that when they are too strong."

I could not look at him. Any previous time it happened... it was never this bad before. Not even my most recent episode that Savanas and Doc witnessed.

Silver seemed to leave it as he got up and offered me a hand. "Why don't I go see if the Admiral is down there and you get some rest?"

I shook my head and shed my coat, tossing it over the back of the nearest chair. It was time to work and I said, "No, he's looking for me. It probably has something to do with the Arcane College. I wouldn't mind the company though." I was unsure if I wanted someone with me or not. Normally I was alone, but with everything going on, it was probably safer for someone to have my back. For whatever reason, I decided to trust Silver.

15

THE SECOND FLOOR WAS EMPTY. I glanced at the name on the note and followed the signs. Artemis chose to remain back in our room on the couch, satisfied the two of us were capable of fending for ourselves. Or at least it was my interpretation.

I continued to mentally kick myself for what happened. Why was I struggling so hard with my control lately? Even with an impatient Archmage breathing down my neck for his requested information, I had never faltered.

I wanted to focus on something else, but this floor was empty. It was late and there were only conference rooms on this floor. Surely meetings would be done by now. It was the best logic I could come up with to keep myself calm.

I was relieved Silver strode next to me. Though I had to nearly jog to keep up with his long stride.

Tugging at the already loose collar of my sweater, I felt like I had been walking for hours. The room was all the way at the end of a hall which branched off at the far end of the main hall. The long walk only made me more nervous.

Looking at the note in my hand again and then the name on the door, I reluctantly knocked, barely making any sound. Being this nervous was not good given what happened.

The door opened and a female Halfling glared up at me. She

wore a Navy uniform, but I could not remember what the bands on her sleeves meant for rank. Opening the door further, she allowed us to enter.

"Good of you to come, though I expected you to be alone." The Admiral stood at a table off to the side of the room - his collar loose and his tie undone. Pouring himself a drink, he said, "Doesn't really matter at this stage I suppose. Oh, and don't mind those two - I can't seem to take a piss without an escort. I'm surprised they didn't follow me upstairs at your office. Come have a seat. Drink?"

Stepping into the room, I looked around - it was empty except for the hotel's furniture. A male dwarf stood on the other side of the door at attention. This room looked as if to be more for relaxing and entertaining a small party than for a meeting.

Doing as requested, I sat down on the couch closest to the door, feeling all eyes in the room on me. I said, "No, thank you, sir."

"A polite Arcane College mage. You must be the exception," the Admiral mused. Swirling the amber liquid around in his glass, he looked briefly to Silver before turning his attention back to me. "Captain Greaves told me how forthcoming you were aboard the *Traverse* with previously unknown information about the Arcane College."

Forcing myself not to retreat from the imposing man in front of me, I fidgeted with my hands.

Silver's hand gently slid into mine and squeezed. Why did he have to touch me so often? The sensation was uncomfortable, but it helped ground me while I waited for the Admiral to continue. I would have to speak later with Silver about personal space.

The Admiral said flatly, "I need you to explain the Arcane College's behavior. I need you to tell me why they changed their tune, claiming he was a rogue mage they demoted and were trying to recall him. They shut up pretty damn quick when I told them you had solid evidence he was responsible."

"Demoted?" I caught onto that first. I retreated into my own thoughts for a moment.

They let mages at lower ranks go if they did not improve their rank within a certain period of time and while there was the rare case of a Human Researcher gaining an actual rank, it never went backwards.

Realizing the Admiral waited for me to continue, I explained my confusion. "Rank is tied to ability. There's never been a demotion.

They've let a liaison be arrested without stepping in before, but never an Archmage."

"Sounds like we have more questions than answers still," the Admiral grumbled. Tossing back the last of his drink, he grimaced. "It's odd - I genuinely believe you are telling me the truth. Think I need to blame Ed for that. It's hard to impress that cranky old bastard. Not to mention what your Director says."

"Thank you, sir." What else should I say? I assumed for the moment Ed and Captain Greaves were the same person. As for what Vince said about me, I still wondered, but I had something of an idea given my conversation with him before I departed.

The Admiral waved his hand at us. "Alright, get out of here. You two probably need rest. I'm certainly calling it a night."

I stood up quickly, I might have fallen back down if I was not so short because Silver had not released my hand. Reclaiming it, I quickly bowed to the Admiral and exited the door being held open for us. Should I report this to Savanas?

Standing in the hallway, I realized I was lost on what to do next. Do I report this conversation? I know I needed to report my latest incident still, but surely she would have gone home to rest by now. I did not want to chance disturbing her with either issue and resolved to mention both when I saw her in the morning.

"Come on, let's go eat." Silver tugged my arm, leading me away from the conference room door.

THE TREK down to the main floor was quiet. My mind was still on the Arcane College's behavior. It simply made no sense. Why hide his rank? Brown claimed to be a Magister before the case even existed. How long had he been hiding under the Magister's rank outside of the Arcane College? And why? Most flaunted their rank.

The Admiral was right in there were now more questions than answers. I had no idea where to start.

Silver stopped and I bumped into his back, not paying attention to my surroundings. I quickly said, "I'm sorry..."

A female Human reporter standing before us was the reason for the pause. She asked before we could continue, "Are you two members of the TIO? Can I ask you some questions?"

Looking around, I noticed a few other heads turned in our direction, curious. I shrank back at the attention - this could be bad.

Silver said calmly, "I am a Paladin of the Holy Church of the Sun, ma'am."

"Oh?" She seemed confused, and said, "I'm sorry. I must have heard the rumors wrong."

Silver gave her a disarming smile, wrapping his arm around my shoulders, and replied, "Not a problem, but if you would excuse my lady friend and I, we have had a very long day and want a quiet meal."

I was too confused by what was going on to squirm out of his loose hold. His wording got stuck in my head and I kept trying to make sense of it. Among other questions forming I wanted to ask.

It was not until we were seated in a corner of the restaurant that I spoke. "Did you just lie to that reporter?"

Silver picked up his menu, not fazed by my question. "No, I said what I was. Just because I'm a consultant doesn't make me a part of the TIO. I didn't say anything about you."

It was a fine line he walked with that. Apparently, the idea of a paladin I had was incorrect. Or perhaps Silver was unique. Though, I suppose I could use the same logic as I was technically just a liaison.

I chided, "Could you not make it sound like we're a couple next time?"

"Did I?" Silver asked, a broad grin on his face. I was going to blame Lockonis and Melody for sticking the idea in my head. Otherwise I probably would not have taken notice of his wording.

Eying him carefully for a moment, I had a feeling his grin meant he was up to no good.

I picked up the menu in front of me. I was quite hungry, which might partially explain the headache.

Silver slid along the semi-circular bench seat. Once he was next to me, he put his arm around my shoulders and whispered in my ear. "We're supposed to be a couple, right? Seems like a good cover. I always wanted to try it from the books I've read."

I stiffened at his touch and said, "That's a bit much, don't you think? Look, let's just eat and then get some rest. It's been a long day and I really don't want a repeat of earlier."

After quickly squeezing my shoulder, his arm disappeared and he smiled apologetically. He said, "You have a point. Does that happen regularly?"

"I've never had that strong of a reaction before. Usually it's small enough no one notices and even those are rare. I usually keep my emotions better in check." I had been going over the menu and had not realized until I said it. I hoped he let it drop. I was glad I did not mention the reaction Savanas and Doc witnessed.

Silver's blue eyes were on the menu in front of him and said nothing. Following his example, I went back to finding something to order. There were too many options that sounded good.

The waiter was back a couple of minutes later.

Silver looked at me as soon as the waiter was gone. Picking up my hand, he first kissed the back of it before holding it to his cheek. I opened my mouth to tell him to knock it off, but something in his face made me hold my tongue.

It took a moment, but I realized Silver was using the motion to hide from the rest of the room as he used the menu before.

"I think it may in part have something to do with your exposure to the strong emotions coming from the souls. You had a lot more exposure and to a much stronger version than Rathal, and he's still struggling with the after effects," Silver said.

"But I can see and understand what is going on. All it did was give me a headache. What about you? If it had divine components, shouldn't it also affect you?" I shot back, keeping my voice down. And why did I not think about that until now? It also meant Retanei was affected.

Silver locked his blue eyes with mine and explained, "No, it wasn't just giving you a headache. I saw what it was doing to you. Retanei saw it. Everyone else has been worried since your last exposure. You keep control of your emotions, which is why you've been able to hold on for so long. However, you were tired and in pain and I inadvertently triggered a reaction to which I am truly sorry."

I did not know how to react to Silver's attitude. I was also trying to figure out what I had missed. I looked down at the patch of silver hair on his chin. It was easier to focus on.

Silver backed off and admitted, "As for me, yes, but not as much as those of you who are arcane sensitive. I fear mine is a little harder to explain, but I usually have enough discipline to handle it."

What he said made a lot of sense. Which was absolutely frightening. If I lost control, I could not imagine the damage I could cause. Looking Silver in the eye again, I asked, "Why didn't you stay away when I told you to?" *Why throw yourself on a grenade?* I pushed back the memories of other times I panicked and lost control - it would only make matters worse.

Blue eyes searched for something. Silver said, "I couldn't leave you like that. And, I don't think you would actually hurt me - even if it was unintentional. I tend to pick up on little things, which works well when dealing with people at the church. However, from the moment I saw you... well, my protective side can be obnoxious."

Silver's thumb was rubbing the back of my hand and it bothered me incessantly, but I dared not move and draw attention to our table. I simply was the type that did not like to be touched.

At least he understood his actions it seemed. Though, it reminded me of something I wanted to ask him. "You said something before, when we were at the crime scene..." I paused to recall the statement. "Not wanting to see the pain about me worsen."

Silver's face changed to surprise and he looked away for a moment, taking a sip of water. "I'm still not sure I understand it. After witnessing what you were previously exposed to, it made a little more sense. There's something around you, dark. Rathal has something similar, but not nearly as strong. When I first saw you, I saw it too. It was such a contrast to how you treated Artemis I knew it couldn't be normal - who you were. Once I looked past it, I could see the pain it was causing you."

And that likely was what got his protective side going. I asked, "Why didn't you say something sooner?"

Silver still would not look at me. "I didn't know what to say at first. When I finally had some kind of grasp of what was happening we were too involved in investigation. When Savanas requested a meeting in the conference room, I brought it up. That was when she told me to add watching you to my duties. Though I had already taken it upon myself."

It might explain why I struggled with my control. Then I realized Silver still held my hand. Looking at our joined hands, I knew pulling away at this point would only draw attention to our table. My hand seemed so small and fragile in comparison. I was much shorter than him, but...

It continued to bother me that I was being treated as if I were glass. Why had Savanas not told me?

I thought about calling her and asking, but Silver's attention turned back to me. His thumb continued to rub the back of my hand and I pulled away. I did not care what attention it might draw.

———

BY THE TIME we returned upstairs, I still had not figured out a way to politely tell Silver to not touch me. Perhaps because I could not deny his presence earlier helped me regain control. Maybe it was an ability of his? Savanas said something early on about keeping the two of us close together.

Then I briefly wondered if she had the power to see the future.

Cleaning up, my mind went over why being touched bothered me so much. By the time I was done, I still had not come up with a logical reason for it now. Not where I knew people would not hurt me.

Silver was not in the common area and I figured he needed to perform evening prayers or something. I had capitalized on his time without much thought to the rituals he was used to performing.

As I rounded the doorway into my bedroom, I saw Artemis sprawled out on the foot of the bed. She perked her head up for a moment before returning to her resting position.

Walking further into the room, Silver sat in a chair by the desk - he was cleaning out my brush. His own hair down and out of its customary braid - it created a silver waterfall. "Don't worry, I didn't use your brush."

I pulled the towel holding the length of my hair tighter around my neck, backing away. Silver did not belong here. "You should go."

Silver raised his hands to indicate being harmless, he strode toward me. "Relax, Ketayl. I'm experienced in a few different healing arts. Some are not magic-based."

My back hit the wall, and my fear was only waylaid by my curiosity. I blurted out, "I don't like being touched."

Artemis sat up and looked at me. She cocked her head to the side, but I did not understand the unspoken question. Would she help me get out of this?

Silver paused and took a step back. He commented, "That explains a lot. You could have told me sooner."

I looked away from him and said, "You should go get some rest. I'll be fine."

Artemis jumped off the bed and nosed her way behind my legs, pushing me away from the wall. What was the wolf trying to do?

Silver took over and nudged me toward the chair at the desk. He explained, "I know you have been having headaches and you need to be able to get a good rest. I used to do this for Maria. It helped her to get some sleep even on the nights of her worst migraines. I'm sure you can tolerate me for a bit if it means a better chance of not having a reaction."

Once I was seated, Artemis sat at my feet with her head on my lap. Absently I pet her with one hand, keeping a firm grasp on my towel with the other.

Eventually Silver pried the towel out of my hand. Maybe he would give up once he realized the work ahead - I had not even dried it yet. The back of my mind reminded me of how long his own hair was and quickly gave up the notion.

Silver used his fingers to gently pull the biggest tangles apart. "You have such long, beautiful hair. A shame you always keep it up."

I worked in a lab most of the time - up was a necessary thing. Even before that, it was more prudent to keep it up as it gave people less to grab hold of. Some of the mages I dealt with were violent and escape was easier without a tail.

I changed the subject, "What happened to Maria?"

"Brain tumor. By the time she got leave from the Elders to go see a doctor, it was too late. She suffered for many years, but she was such a strong person and fought her way through it. There are unfortunately some things our magic cannot heal," Silver stated so matter-of-fact it threw me off.

I asked, "They won't let you see regular doctors?"

Granted, the Arcane College was the same way. They had alchemists, but unless it was life threatening, we were to deal with it on our own.

"No. I'm afraid most of the Elders still adhere to the old ways. I may be the same age as many of them, but I do not see the purpose in holding onto ideals so outdated they endanger people's lives. Perhaps the next generation will not be so blind."

Silver started brushing my hair from the bottom, pulling as little as possible. I was not so gentle when I did it myself.

"I can dry it. It would only take a moment," I offered.

Silver never paused in his work and said, "No, you need to reserve your strength."

I crossed my arms under my chest and sat still. My eyes glued to a point on the wall. Fine, Silver could brush my hair. At least then it was one less thing I needed to take care of.

It had been a while since someone else brushed my hair. Normally I would not let anyone else near me, though Mother insisted on trimming my hair about once a year.

Why was I even letting him? Because we had similar pasts? Because I thought some give on my part to help ease the transition to working within the TIO would help him? Because so far he had been open and honest with me? Because I felt I owed him after the danger he put himself in?

But Silver was not a member of the TIO. After this, he would return to his church and normal way of life.

I fidgeted, pulling up the strap of my tank top up that had slid down my shoulder. The mint green pajama set was a gift from Mother. I found I missed her right now. Her wisdom was something I came to rely on. I made a mental note to call her as soon as I got back to the main office.

Needing to break the silence, I asked, "Are you considered an Elder?" Age often defined status, but an Elf among Humans who had not even reached the age of true adulthood...

"No. The Elders at the Central Seat did not wish me to walk the path of a paladin, but my mentor's father fought their initial decision saying the paladin order would die out if we did not accept those who showed genuine interest, even if they were not Human. I would certainly never be allowed to sit as an Elder," Silver said, his voice even.

I wished for a mirror so I could watch Silver. At least it would beat staring at the wall. Considering it, I reached for my tablet, needing something to do.

Silver moved it out of my reach and chided, "No more work right now. Savanas' orders if you will."

Crossing my arms again, I stared back at the wall. Being ganged up on like this was unfair and to have even Artemis working against me...

"You certainly are a stubborn one," he laughed. "Too bad you don't live in the area. It would be nice to get to know you when you aren't working yourself into the ground."

Channeling my sister's more childish behavior for a moment, I stuck my tongue out and retorted, "I'm always working."

Silver laughed. He put the brush down on the desk. Finally, he was done and I could get out of this mess.

I went to get up and strong hands pulled me back into the chair. Silver said, "I'm not done yet. I'm sure you you feel fine, but it'll come back in the middle of the night." He started rubbing my head. "Tell me if something hurts. My mentor got so mad about me doing this for Maria, but I was the only person she trusted to not make it worse."

"Why do you refer to your mentor and his father that way, but call Maria by name?" I did not mean to pry, but it slipped out as his fingers began loosening tension I did not know was there.

His fingers moved down to my neck and shoulders, and I really did not care anymore. The release set my mind at ease for the first time in a long time. I did not even care about being touched at this point.

He answered my question anyway, "Maria was one of the few people I could truly call a friend. My mentor only did as his father bid him, and it would be improper to refer to my mentor's father as master since he is deceased. May I ask what made you upset this afternoon?"

I tensed up the moment the question dropped. Sitting up, I debated if I should tell him or not. "Well, I, uh..."

Pulling me back to relax in the chair again, Silver hushed, "No need to answer if it would further upset you." He ran his fingers through my hair before repeating the process of alleviating the tension.

It was not fair to him, given how much he shared, but speaking of things still raw to me was something I did not think I was ready for. "It would be a long story that is too soon for me to tell."

Silver said, "Fair enough."

16

When I woke the next morning, I had no idea how I ended up in bed. Artemis laid curled up next to me, snoring softly.

What time was it? It was still dark. Being winter, it was dark a lot - especially as it approached the Winter Solstice. The holiday was a couple of weeks out still, and I wondered if I would be done in time to go home. Rarely had I such a longing to be among family.

Granted, I was not looking forward to my sister dragging me around to shop for dresses. She had been threatening me since last year when she got fed up seeing me uncomfortable in my formal mage robes.

I slid out of bed as carefully as I could to not disturb Artemis. Her head perked up anyway, and after a moment, went back to her previous position. The room was chilly after getting away from the furry heater.

Searching for my phone, I found it still tucked in the pocket of my jeans. There was still time before dawn when Silver would be performing his morning prayers, or at least that was what I could infer.

I rubbed my arms thinking about last night. I was going to be grateful to put distance between me and Silver once this was over. I knew he was only doing as he was trained, but it still bothered me.

Going about my morning routine, I thought about the upcoming holiday to get my mind off of last night's events.

While a universal calendar had been adopted, setting the new year about a week and a half later, the Winter Solstice was the Elven celebration of a new year. A time for renewal and to let go of things past - to look with hope toward the future.

I had not participated in the burning of the scrolls previously because I never knew what to write. My sister, Kitteren, told me I could write anything I wanted. The Gods would receive the prayers at their Great Feast where they would be gathered.

It just seemed a waste to bother supreme beings with inconsequential desires.

Kitteren had more faith than I did. I only seemed to understand what I could see. Magic and science were so alike I barely noted the differences between them.

The lights which accompanied the Winter Solstice should be lit at this time of day. It was something I loved about the holiday. They were so beautiful and elegant. I would spend so much time in Great Tree wandering around, looking at the light displays.

As soon as I was ready, I headed out to the little cafe nearby without bothering to leave a note - Silver would figure it out. It was the first day of the weekend and I hoped it would not be busy.

Artemis followed at my side. I guess I was not getting away without one escort.

With my tablet in my pocket, I thought about where to direct my search. There must be a way to scan for a specific arcane signature. If we could get the Archmage in custody, the rest of the case should fall into place, right?

I was pleasantly surprised to find the cafe mostly empty upon my arrival. After I stepped through the door with Artemis, I suddenly worried maybe pets were not allowed.

"Ah, welcome once again! And you brought a friend I see," the older Elf I ordered from yesterday greeted.

I apologized, "I'm sorry, I didn't even think she might not be allowed. My friend left her with me for the evening."

He paused for a moment, before asking, "The Dark Elf I've seen her with? Such a fine young lady that one is. Come, what can I get for you on this cold winter morn?"

Once I had gotten my order, I found a quiet corner with the

biggest plush chair I could snuggle into. It was warm and I shed my coat, hanging it over the fat arm of the chair.

I pulled out my tablet and I saw I had new messages waiting for me. It would probably be prudent of me to respond to the ones I could before getting too involved with my research.

It became busy quickly as it got closer to dawn. I had long since finished my meal and was finishing up the last response when a male voice asked, "Is this seat taken?"

Not wanting to lose my train of thought, I held my hand open toward the seat, signaling it was free. I was trying to describe where something was in the lab for Lockonis. Thinking about it, I was going to end up spending weeks getting the lab back in order again.

The voice spoke again, "It has been difficult to speak with you, given the company you keep. Do you understand the debt you owe us?"

My head shot up. Sitting across from me was Archmage William Bernard Brown. Older than I last remembered. Despite the plush chair he resided in, his body was stiff and rigid, wearing similar green robes to the ones we found. Suddenly, it was hard to breathe.

Brown continued, "You owe us your life and yet you would aid those who blindly follow false gods? Discarding your sacred robes and consorting with the unenlightened? Dabbling in their *technology*? Pathetic. But I suppose it is to be expected of one of your race."

I could feel the blood drain from my face and froze. Panic quickly started to settle in.

"I am ordering you, as an Archmage of the Arcane College, to end your involvement with the Terran Intelligence Organization," he said and suddenly Brown disappeared as if he was never there. The tightness in my chest refused to subside and I could not get enough air.

I fear I jumped a mile when the older Elf I spoke with earlier knelt down to get into my view. "Are you okay, child?"

I looked around - others were staring in my direction and even Artemis was on my lap to get my attention. She nudged my face with her nose.

I bowed my head, embarrassed. I told him, "I am now. I apologize for causing a disturbance."

He sat in the chair Brown vacated and commented, "Forgive my intrusion, but it looked like you saw a ghost."

Rubbing the bridge of my nose, I considered his comment. I

found no arcane remnants in the chair he now sat. There was another mystery I would have to deal with. I said, "Perhaps I had."

He smiled and suggested, "Why don't I keep you company for a bit? Help keep the ghosts at bay. Don't worry, my wife can take care of our guests. I fear she is far better at it than I am. She says I talk too much."

I smiled for him, looking down at the tablet on my lap and said, "I'm afraid I'm not much company."

He smiled and picked up a magazine to read.

I could feel my control locking back into place. I may have to give more thought to Silver's theory. If he was right, then I was a walking time bomb.

WHEN I RETURNED to the hotel, I spoke none of what happened to Silver. He was highly upset I left without him. I was not even sure if I should mention it to the others. The company I had been keeping... Who?

Telling anyone could put them in danger. How could I leave? They would not so readily let me go. If I disappeared, someone would go looking for me. How was I supposed to follow those orders?

Should I follow those orders?

I drove us to the office again and other than Melody who greeted us at the front, no one else was in. The others not being present only gave me more time to debate who I should tell what to and in what order. There was also my reaction last night Savanas would want to know about. The conversation with the Admiral. What Silver told me about what he could see...

Silver asked if he could go spend time in meditation to see if the Gods would help guide him. Letting him do as he wished, I paced - my feet not keeping up with my mind.

Retanei had not come back by the time we left and Artemis stayed downstairs with Melody. Where was everyone else? I know they all needed to rest as well, but someone always seemed to be here. At least Savanas did anyway. I thought about seeing if Doc was in to at least have someone to talk to.

No, he would not be able to help. And why this urge to talk to someone?

Brown waited until I was separated from the others. Even if I obeyed his orders and left the case, the others would pick it up in my stead. But it was not only the case he ordered me away from, but the TIO as a whole.

Surely he knew the others would still continue the investigation without my presence. Why would he even bother? I was only a Researcher. I would not be able to stand up against him.

But did I owe the Arcane College? The TIO? Both? Neither? I did not know. All this was doing was aggravating me. I could feel another headache starting I could tell was going to be a bad one.

Digging into my pocket, I pulled out my Arcane College pin and stared at it, hoping it would give me some sort of insight. But it was a pin, and outside of the library stored in it, it could not tell me anything.

Never before had I wanted to throw my pin as hard as I could. I clenched it tightly in my hand considering the motion. "Ow, damn..." I clenched a little too tightly. The sharp points cut into my hand.

Before the pin hit the floor, Retanei stood in front of me.

"Ketayl, look at me. Look at me!" Retanei said in a panic and then ordered, "Someone, get the first aid kit."

"Damn good for nothing paladin, where is he?" I heard Savanas to my left.

Everything was surreal. Even if this was not real, I could at least answer Savanas. I pointed in the direction of the conference room.

She strode purposefully through my field of vision.

"Good, Ket. That's it. Take deep breaths." It was Retanei speaking, but I felt someone dabbing at my hand and hers were on my shoulders.

When did I sit down?

Retanei spoke again, "Brad, can you bring Artemis up here? I need her abilities."

"By the grace of the Gods, what happened?" This time it was Silver's voice entering into the conversation.

Rathal's voice cut at him, "You left her alone."

"I kept her in range."

Their argument made no sense. And it only added to my quickly growing headache.

Rubbing my temple with my free hand, I lowered my head and

closed my eyes, trying however I could to pull myself back under control.

"If you two want to argue, do it elsewhere. We have a situation right now," Savanas' voice warned.

Someone stroked my back - I wanted to tell them to leave me alone, but I still had no idea what was going on. "Just hold on, Ket. Artemis will be here at any moment."

"Artemis?" I knew who she was talking about, but not why it was important for the wolf to be here.

Opening my eyes, I understood what everyone was in a panic about. Streaks of raw arcane energy moved over my body like lightning. Or water. I was not quite sure, but it was fascinating to watch. It was stronger this time by far.

The iridescent colors moved, collided, separated. I should be worried about this. Something told me the last part, but I held my uninjured hand up, watching the colors dance across the palm and there was no sense of urgency. No sense of wrong. Just curiosity, and in it, understanding.

The hands holding my shoulders switched suddenly, but it did not bother me - I was too preoccupied by this new sensation. My control was at its limit, but I was not in a panic.

It made sense now. Brown had not known I was an Arcanist. When he sent the puppet and I reacted, I was able to channel the emotional energy into my connection with the arcane. My further exposure set me off balance because I had not fully understood what was happening. What he did this morning tried to prey upon that.

I watched as the colors converged and sat in the palm of my uninjured hand. It was so pretty, but it was scaring the others. Closing my hand on it, I pulled it back into myself and looked up.

Somewhere along the line, Artemis got upstairs, but kept her distance. Retanei could not get her to come closer. Magic in general often scared animals.

"Are we good?" Savanas asked. She stood there with her hands on her hips and did not actually wait for a response. "I want answers from both of you. Now!" She was angry to the point of it emanating off her. "You first," she said as she pointed at Silver.

He was the one who took over attempting to bring me out of it. The look on his face told me whatever he did last night had not worked this time.

Savanas said, "I told you to stay near her. What were you doing in the conference room?"

Silver did not look up as he took over tending to my hand. He answered calmly, "I was meditating, looking for guidance. Ketayl was still in range."

"Range of what?" Then I realized I had spoken aloud.

The pain in my hand made itself known now that I came out of whatever state I was in.

Silver explained, "Me. Well, whatever it is about me that disrupts people's ability to scry in my general vicinity. The only time we were separated was when she left this morning before I got up."

"Why did you leave without Silver?" Savanas' question was directed toward me.

I had not thought it possible to feel exhausted and like a live wire at the same time. I said, "I didn't know I was supposed to stay near him. I just went to the cafe near the hotel."

"The Hidden Flower?" It was Retanei asking this time, "Did Artemis go with you?"

I looked up at Retanei. The concern on her face was blatant. I said, "Yes."

Savanas leaned back against the desk behind her and crossed her arms. "Fair enough. We did keep you in the dark on that. Didn't want to give you one more thing to worry about. Now, I need you to recount for me what happened while you were there."

That, I was not ready to share. "Um, it's really not important, is it? I got something to eat, checked my messages..." I trailed off, hoping the two women would accept it. Something squeezed my chest again.

I turned my attention to the others. Silver still had my hand. Rathal stood leaning against his desk glaring at the paladin. Darius and Brad stood on the other side of the short walls observing.

Savanas looked to Retanei and raised an eyebrow at her.

Retanei said, "She's squirming. Ket, you don't squirm unless you're being pressed for something you don't want to talk about."

Mentally I cursed her powers of observation.

"Please don't..." I begged. It was getting hard to breathe again. The source of the pressure was external and it gave me something to focus on with a detached level of curiosity.

Silver grabbed my wrist to hold my injured hand in place. I grit my teeth at how tight his grasp was - it hurt. He said, "You need to stay still."

"Ketayl, tell me." Savanas glared me down. After a few moments of staring at me, she said, "Darius, Brad, go down to the Hidden Flower and interview anyone who saw Ketayl. Rathal, get Vince on the line. I don't like it when one of my own is too afraid to talk."

I noted the quick departures of the agents and Rathal sliding into Savanas' chair. Silver still knelt next to me, his firm grip on my wrist. Retanei and Savanas were like statues, barely moving in their observations.

Fear? She was right. It was fear. I knew Brown was not here, but I could still feel his cold, dark eyes - feel the power he had over me.

I shut the world out for a moment to collect myself and turn my attention again to the hold on me.

Following the worn thread from myself, I looked at my pin which had been hastily thrown on Savanas' desk. That was where it ended, but besides my personal modifications, there should not be anything arcane related about it. It was a puzzle that kept my attention.

The thread became visible when I first handed it to Silver. Was it his aura? Divine on a pin for the arcane? That made no sense.

"Care to tell me what is so urgent and what you're doing to my Arcane Investigator?" Vince's voice came from the direction of the large screen on the wall.

I could not bring myself to look up and see his disappointment, though his wording struck me as odd.

"I'm here!" It was Lockonis. She sounded out of breath. "What in the Hells happened?"

Savanas moved to stand center before the screen. "This is only theory, but I'm thinking someone threatened Ketayl. She's too afraid to tell me what happened and I need more information. My instincts tell me Arcane College."

There was a slight pause before I heard Vince say, "Fletcher, have the team get a Shrike ready to go to Ocean's Edge and get me someone from the Arcane College Circle of Magi." There was another pause. "I will not tolerate this."

Lockonis jumped in and begged, "Ketayl, please."

I looked up at the screen and the fear Savanas spoke of kicked back in. "I can't. He knows." I pulled hard against the thread. I almost did not have enough air to speak.

There was no way it could have been my library.

Taking a deep breath, Lockonis stared at me as best as she could through the feed. "How?"

"Nothing behind. Only me." I had no idea how I was breaking past the stranglehold with Lockonis.

Perhaps because I could say less and speak on a different level with her. Her ability to piece together a full picture with seemingly random parts was something I strove to understand and learn.

"Dammit." Lockonis cursed and paced back and forth behind Vince's chair.

Savanas stepped in during the pause. "It happened while she was separated from the rest of us except for Artemis. It was my fault I hadn't told her to stay with Silver. For whatever reason, he stops people's ability to scry. If Brown was targeting Ketayl, I wanted her out of his sight. I have a couple of my people on their way to the place it happened."

"Ketayl, I need details." Vince sat forward in his chair looking far deadlier than I had ever seen him. "What did he say to you?"

"Please, don't..." I could feel the thread getting tighter around me. "I can't..." I could not breathe again and it made me panic. Panic was bad. I knew what happened and I did not want to hurt anyone here. I should run until I calmed down.

"That's an order," Vince said.

Silver rubbed my arm. He still knelt next to me. I then realized my hand stopped hurting. I desperately tried to tug my arm out of his grasp, but he held firm.

He whispered, "Please."

The thread snapped and I forced myself not to physically react to the sudden release. It was as if an elastic broke. I stared at the pin for a moment to see the broken thread. It was searching, but I was too far away.

Taking a deep breath, I started more calmly, "He said I owed the Arcane College a debt."

"What?" It was Lockonis. She stopped her pacing.

"That I owed them everything. He ordered me to leave the TIO. I think..." I lost my voice.

"Oh, he's mine." I saw a flash of fire appear in Lockonis' hand quickly. She had a habit of doing that when she was mad, and for once, I did not feel the need to look for a hiding place.

I heard Savanas mutter an "Oh no." under her breath.

"Continue," Vince said patiently.

"The puppet. I don't think he knew I was an Arcanist. I didn't fully understand it then and I hadn't much exposure, but I was able to channel the emotional energy into my cast, which burned off most of the effects. I'm not sure if he knew I had been exposed again to a higher concentration. He wanted to unbalance."

Lockonis took a moment before rewording my conclusion, "Brown wanted to use you to cause another incident. Two birds with one stone. Gets rid of you and creates more chaos for the cause."

"With Artemis there with you, she was able to hold off the effects, but then she stayed downstairs with Melody thinking you were safe," Retanei said and knelt down to pet her companion.

Vince took back over the conversation. "I have a few calls to make. Lockonis and I will set out for Ocean's Edge as soon as we can."

The call was over and I had four sets of eyes on me. It was going to be a very long day.

17

————

Retanei pulled me into the conference room, away from Savanas and the others.

Savanas' temper was barely kept in check after finding out I delayed reporting my reaction last night. Thankfully she was distracted for the moment breaking up the argument that had broken out between Rathal and Silver. I was sure once she finished, she would be coming to deal with me.

Retanei ordered Artemis to stay with the others, hoping her calming presence would help.

Chaos, is what Archmage Brown wanted, and it stalled us. There was nothing any of us could do until it was resolved. Silver eluded to the idea everyone affected would be different in how they burned off the effects. I focused whatever was causing me to be unbalanced from the arcane remnants the first time into casting. I contemplated Retanei's early desire to go hunting immediately. Was that how she burned off the effects?

"Sit down, take a breather," Retanei said and moved to get some water out of the nearby cooler. Placing the cup down in front of me, she admitted, "I still don't understand a thing about what just happened. However, if Brown wasn't my next target before, he certainly is now."

I smiled at her candidness. I said, "I could try to explain, but my understanding of it is still more instinctual than intellectual. I... didn't wanted to get the Director involved." I had failed and now he was coming to clean up my mess.

Retanei moved to the window. She said, "Don't blame yourself - it was going to happen regardless. You were just the final catalyst. Vince was thinking about coming out here himself when the Arcane College first got involved. Keeping Lockonis from frying this guy alive when we find him is going to be hard. I'm pretty sure Savanas will be requesting vacation time shortly after we wrap up this case."

That was right, Lockonis had been Savanas' partner before. Lockonis could drive anyone crazy. I thought she did it to hide her true self. In the call earlier, it was the most raw I had seen her. Well, besides the phone call yesterday, but seeing her face was a different thing.

"Ketayl, I'm sorry," Retanei said quietly. I looked at her, not understanding. She was still staring out the window. "I wanted to ease your burden with this case, and the only thing I did was to put you in harm's way. Early on I decided to let you focus on what you do best, which is why a lot was kept from you. Then this mess with..."

"There's enough blame to go around - I agreed with the plan," Savanas cut her off as she strode in. "Artemis is currently staring the hotheads down. I guess Elven men under the age of adulthood really are immature. Before, I thought it was just Rathal." She took a deep breath, obviously exasperated. "What we need now is a solid plan for all of us. Brad and Darius should be back soon."

Retanei folded her arms across her chest as she leaned back against the strip of wall between the windows. She commented, "You know they're going to have to fight it out. They've been circling and hissing at each other since they were first put together in the same room."

Savanas rubbed the bridge of her nose and said, "I know." She looked at Retanei, weary plain on her face. Her voice cracked when she asked, "Why is this happening? How do I deal with someone who can break my team with no effort?"

What else happened I did not know about? I had seen little of Brad and Darius, but nothing seemed amiss with them. Rathal, despite his behavior, was still competent in his duties.

Savanas looked lost. It was something I never thought possible.

"Your team is still in one piece and you know it. Maybe a bit worse for wear, but still solid," Retanei corrected.

Taking a deep breath, Savanas pulled herself back up. She said, "You're right. One of these days you're going to tell me how you do it. Especially when even you were affected by that stuff."

Retanei smirked and said teasingly, "Well, first of all, I turned down the offer to head a branch. Second, hunting helped me regain my focus and perspective."

I found her admittance to that fact interesting. She rarely spoke of herself and less if something was bothering her.

Savanas shook her head and laughed. I was lost, but kept quiet. Obviously they knew each other better than I thought.

"Sorry you had to see that, Ket. You ready to deal with your boys again?" Savanas asked me.

I raised an eyebrow at Savanas, not sure why she chose that phrase to describe them. I downed the last of my water and got up. Might as well get this over with. At least she spared me the interrogation.

Walking past Savanas, I heard her ask Retanei quietly, "Is she really that oblivious?"

There was no verbal response. While I knew they talked about me, I supposed I was oblivious in the fact I had no idea what she meant. I took a step to the side once I passed through the doors, not sure how to handle the scene in front of me.

Silver and Rathal sat across from each other with Artemis growling at them.

"I leave you guys alone for not even five minutes..." Savanas complained.

"Well, if this moron hadn't..." Rathal angrily said. He was half out of his seat, an accusatory finger pointed at Silver.

"I already heard your grievances against him. And don't you dare start either or I'll take you both downstairs and knock your heads together. Speaking of... Ket, how's your firearms handling?" Savanas turned back to me.

I had been contemplating returning to the conference room.

It took me a moment to find an answer, "I'm not overly fond of them." The noise and the recoil kept me from wanting to practice much.

Savanas did not seem to like the answer. She said, "We'll wait until Darius gets back then." Looking at the two male Elves, she ordered, "Take yourselves downstairs to the gym and work it out. Retanei, keep an eye on them so they don't kill each other. Chaos is what this guy wants and I don't want to give it to him."

As soon as Brad and Darius returned and gave her their report, Savanas sent us downstairs. It was something short of amazing how many questions Darius managed to ask me on the way down. I had few solid answers.

"Well, you're not as used to them as we are so... something with a full metal frame?" Darius looked at Brad who accompanied us.

Brad shrugged and said, "You're our firearms expert. We should have her shoot a few and see what fits, but I wouldn't count out some of the polymers. She might just need her grip adjusted."

Darius would pick up a gun and then either put it back down in the safe or on a tray he was carrying. He said, "Oh, yeah, we got that little one in recently for backup carry. It's a little snappy, but the recoil is manageable even for new shooters. Then there's the modular one. That would make it easy to fit to her hands."

They kept going back and forth debating the pistols. I really did not want to carry one, but I was not going to argue against Savanas' decision. I understood her choice - my own personal firepower was questionable right now and I was no Warmage. Even under normal circumstances I would not be able to go up against an Archmage.

The room we were in separated the indoor range from the physical training facility. It looked like Rathal and Silver were attmpting to kill each other. Insults flew as well as fists, but was muffled to the point I could not make out what was being said.

Retanei watched with Artemis curled up at her feet. The fighters wore the standard exercise clothes the TIO provided. As long as their injuries were not severe, they could be healed quickly.

Speaking of... I looked down at the hand I injured earlier. I had not realized at the time Silver used his power. If I had paid more attention, I would have made him stop - healing me then was too dangerous. That and he did not need to waste his energy on me.

With some relief, Savanas had taken my pin. It felt awkward as I was used to it always being with me, even if lately only stuffed in a pocket. I was afraid of what secrets were still hidden in it.

"How goes the search?" Savanas asked. She came in carrying a file folder. I was not sure why she also held my coat.

Darius was deep in another safe when he answered, "I've got a small selection together to start. Just getting ammo and we'll have to figure out how she's comfortable carrying."

Savanas picked up one of the pistols on the tray and commented, "You cannot be serious with this one. I might like something that packs a bigger punch, but Ketayl's training time is limited."

Brad was the one who spoke, "That one is my fault. The recoil isn't bad, but you're right, this big of a caliber might scare her."

Darius finally backed out of the cabinet, his arms loaded down with different boxes of ammo and extra magazines. He said, "Told you. Oh, is that for me?" He eyed the file Savanas carried.

Brad took the items from Darius. Once his arms were free, Darius read the file. He commented, "Not so limited. I thought you were going to tell me she only had basic pistol. Looks like she's gone through concealed and a couple of the more advanced courses. Limited range time though. No rifle, but it's not an issue."

I did not want to admit the only reason I took an interest was the idea of combining the use of the arcane with a firearm, which I managed mild success with.

That and my sister liked to drag me down to the range every so often.

"I brought Ketayl's coat. It may pose a problem with drawing compared to the standard TIO coats." Savanas turned to me saying, "Since you gave yours to Silver."

I explained, "He didn't have a coat."

Savanas said, "I know, and we don't have spares. It's not like we go through them quickly."

"Rathal always seems to ruin jackets though," Brad commented. "We've got a surplus of those, but it's too cold for something that lightweight."

Darius paced, reading my record. "Just because he seems to find fights as the temperature heats up…"

Tossing my coat to me, Savanas crossed her arms and leaned back against the counter. Her attention turned to the physical training area. "Rathal's a hothead. And it looks like he's met his match with

Silver," she said, "Rathal might be a good scrapper, but he's going to have a hard time outlasting Silver's stamina."

"The guy trains in his armor," Brad said while he loaded the magazines, "Silver has to have a leg up in strength on him also. Rathal just moves damn fast."

It was cold down here and having my coat was a good thing. I slid it on, leaving it unzipped.

"Come on, Ket, let's get you started. We can leave these two to analyzing the fight," Darius said and signaled me with his head. His hands were full with the tray.

I quickly opened the door for him, not wanting to be rude, but also not looking forward to this quick training session.

RATHAL AND SILVER were still fighting when Darius was satisfied with my choice and handling. I admitted, Darius was an excellent instructor and I felt more comfortable, but not so much I wanted to carry.

I watched the two silently through the window, rubbing my hands and wrists. The recoil on a couple of the pistols really hurt. I lost count of the number of rounds I shot.

The two fighters were randomly swinging punches at each other when they got close. Both covered in sweat and exhausted. Shirts tossed carelessly aside.

Rathal's hair was mostly out of the little ponytail he kept it in. The glint of metal around Silver's neck caught my attention. A small golden sun swung on its thick chain.

"Who is winning?" Darius asked.

"Neither," Savanas said and kept watching through the window. "They're too evenly matched. As much as I'm curious how they would be with their weapons of choice, I do not want to clean up after that."

Rathal made a run for Silver who got under him. He picked up Rathal and threw him down to the mat. Silver then collapsed onto his rear and did not move to get up. Rathal stayed where he landed. They were both alive, but too exhausted to continue.

"I think that counts as Silver winning," Brad said and smirked at Savanas, "I told you I trained with this guy. Rathal's speed isn't enough."

"No way. It's a tie," Savanas tossed back before grumbling and digging into her pocket for her wallet. She handed Brad a bill. "Damn, I really thought Rathal was going to have enough to wear him out. I should up his physical training requirement for losing."

I followed Darius so he could figure out a holster for me. The show was over and I wondered why Savanas and Brad still hung by the windows.

Looking into the physical training area, I never wanted to see either of them hurt. Whatever was going on between them was not resolving itself otherwise. Silver was now sprawled out on the mat, breathing heavily and Rathal had not moved. They were talking, but I still could not hear through the thick glass and soundproofing on the walls.

Retanei seemed unconcerned about them and just watched. There were a couple of bottles of water next to her I did not remember seeing before.

Savanas took an interest in what Darius and I were doing. "Good. I can't arm our consultant, but at least I can make sure you're covered. Surprised me when I saw your file. Most mages opt out of firearms training or take as little as possible. Not that we have many mages on staff. Lockonis outright refuses, but she's in a class all her own."

I shrugged, still not wanting to get into detail about my motivations. It would only cause more problems right now.

Savanas said, "In any case, I got a call from Fletch. They've been delayed due to a stalled storm system over the Chained Lakes region. They'll wait it out until the end of the day, but I have a feeling they'll take the long way around. Especially if the storm starts to move our way. We get enough crap coming down from the north. Ah, they live." Her attention was once again back to the physical training area.

Silver and Rathal struggled to get up, but Silver managed to stand first. He offered a hand to Rathal. Rathal took it, got up, and patted Silver on the shoulder, smiling.

"All's well that ends well," Brad commented.

Retanei finally moved and handed them each a bottle of water, pointing toward the side where it looked like there were changing rooms. Both were laughing and talking, acting like the best of friends. It confused me - they had not liked each other from the moment they met.

Savanas watched the two carefully. She said, "I can't speak for

Silver, but Rathal at least looks more back to normal. I'll have to remember not to be too hard on him."

I made a mental note to ask Retanei what happened. If this was what the two were like under normal circumstances, I shuddered at the thought of what the arcane remnants might have turned the city into.

After a couple of hours, we took a break for a late midday meal. Savanas ordered Brad, Darius, and Retanei to get some rest. Artemis was again left with me. I was not sure how well that would work. If I had another reaction Artemis was too scared to come near me.

Yet her presence was why I did not at the cafe. She was able to use her gift before anything manifested. I still wondered how it worked exactly.

The extra weight from the pistol strapped to my thigh bothered me and I thought about begging to be rid of it. I was pretty sure if I had to shoot someone, I could, but I was no marksman - I could as easily graze them as I could kill.

It was early evening when Savanas got off the phone and announced, "Retanei's up. You two call it a day." She pointed in our direction without looking up from what she was writing. "And be prepared for a possible wake up call."

Silver looked at me and then back to Savanas. He said, "I don't understand."

This time Savanas stopped and leveled a look at Silver. She snapped. "It's simple. We've got a lead, and Retanei is following up. If she finds something, we move. You'll need your armor if she does."

"What about the Director?" I asked. It seemed strange after the last call we would not wait for him.

Savanas said, glaring at me, "I don't want to miss any window of opportunity we get. Now go."

18

LEANING against the cold window in the backseat, I yawned, still tired. I had gotten more than enough rest when Savanas knocked on the hotel door, but the nightmares kept it from being effective. More than once Artemis nudged me awake. I was grateful for her vigilance - the last thing I needed to do was wake Silver.

I was also relieved Silver had not repeated the previous night.

Savanas was in such a rush I did not have the chance to put my hair up in its normal bun. I simply bound it in a loose ponytail over my shoulder. Silver finished braiding his hair on the drive.

When Savanas picked us up, she swapped vehicles. Silver's armor was not going to fit in the back of her car and she wanted as few vehicles as possible.

Silver sat in front of me. Big Black laid on the seat next to me and the very large dog still made me nervous, though Artemis somehow managed to squeeze between us, half her body across my lap. She was heavier than I thought, though I could not complain about being cold.

Savanas told us we were going to meet the others at a farm outside of the city. She knew the owners and it would put us slightly closer than the road to our first destination, but it would still be a lot of walking. She left out where our destination was.

When we arrived at the farm, Retanei was nowhere in sight, but

Brad, Darius, and Rathal worked out of the back of another vehicle. They were busy donning armor, arming themselves, and testing their communications equipment.

As Silver donned his own armor, I found a certain level of fascination between the armor everyone wore. So much had changed in armor with technological developments and yet, it was all based on the same concepts.

Darius held out a thinner vest from the ones the rest of the Ocean's Edge team wore. He told me, "Put this on under your coat. It shouldn't hamper your movements if you need to cast, but stay behind us - it can't take a hit like ours."

Taking the garment, I did as I was told, shivering as the cold took a bite at me the moment I opened my coat. Silver had still been wearing my TIO coat until he put his armor on and Savanas tossed it at me. Guess I would notget the extra coverage on my legs from mine. I quickly folded up my personal coat and stored it. Then I started trying to figure out how to put on the armor I was given. Shivering made it harder.

Savanas came over to help. She also checked to make sure I was armed and helped me put on an ear piece. She was a little rough when she put my issued gun back in the loaned holster wrapped around my thigh and I grabbed the truck to keep my balance.

She finished by putting a necklace with a small tear drop gem around my neck. "I hope this will work if we need you to copy information on the fly."

It was too dark to make out what the gem was, but I doubted there would be much information to copy. I said, "It shouldn't be a problem." I was fairly confident in my ability to make it work.

My tablet was also in my bag and I could go straight to it if I had enough time. It was not the best solution as it bogged down the system, but it would work. Though depending on how much there was and if I had a network connection, I might not have enough space either.

I pulled my hair out of the loose ponytail, pulling it back behind my head. My hair elastic broke when I went to put it back in. Any spares I had were back at the hotel. I knew it was worn out, but I thought it would last a little longer. I hoped this was not a sign of how things would go this morning.

Savanas still stood next to me, securing her own gear and took a moment to spread my hair over my ears. "If we had taken my car, I'd have an extra hair elastic you could borrow. At least you'll be able to stay warmer this way."

As we set out, I used the light from the building we were parked next to so I could observe the others. Savanas had two swords with curved blades slung on her hips. The one on her left side was significantly longer than the other. Big Black followed at her side. Rathal carried what looked like a fat arrow, but the head was more like a dagger. Darius seemed content with the large gun he carried. I could not see anything more than the standard sidearm on Brad. Artemis followed beside me. It felt weird having Retanei's animal companion constantly at my side. It also made me worry for Retanei being out here alone.

"Where's Retanei?" I asked as the forest loomed closer.

"She'll rendezvous with us," Savanas said.

I bit my lower lip. She avoided answering my question. Why did they have to keep doing that?

Silver, who walked next to me, was only focused ahead. I had not expected his armor to be so loud. Or maybe it was the dead silence of the night.

I wished I had more information. I also hoped the walk would warm me up. My TIO coat still contained some of Silver's residual warmth when I put it on, but my legs were freezing. Had I thought enough ahead, I would have worn tights underneath. Though I was not sure I had packed any. I preferred to wear them when I wore my slipper-like shoes, but I had been wearing boots while I was here, which meant socks.

Then I wondered why I was thinking about any of this. I should be focused on the task ahead. We would not be here, walking in the cold and dark without reason.

As we walked, no one spoke and I was too afraid to break the silence. I busied my mind with what I should expect, but I had no idea what to expect. Would there be another arcane bomb? The Archmage himself? Who would be there with him? How fanatical were they?

At some point Silver took a position a few steps ahead. It took a moment for me to realize his armor had taken on an unearthly glow - as if it reflected the light of the moon. Perhaps it was some type of enchantment. I filed the thought away to ask him later.

The others spread out. Savanas and Brad were far to the front on either side of us. Rathal and Darius had fallen back.

The forest was thick and eerie making me itch to cast a light spell. The moon above barely provided enough illumination to see where I was going. The sounds of the forest and things I could not see made me uneasy.

Savanas kept us moving until we reached a familiar clearing. On the other side, a shining set of silver eyes watched us. I took a step back, but then she stepped forward enough to be seen.

"Retanei..." It came out as a breath of relief.

Artemis trotted to her. I forgot Retanei's ability to see in the dark also changed her eye color, which the moonlight had illuminated.

Here there were signs of a camp. Trash littered the area around a fire pit.

The other thing that caught my attention was the arcane spells used. They gathered here and then teleported. It was a big group too. The arc was the same, telling me it was a mass teleport.

Kneeling down at this end of the remnant, I touched the ground with my gloved hand, gently moving the tall, snow-covered grass for the hidden element. I gently shifted the arcane mites out of the way.

"What do you have?" Savanas asked and knelt next to me.

"It's the Archmage's signature. He tried to bury it." Not many mages were even aware they created a signature when they cast. It must have been him watching us the first time at the Waking Dawn. He directed his cast directly against the solid ground to hide it. It was a good attempt, but obviously not enough.

I started to think the Archmage had not known before observing us that I could see the arcane. However, because of Silver's power to cover an area from scrying, he would not know about my ability to follow a teleport line either.

Savanas pulled the camera out of my bag and waited for me to point her at the signature.

Separating my fingers into a V shape, I surrounded the small signature for her and said, "Mass teleport heading that way." I pointed in the direction of the arc.

"Gods..." I heard Silver whisper and turned my attention to him. "The church is in that direction. How far?"

Closing my eyes, I tried to follow the arc, but was unsuccessful. I repeated the process, using more of my power to follow it as if I was teleporting, but failed at the same point again. I shook my head this time because the extra power bounced me back off the barrier and it took a moment longer to re-orientate myself.

Taking a deep breath, I looked up at him and said, "I don't know. It cuts off after a bit. There is some kind of barrier."

Silver started to move, but Rathal grabbed his shoulder. Rathal said, "No, we stick together, and more importantly, you stay with her."

Some part of my mind thought it was the most rational thing I had heard out of Rathal yet. I disliked being the one he pointed at.

I took my camera from Savanas and set about documenting. It gave me something else to focus on for the moment. What changed between the two of them, I did not know nor did I have the time to find out.

Savanas scratched the back of her neck - an unusual movement. She said, "Things are starting to make sense and I wished to the Gods they weren't."

Darius asked, "How far to the church?"

Retanei looked in the direction of the place in question and considered for a moment. "A couple of miles."

"Alright, enough chatter, let's move," Savanas ordered and did not wait for anyone to respond. "Retanei, once we're back in the forest, scout ahead."

The moment we hit the tree line, Retanei and Artemis were gone. Savanas set a grueling pace. After a while, I had to stop and lean against a tree to get some air.

"Hey, guys," Darius said, stopping by my side.

The ones ahead turned back toward me. Reaching into a pouch on his vest Darius handed me a bottle of water.

I wondered how on Terra Silver could move at such a pace in his armor and the others carried far more than me. I was only slowing the group down. My bag felt like it weighed at least double what it should. Skipping physical training had caught up to me.

I gladly accepted the bottle of water, downing half of it quickly. I said, "Thank you. Sorry." I was still trying to catch my breath.

Savanas approached, her arms crossed. I could not make out the expression on her face. She said, "It's as good of time as any. We're getting close to the church and I want a plan of action in case we find something."

She pulled out her phone and brought up a map. It was a satellite image of the region and I could see the parking lot and the road which sat between the church grounds and the ocean. It would make sense, I reasoned, for a Holy Church of the Sun to greet the dawn.

Savanas continued, "First, we'll observe the grounds. Silver, you're going to be the one who can tell us if something is out of place. If everything is fine, we'll continue on. If not, we're going to need your permission to search the grounds."

Silver nodded. His face was hard in the glow from the phone.

"We'll split into groups of two and search each building. We'll be approaching from the backside of the grounds so we'll deal with the cathedral last. Brad, Darius, you two will take the north side buildings. Rathal and I will go through the west and south. Silver, keep yourself and Ket out of sight. She'll be able to hear if we need backup. Can you tell me what the buildings are so we know what to expect?" Savanas ordered, looking at Silver expectantly.

Silver stayed silent a moment. Then he pointed and said, "This large building in the center facing east is the cathedral. This one on the north side near the parking lot is where the offices are located. Behind it is the training center. The long one here to the south is housing - there aren't many residents at this time. Only the first floor should be occupied - I'm the only one living on the second floor. And this," he pointed at a small building to the west of the cathedral, "is where we prep the dead before the funeral and burial - unless something happened recently to one of the paladins, it's likely empty. The graveyard is behind it. The docks are mostly empty at this time of year."

"What do you mean?" Rathal asked.

Silver pointed at a small building nestled between the forest and the water. He said, "Paladin Parker keeps his boat in the water inside the boat house year-round. He'll usually go fishing after the first light service." He looked up at the sky and commented, "We're getting pretty close to dawn. There will be people moving about getting ready for the first light service. Likely you'll find my mentor in the graveyard before his wife's grave."

"This is the busiest service of the weekend, isn't it?" Brad asked as he looked over the map.

"Yes," Silver did not even hesitate. "The second day of week's end has the highest attendance for first light. The parking lot will be full."

I sincerely hoped the group had merely moved through the

church's grounds - otherwise this could be a repeat of what happened at the Waking Dawn and I was not sure I could handle another.

WHEN WE ARRIVED at the church grounds, I was grateful for the rest. The others took off the moment Silver said something was wrong and granted his permission for them to search. They moved too quickly for me to tell them I found the tail end of the teleports, though the line was blurry as if looking at it through water.

Silver impatiently waited with me inside of the tree line where winter still had its grasp. He paced back and forth with his sword drawn. Occasionally he would flip his sword around in his hand - his eyes always on the church grounds.

At least he kept his distance so I did not accidentally get hit.

As I huddled to try to keep warm I could see what Silver said before about the grounds. Flowers bloomed radiantly even in the night. It looked like spring and more importantly, warm.

Why would they not let me wait where it was warmer? The movement of me rubbing my legs to try to keep them warm was more likely to draw attention.

It was extremely quiet. Given what Silver briefly described about the activities we should have expected, there was not a soul in sight.

Silver stopped and stared at the graveyard. Following his line of sight, I saw a freshly dug grave and asked, "Did someone recently pass?" His mentor was not there either. I worried something may have happened to the man. While I may not have known Silver's family, I understood the death of any of them would affect him. In our conversations, I could hear how much he deeply cared for them.

In the back of my mind, I was glad I was given the ear piece I needed to push a button to talk. I would not have wanted to interrupt the other's active communications with conversation. I gave up on counting how many times the others said "clear."

Savanas and Rathal finished clearing the west building. It did not take long for Brad and Darius to clear the outside training yard, but they were still working their way through the attached building.

Silver turned to me, worry plain on his face. "No one has been buried over there since Maria's funeral. The only reason to disturb a lot in that area is if my mentor has passed." I pondered that for a moment before he elaborated, "The lots are by family. Maria and my mentor were not able to bear children. My mentor's father may have adopted me as his own, but because I am not related by blood, I wouldn't be placed there either."

This conversation had become morbid quickly. I asked, "Would there be a reason to disturb an occupied grave?" It was different than the customs of both Elves and the Arcane College who disposed of the dead with fire.

Then the all clear on for the training center came through.

"No," Silver said.

The wait was maddening for me and I could only take a guess at how Silver must be feeling. It was so quiet. The predawn cast an even more eerie glow across the grounds than the moon in the forest.

"I found them." The call was not from either of the groups - it was from Retanei. I did not know she was linked in our communications. She warned, "Prepare yourselves." Her voice sounded hard and forced.

Savanas' voice rang through next, "First finish off the searches in the outer buildings. I don't want any surprises. Ket, how are things on your end?"

How did she know where Retanei was?

I had not expected to be addressed. Pushing the button on the ear piece, I replied, "Quiet, I found the tail end of the teleports - they came in behind the west building. Silver says there is a freshly dug grave out of place."

"Check it out and come along the southern building, we'll meet up with you."

I relayed the information to Silver. The call came through for an all clear on the offices and that team was heading for the cathedral's north-side entrance.

Confirming whose grave was disturbed, Silver set off at a pace which forced me to jog to keep up - I was not able to read the name on the stone. Not in this light and from the distance he kept from it.

Feeling a stitch starting in my side, I was not sure if I should be cursing being short or because I was not in as good of shape as everyone else. The sun also chose at that moment to break the horizon and I had to squint until my eyes adjusted.

We met up with Savanas and Rathal, then the latter split off to head for the south-side entrance. Savanas led us around to the front of the building. I took a moment to look out over the water - it lapped lazily at the shore. It was so peaceful and quiet. Even the clouds had cleared allowing the sun to shine radiantly as it rose.

The cathedral stood tall - it was mostly white, the spire at the front of the building held a giant golden sun at the top. It was designed the same as Silver's necklace. Another sun, in stained glass, sat on the front well above the entrance. This building must have at least three floors. It was both grand and intimidating at the same time.

Before we set foot on the stone stairs, I heard Rathal through the ear piece, "Gods preserve us."

Brad and Darius echoed his sentiment, though it sounded like hushed prayers under Brad's breath that followed. The three stated they saw none of the targets inside. Retanei remained silent.

Savanas rushed forward, the large, heavy doors doing little to slow her down. In the vestibule, she leveled a look at the two of us and said, "I'm going in first. I'll call for you. Do *not* enter before I tell you to." She could not have known what was in there, but she knew her people. It told me more than I wanted to know.

I put my bag down, needing to be free of the weight. It gave me a moment to rest.

The look on Savanas' face as she peeked through the heavy wooden doors told me even more. I never imagined there would be anything which could make Savanas pale instantly. The smell of blood and death quickly wafted through the crack and assaulted my senses.

I also sensed heavy arcane usage inside. There must have been another barrier on the doors. All of it together turned my stomach and I found myself kneeling in the vestibule, trying to breathe and hold back the urge to vomit. Silver knelt next to me and rubbed my back.

I thought we already talked about not touching me.

"Ket?" Savanas let the door close allowing me relief. "What's going on in there we can't see?"

Taking a few lung fulls of air first, I managed to press the button on my ear piece so the others could hear. I said, "There's a lot of arcane usage. Without seeing it, I couldn't tell you exactly what, but it's dark. Similar to the necromancer's spells."

"Oh, honey, you don't want to know how dark," Darius said, his voice was hushed.

Silver moved on my statement and threw open the doors, stepping fully into the cathedral's main chamber. Savanas cursed at him from where she darted to the side.

I was once again assaulted by the darkness emanating, getting more of the effects than previous, but now also had a visual to push my limits further. Silver took up most of the doorway, but not enough to block it completely.

My eyes were set on the pews where people lay - the life having been stolen from them, their blood coating the light wood and white marble floor. It was carnage.

Suddenly I was breathing fast, but I could not get enough air and the room started to spin. Closing my eyes, I huddled down closer to the floor, putting my head between my knees. I was supposed to be a professional - I have seen plenty of gory crime scene photos. Why was this so much different?

Part of my mind told me it was because I was never actually there. I could not smell the blood and death, taste the air upon which it rode, hear the screams of those who died...

Picking up my head, the room swam, but I forced myself to focus. I said, "It's the same." It came out as a whisper. Unwillingly, I soaked up the raw, twisted arcane energy and felt a level of filth like never before. It added to the difficulty of keeping tight control.

Savanas knelt next to me. I heard her telling me to stay here and that Rathal was on his way.

Grabbing her arm before she could go anywhere, I pulled myself up, remembering what Archmage Maewon had told me about necromancy.

I told her, "You're going to need both of us." Gritting my teeth, I strode forward as steady as I could. This madness needed to end.

I could feel the power surging through me. I struggled to focus and hold it. Silver looked back at me and I nodded, letting some of the excess flash as pure arcane energy in my hands. The quick burn off helped me regain a measure of control.

His look though was of barely contained rage. I should have asked for more detail on how the exposure affected him.

Necromancy was the darkest sides of both the arcane and the divine twisted together. Neither of us could delve into the other side of the puzzle without potentially losing ourselves to the madness Archmage Maewon spoke of. It did not mean we could not work together.

Standing beside Silver, I took notice of a casket at the altar. It was clean and open, but I could not see inside. I could sense a source of arcane power now that I stood past the doors. I said, "He's here."

"There's more than one. Both are twisted. Let's end this." Since I could not pick up on the second presence, my guess was they were solely a divine caster. I hoped we were not dealing with more than two.

Rathal arrived, out of breath, and Savanas ordered him to call for backup. I followed Silver, who picked a path down the center between the pews, trying not to step in the blood slowly painting the floor red.

The light of dawn came through the stained glass, painting the white walls in color. It was beautiful, contrasting sharply with the death and dark arcane energy.

I heard the doors shut behind me and took note of Savanas and Big Black heading down toward the door on the south side of the building. Brad and Darius each slid inside and moved in opposite directions along the north wall. I heard the door at the back open and close again.

As we approached the altar, Silver stopped and bowed to the large sun statue hanging at the back.

As soon as I took the couple of steps up to the altar, I could see inside of the casket. It was as I feared, the dark-haired woman looked to have been deceased for a while. I guessed this was Maria by the anger on Silver's face.

Time buried had started to decay the corpse. She wore a circlet and armor almost identical to Silver's. A sword was held in her hands, the blade pointed toward her feet. A familiar looking shield once likely rested on top, but it had shifted in the casket.

The spells used were similar to the Waking Dawn, but this time the energy was being gathered. Thin, black tubes were flowing into Maria from the congregation - they pulsed with energy. Looking back at those who gathered for the morning celebration, I saw a spell I feared I researched. Before they were only visible in Silver's aura, but black tendrils marred the walls and up over the second and third floor balconies at the back. This building must be soaked in the same aura as Silver's.

The tendrils held the parishioners in place. It was a variation on a combat spell to ensnare one's opponents in a certain radius. I vaguely remembered fulfilling the request for locating such a spell, but it had been several years ago at least.

"Ah, James, we have guests." His voice sent a shiver through my spine. My head whipped back around and I was not sure what I felt. Fear? Anger? Blood lust? I held myself back from reacting.

Behind me, I heard swords draw and a couple of firearms being brought to the ready, but I dared not turn around to look. Brad, who stopped on his way to the altar seemed unsure who to direct his aim at.

Brown and James emerged from a side room off the altar along with several other Humans. Brown was surrounded by a magical bubble. The unidentified men all wielded blades of varying length - many of them still dripping with blood. Most of them wore a gun on their hip as well.

"Sir, why are you taking part in this madness? Why would you aid this evil?!" Silver asked, sounding more betrayed than angry. He directed his attention toward the man clad in similar armor to his own. Why was Silver directing his attention at his mentor instead of Brown? Was he the bigger threat?

I realized I knew little to nothing about a paladin's abilities. While I saw the Archmage as the biggest threat, I could be wrong.

James strode forward, with an elated expression. Blood liberally coated his armor and dripped down his sword. He said wistfully, "Soon my beloved will return to me."

Silver stood between me and his mentor. Big Black growled. Shaking, I pulled my gun.

Perhaps not the most intelligent thing, but this was an Archmage I faced. In an arcane battle, I was not going to win. If I could get him to drop the bubble...

The paladins ignored me. Brown was not. The others with him seem to be picking their targets. "Initially I had not wanted your friends involved, but you brought this upon them by continuing to interfere. And who am I to turn down more power?"

Gritting my teeth against the pain and suffering around me, I struggled to keep my focus. I said, "I don't take orders from you. The Arcane College labeled you a rogue mage."

"Please, what can a little fairy girl like you do? You, a mere Researcher, who can barely keep your control in here," Brown scoffed at me and walked toward his sacrifices, extending his arms. "Isn't this beautiful? All of this for love. But you wouldn't be able to comprehend that."

Fairy... I wondered how much about me he knew or if he only repeated the racial slur.

The men with him grinned and spread out to surround those of us on the altar. A few headed for the rest of the team but stopped before they stepped off the raised platform.

I could feel the anger rolling off Silver. He directed toward James, "Sir! You would kill all those here for your own selfish desires? Even Maria would not..."

"Don't say her name! You have no right to address my beloved that way!" James yelled and launched himself at Silver who easily blocked the enraged attack. "This one is mine!"

Then chaos erupted and the other men attacked. I found myself being dragged back, behind the casket. Gunshots rang out and the couple heading for Savanas and I dropped. Big Black was attacking a third and Artemis appeared in a streak of gray to assist.

The casket sat upon what looked like a heavy, sturdy stone block. Savanas forced me to crouch down on the far side from the paladins fighting it out. She said, "Tell me you've got something we can use."

The move turned me to face toward the doors we entered. Rathal's fat arrow had become a lance and he took on two more along the south-side wall. Brad and Darius were aiming to take down the remaining four, but were unable to get clear shots as the men used the pews for cover.

I closed my eyes for a moment to clear the images and focus on Savanas' words. I frantically searched the area with my own power to gather information about the spells going on and felt hopeless.

Shaking my head, I said, "I don't know enough about Brown's bubble yet to shatter it, but I wouldn't recommend shooting it - the kinetic energy could make it stronger. If you can give me some time..."

My head hurt and it was getting more difficult to focus. This was far stronger than the spell used at the Waking Dawn. The voices I heard before screaming in pain and anger faded against the pounding. I also stopped hearing the voices in my ears. My grip on the gun was lax.

"I'll come up with something if you can give me some time," I said.

Savanas tugged on my ear and smirked, twirling her blades as she got up. "This could be interesting." The longer blade was in her right hand.

Holding the gun in my left hand, I picked up one of the black tubes with my right. It pulsed with dark energy. It did not feel like pure arcane, but without Silver, I could not tell if it was mixed with divine. The energy flowed from the parishioners to the casket. There was a small set of tubes with energy flowing out of the casket into Brown's bubble. They were almost hidden among the others.

I tried to ignore the fight going on between Silver and James, but with sparks flying from their strikes, calling it difficult was an understatement. I pushed the sounds of the others out as well, including the occasional "thwap" of an arrow hitting home. Knowing Retanei was also in the fight helped. Part of my mind had been concerned the ones Darius and Brad were fighting would take a shot at me.

James shouted, "She always had a soft spot for you, didn't she, Silver? Well, you can take her place!" It was one of many insults James spouted. The two paladins got dangerously close. I quickly dropped the tube and scrambled to hide. Then I noticed where my friend was as I caught a flash of black and silver-white on the top balcony.

I took a moment to figure out where everyone was in case I needed to run. James fought like a crazed man. Silver's movements were full of passion, but calculated. I was glad someone was able to keep their head about them.

Rathal, on the other hand, looked like a man possessed. I watched as he thrust his lance through one man's chest and then swung it with the dying body still attached into the other.

Arrows stuck out of two more bodies lying in the middle aisle. Retanei lent her aide to Brad and Darius. Brad was in close combat with one of the men while Darius kept trying to get the other in his sights. Big Black and Artemis finished with their opponent and went to help Savanas.

I was useless here - I could not help any of them. I did not even know what I was looking for. I had a gun in my hand and...

Why was I here? Why was I useless? This was not my first fight, despite what the others may think. It was not the first time my life, and the lives of others, had been on the line.

But I was not that person anymore, was I? I put her behind me decades ago. I was not the scared little girl acting on instinct. The myth had become just that.

"Oh, please, like your little toys could hurt me," Brown said, bored. It shook me out of my moment of self-doubt.

Brown did not move as Savanas launched a series of attacks. It looked like she was dancing with the two blades. Something was wrong about his lack of action, but the pounding in my head and my barely controlled power made it difficult to focus.

A gunshot sounded out again. Another of the enemy was down. Darius turned his attention forward, though he was at the far back of the cathedral. I looked at him, scared.

Then Brown ordered, "Ketayl, stand."

A wave of magic hit me, and I recognized it as a command spell. It broke over me like water.

The paladins had moved to the far side of alter, still fighting fiercely, so I took the chance to stand up. I needed to see what was going on.

"Eliminate this woman," Brown said and pointed at Savanas.

Brown must not have known his command spell broke. My panic gave way to confusion.

"Damn, that's hot," Savanas said, turning her pocket to empty it. My Arcane College pin fell out, glowing. She looked in my direction with worry.

Even the paladins slowed. Brad had his opponent in a headlock and held him there as he watched. I caught Darius out of the corner of my eye raising his weapon, unsure where to point it.

Brown did not seem interested in the actions of the others. My pin reached out to me again, but it could not find me - I was too far away.

Savanas kept her attention between Brown and myself, unsure where to direct her blades. Her voice warned, "Don't do it, Ket. Don't do it." Her expression showed she would fight only if she absolutely had to. Big Black growled at her side, teeth bared. Artemis whined at me.

"I GAVE YOU AN ORDER!" Brown roared.

Everything cleared as time slowed. Arcane power zoomed around me, pushing the limits of my capacity. I felt my hair lift off the back of my neck as if picked up by an unfelt wind.

It had become clear - the Archmage needed Maria as a valve to slow down the energy he was collecting. Overloading the bubble was an idea I could run with.

I summoned pure arcane energy to my hands, channeling them into the gun I gripped. The iridescent colors swam wildly in anticipation as I struggled with the combining spell I had created.

Bring my gun to bear on Brown, I fought through the overpowering energy to tell him: "You. Don't. Control. Me."

Before I fully registered the movement, I fired. Time still had not regained its normal pace - I caught the ejected casing twirling lazily through the air out of the corner of my eye. Brown had a look of disbelief on his face, which was changing to anger when he figured out I aimed at him. Savanas had brought her swords up to deflect - a shocked look on her face. Brad was barely in view, his opponent down and had started running for Savanas.

The overload of energy caused it to crack and threaten to shatter. I burnt out the arcane side of his spell. I could also smell the melting metal and feel the heat in my hands and reflexively let go of the gun. The added kinetic delivery had the effect I hoped for. Unfortunately, I was only able to use it once. Part of my mind noted I infused the bullet with too much raw arcane energy, damaging the gun.

"Defend me!" Brown cried as time returned to normal. I could tell he scrambled to find the power to reinforce his bubble. It was his turn to panic.

James immediately complied, knocking Silver back with brute force and taking a stance to engage whoever attacked first.

Big Black took the momentary distraction to launch himself at James, but the paladin was faster and cut down the big dog mid-flight. Artemis let out a howl and would have attacked if Savanas had not grabbed her.

I heard Savanas also cry out for her companion, but she did not move from where she held Artemis. Taking a chance to glance at her for a split second, anger rolled off her. I feared she might do something reckless.

Staggering a moment to regain my balance, the attack I launched took more effort than I anticipated. To fully shatter his bubble, I would need considerably more power. There was plenty here, but it would take time to collect and more personal energy than I had to be able to control and focus it.

"Her, you fool. Eliminate the mage," Brown pointed at me angrily.

James took a step before a shield slammed into him.

Silver stood to my left, holding his arm up, having caught his shield when it flew back. He stepped in front of me and brought his shield down into a defensive position.

"Forget them. Come to me," Brown said. He was scrambling. I did not have enough knowledge of necromancy to figure out what he planned.

Silver's mentor obeyed instantly, his eyes glazed over. He was merely a puppet at this point. There was no will of his own.

I stared in disbelief when James was able to easily walk through the remains of Brown's bubble. That told me the rest of the puzzle.

Leaning forward to the paladin in front of me, I said quietly, "Silver, can you..."

I stopped short when Brown pulled a dagger out of his sleeve and slit James' unprotected throat. Blood sprayed wildly, coating the inside of his bubble, strengthening it.

I thought I was going to be sick, but could not look away.

Brown sneered, "You have failed our masters and must pay the price. However, if your death can help me eliminate the undeserving, perhaps they will grant you mercy in the afterlife."

James' face changed to betrayal and whatever he tried to say came out as a gurgle. As his dying body collapsed to the ground, I could see an angry soul taking shape. It went to lung at Brown, but a black tendril shot out of the casket next to me and bound the soul in place.

With Silver close to me, I was able to see the connection more clearly - his aura being stronger, but the pounding in my head was gaining strength again. I did not have much time left.

Brown commented, "James so wanted to see his love again - be with her again. Had he not failed me so, I might have even let him go on believing she was back for him. A shame, it would have been entertaining for at least a while."

In my moment of clarity previously, something nagged at me about Brown's lack of action. So far he only spoke and walked. Why not show his superior power? He was an Archmage after all.

Of course, Brown was a traditional mage - it took all his concentration to maintain the bubble. It kept him protected from the effects of the room. His spell also kept him from casting anything else. He must have run out of stored spells.

The tendrils snaking from the casket to Brown pulsed stronger with energy. I knew it was only a matter of time before he would be free to attack us himself. For all his grand speeches, he was just trying to buy himself more time.

Brown recomposed himself. He warned, "Boy, you need to move away from that mage. She's likely not going to be able to hold on much longer. When she does lose control, it will be beautiful to watch. I have no grudge against you, but with your considerable power, I needed you to be sent away. And how better than for an organization to have desperate need of a divine caster?"

He was right - my control had been at its limit for a while. The burn off from attacking Brown helped, but it was not going to be enough. The big picture was quickly forming itself in front of me. The bombing of the Waking Dawn had been to get rid of Silver, who was becoming suspicious, so he could come after the church. The bombing was also a distraction as well as to drive people who were seeking solace and guidance to the church.

The thought made me sick.

Brown's attention turned back to me. He smiled in such a way I felt dirty, "Such a lovely creature. I thought about making you my assistant, but I cannot trust one who can so easily outlive me. And then to find out you were an Arcanist. Oh, how delightful that was. I am impressed you are still here after my warning. Though that little show of power before must have put considerable drain on your very limited resources."

Silver practically growled. Savanas moved farther away, looking like she was mumbling to herself. Why did I not hear any of it over the ear piece? Then I noticed my ear piece was missing. Had I lost it in the fight?

It did not matter at this point. If I could not break his stolen source of power, none of us were making it out of here alive. Stepping back in fear, I bumped into the casket.

Maria, of course, his prize - it probably mattered not whose corpse he used, but she had been enough to convince James to join them.

I sent out a prayer to whoever might listen that Silver would forgive me for what I was about to do.

"Your resources aren't endless either," I shot back at the Archmage. Focusing as much of the raw power as I could, I unleashed the hottest flames I was able to conjure on the casket, quickly grabbing the bundle of tendrils leading back to Brown. Wrapping them around my hand, I sent another wave of fire along the black tube, cutting through the bubble and burning Brown's reinforcement in a violent flash.

It knocked him down and weakened his bubble, but he was already getting back on his feet when Silver threw his shield, shattering the remains of Brown's bubble like glass. Savanas moved in an instant, driving both of her blades into Brown's torso as multiple arrows pierced his back.

Collapsing next to the casket, I did not even care about the overpowering heat and the smell of burnt flesh on top of the blood and death in the cathedral. I was too damn tired.

My attention was drawn to the upper balcony as Retanei stood there with bow in hand and another arrow already nocked and drawn.

I tossed her a thumbs up and leaned my head back against the stone.

Looking up, I watched Silver stare at the casket of flames. From my angle, I could not clearly see his face. I probably should be worried about being so close to him right now.

Savanas extricated her blades from Brown's corpse and knelt over Big Black, tears falling freely. She wiped her blood-covered hands on her jeans before petting her fallen companion.

I looked over at Brown's corpse. His soul was desperately trying to get back into his body.

Suddenly a shadowed figure appeared and grabbed the soul, disappearing just as quickly. I blinked a few times, wondering if my mind had made it up. Glancing around, no one else acted as if they saw it and figured my mind conjured a fitting end.

Brad asked me questions to assess my condition, but my head still pounded. I probably should get out of here and to a safe distance before I lost control. Just damned if I could move.

19

RATHAL APPROACHED ME, the wild look still on his face and lance still in hand. His hair had fallen out of its short ponytail and was plastered in places to the sides of his face with blood and sweat.

Dropping his lance, Rathal bent down to pick me up. I did not have the energy or care to fight him. He looked at Brad and tilted his head toward the doors we entered through.

Once we were out in the vestibule with the doors firmly closed, I took a deep breath of clear air. Rathal put me down in the middle of the room. I did not have the strength to remain sitting and rolled onto my back, pressing the heels of my hands against my eyes - my head hurt so much.

Once out of the main chamber of the cathedral, the pain in my head eased slowly. It would take some time to be rid of it completely, but I was no longer concerned about losing control as I was pretty drained of arcane energy. I had no idea how I was still alive.

Brad resumed his attempt to check both of us for injuries. I paid no attention to the exchange between him and Rathal. After a few minutes, he went back inside.

The silence was nice. I let my mind go blank and closed my eyes.

I'm not sure how long I soaked in the quiet before Rathal broke it.

"You are damn crazy," Rathal laughed. "Gods, I have never seen anything like it before, and I will be more than grateful to never see it again. I seriously thought you were going to turn on the boss lady."

I groaned and rubbed my face, dropping my hands to my sides once I figured out it was not helping. I had not realized in my confusion what it looked like to the others.

Rathal lightly punched my shoulder and said, "Don't worry about it. Just rest and when you're feeling up to it, I have a bottle of water for you. Brad said to drink it. I'm sure mother hen will be back to check on you soon."

I did not remember hearing Brad referred to that way before. For some reason I thought it was sweet.

For a while I stared at the ceiling in the vestibule. It was pretty. There was a big golden sun in the center radiating out its light. It was simple in its elegance. It hung from the ceiling and I wondered if there were lights behind it to add to the effect. Focusing on the ceiling helped bring calm and with it, control.

Rathal got up and peeked inside. As soon as he cracked the door open, I got hit with the same effect as earlier though not nearly as intense.

Turning my head in his direction, I asked, "What's going on?"

The door closed and I could breathe easily again. Forcing myself to sit up, I waited for an answer.

"Savanas, she's up," Rathal said and handed me the promised bottle of water. "Silver is releasing the souls of the dead. We should be able to reenter once he's done. The others are cataloging evidence. Doc will be here soon with backup. How are you feeling?"

I contemplated the question for a moment and hid the delay behind taking a drink of water. I tried to lighten the mood and said, "Like I got between you and Silver fighting." While the hurt was not physical, I felt beat up from the time I spent in there. "I lost my ear piece. I'm not sure when."

The door opened and I steeled myself against the momentary onslaught.

Savanas knelt down next to me. She still had blood splattered on her, mostly around her hands. It looked like she tried to wipe her face at some point, but had only smeared the mess further.

Savanas must have heard me over Rathal's microphone and said, "I'm guessing you didn't notice when I pulled it off you after I got you away from the immediate threats. Even I could tell you were struggling to keep your concentration. The last thing you needed was our chatter in your ear. Rathal, if you can get it out of my coat pocket? I'm kind of a mess. Also, change to passive communication - we're getting tied into the team that's on their way." Her tone was solemn. I did not know how close she had been to Big Black, but I remembered when Retanei lost her last companion. I thought I would lose Retanei. I think what kept her going was she had already started training Artemis.

Rathal flipped a switch on his ear piece before he dug in her pocket. He smirked and said to Savanas, "Just remind me not to piss you off. It's been a while since I've seen the blade dancer in action."

"Oh, shut up," Savanas shot back, smiling a little, and then turned her attention to me. "I need to know: why did your Arcane College pin heat up like a hot iron when Brown ordered you?"

Taking another drink of water, I took a moment to contemplate what I wanted to say. "I'm not sure - I've never seen it do that before. I knew he was trying to use a command spell, but it broke when it hit me. I might have had too much built up power." I did not want to talk about the thread. That would require more questions than I had answers. I was formulating a couple of other theories, but was not ready to share.

"Wait, you were never under his control? You were acting?" Savanas asked, surprised.

I clarified, "Confused, and then angry. I was able to fully focus for a moment."

"I'm just glad it wasn't me. I don't think I would have survived that attack," Savanas said and brushed a stray lock of hair out of her face with her shoulder. "Vince and Lockonis are on their way also. They apparently landed as we began searching the church grounds. They should be arriving with Doc. Ket, once Silver is finished, I'll need you in there to work with him and make sure we have everything. Retanei is taking images, but she's not sure she's getting what you need."

The thought of facing Silver frightened me. "I don't think that's a good idea..."

"Too bad. He wants to talk to you anyway," Savanas stated firmly and got up, going back into the main chamber of the cathedral. She left so quickly I barely felt the brush of the effects from inside.

Pulling my knees further up, I buried my face and groaned, "Silver's going to kill me."

Brad and Darius came into the vestibule for a few minutes to touch base with Rathal. Brad took a quick check of my vital signs again and questioned Rathal about my state of being. With the number of people dead, it would be a while before Silver finished.

When Doc arrived with the others, he saw to the two of us first. Savanas came to catch the newcomers before they entered the main chamber. I spoke with her briefly before the others came in and expressed how sorry I was I had not been able to act sooner to save Big Black.

Savanas surprised me by saying it was his choice. Going down fighting was better than slowly letting old age take him. He apparently had not taken well to retirement.

The vestibule filled up quickly and I found myself against the wall so I could remain seated. Vince and Lockonis stayed on the other side of the small room. He spoke with Savanas as people organized themselves and sorted out who needed to wait and who could go in now.

Lockonis watched me and after a few moments, I looked away. I messed up.

I was also a mess. The shorter ends of my hair near my face had plastered themselves against my cheeks - it was hot in here with my coat on.

Sliding out of my coat, I took the time to fold it as neatly as I could and put it aside. I dug through the bag I abandoned in here, looking for something to keep me occupied.

Rathal still wore his armor so I left mine alone, though I really wanted to shed it also. I had a short-sleeve shirt on under my sweater, but shedding any other layer would require removing the armor.

Suddenly there were people leaving out the front door as others gathered near the doors to the main chamber.

Lockonis held the door to the outside. As soon as she closed the door behind the last one, Vince led the other group inside.

Gritting my teeth against the coming onslaught, it felt almost like a strong breeze compared to its previous power. I was grateful, but it also meant Silver would be done soon.

Lockonis came over to us, rubbing her temple. She commented, "Well, that was a head rush. Hope you two don't mind I let you continue your rest here. You've both already been exposed - those poor buggers outside haven't."

"That was nothing compared to earlier," Rathal said, but looked visibly ill regardless. "Pretty sure I worked out most of my effects during the fight. Haven't fought like that in a long time. Not sure how your girl here kept her head about her."

I had no response - sheer will power felt overconfident.

"What about you?" I asked Lockonis. It would be extremely dangerous for someone like her to fall to it.

"Something that low won't phase me. Too many mental barriers built up. Yay for Warmage training," Lockonis tried to cheerfully say, but simply looked exhausted. "Ket, I need to know."

I was pretty sure I must have been looking at her like she had two heads - I had no idea what she was talking about. "Know what?" I asked. About Brown? About what happened in there? About Silver? About... there were too many options.

"About what I told you," Lockonis said cryptically.

I was still lost so I took the first thing that came to mind and asked, "Regarding Silver's order?"

Shaking her head, a small smirk appeared briefly on Lockonis' face and she said, "Never mind - you're too tired. As dangerously low as you are on energy, you've got to be hurting." Lockonis had some ability to see the arcane, though not as clearly as I did.

Brad came through the doors, and then said, "Silver is done. Vince asked you three come in to monitor the last of the effects before we bring in the rest."

Rathal helped me up, though I told him not to, and the three of us made our way into the main chamber. An echo of the effect remained. He pointed at the altar where Silver stood and said, "Go ahead. I think we can handle the task."

Silver stood before the casket - the flames were gone. He held his sword loosely in his right hand, his shield hung on his left. It was the one time, I realized, his braid hung down his back. Usually it was over his right shoulder and this... it was wrong. It made him look heartbroken.

I came up on his right, staying behind him a step and said nothing. I stood and looked around him into the ashes in the casket. I wished I could find the words to explain my actions.

"Thank you," Silver whispered. He turned to look at me, and I could see the deep sorrow in his eyes.

All I could do was simply nod. I was unsure what he thanked me for. Typical Human custom was to bury the dead - I defiled that.

Silver turned back to the casket and said, "This is how Maria should have been remembered - as bright in death as she was in life." We stood in silence for a moment before he spoke again, "I have a favor to ask of you."

"What is it?" It was hard to stand here - the death around us over-powering. I felt a little better as I was able to regain a small portion of my arcane energy, though slow as it was. It was not the dark energy as before - this was pure arcane.

Silver asked, "When this is over, could you play for those who have fallen here this day?"

Turning back to the dead, I took note of all the people, children and babies included, who were sacrificed. I turned away, the sadness threatening to bring me to tears. I could not risk getting emotional, even as drained as I was. I debated turning him down on the principle I disliked playing in front of others, but found myself saying, "Of course."

As we stood there in silence, I turned to watch everyone else working. I needed to do something, but I did not want to leave Silver like this either. It would be wrong after everything he had done for me.

Lockonis was up on the second floor balcony with Retanei and Rathal and a few new people. I assumed Artemis was with them, but the wall was too tall to see her. Doc was on the main floor in the back slowly collecting the bodies with the help of others, including Brad and Darius. I heard them calling for more assistance. Vince was off to the side, talking with Savanas who was being animated in whatever she was saying.

Something with a faint arcane energy source caught my attention and I excused myself. Silver followed me anyway.

I wandered aimlessly for a few minutes, trying to get my bearings. There was an antechamber off to the right of the altar I was being drawn toward. As soon as I reached the doorway, I stopped and covered my mouth with my hand, looking away. This scene was more gory than the rest. This man had been stabbed multiple times - there had been a fight in here.

The male Human wore blue and gold clerical robes and looked young. The top part of his shoulder-length brown hair had been pulled back, the ends hanging in his own blood like a paintbrush. His sword and shield still held.

Out of the corner of my eye, I caught Vince and Savanas making their way over. Retanei and Lockonis had come down to give them an update at some point and followed.

Silver's hand gripped my shoulder. He said, "Paladin Marsh." He gently moved me out of the way and knelt next to the fallen man. "Brother, I may have called you a windbag, but I never wanted to see you silenced."

Entering the antechamber, something was still on the edge of my senses. I said, "He doesn't seem to have been part of the necromancer's spell." I doubted it was much relief.

"No, he fought, but without looking at the security video I wouldn't be able to tell you exactly what happened," Silver said and looked at the people gathering behind me. "Paladin Marsh would have set up a camera to record the service on the balcony. He used it to improve his sermons. He could go off on passion-filled tangents rather easily."

Retanei nodded and said, "I saw it when I had gotten up there and left it recording. I haven't taken a look at the footage yet."

Lockonis came in looking around. She asked, "Ket, you picking up anything in here?"

"Yes, but I can't tell what," I admitted. Must have been because I was too drained still. Even the simplest of spells would put me at dangerous levels.

Both of us converged on the corner hidden by a changing screen.

"Oh Gods..." Lockonis said.

She beat me to it by a split second and I felt my face pale when I saw the same type of arcane bomb that destroyed the Waking Dawn.

Lockonis ordered loudly, "Evacuate everyone NOW!" I never witnessed her take such a commanding tone before.

In her rush to start the evacuation, Lockonis bumped into me and I knocked the changing screen over. Instead of following the others, I knelt before it to see if there was a way to disperse the rapidly building energy - it would explode soon.

"Ketayl!" Lockonis yelled in a panic.

The others relayed the evacuation order and had begun to retreat when they stopped to see what was happening.

It was the only choice I had - the energy was too close to release to get everyone out. Even we were too close.

Grabbing the bomb, I gathered everything I had left, digging as deep and pulling as hard on whatever arcane energy was around me as I could before teleporting a short distance to a place I saw on the way in. It would be far enough away from everyone else. I threw the arcane bomb as far as I could before falling in the freezing cold water.

I was done. I could not find the strength to get back to the surface. I prayed to whoever would listen that it was the only one.

Something hit me hard - the bomb had detonated. I was knocked out of the water and hit the ground, rolling. I thought I heard screaming, but I hurt so badly all over I could not tell who it was.

I also heard muffled voices - they sounded urgent. If they wanted me to research something for them, it would have to wait - I needed sleep.

20

THE FIRST THING that pulled me from the blissful darkness was pain. More than I ever felt before. Pushing through the haze clouding my mind, I forced myself to open my eyes and find out the cause. My mouth was dry and something forced me to breathe at awkward intervals.

"I wondered when you would come back to us," a male voice said.

I recognized the voice. It took a lot of effort to turn my head toward it, and I was not sure why Vince sat there. He had a book, or at least it looked like a book. The whole picture was blurred and out of place. Maybe I was not awake yet. Why had I wanted to sleep before? I hated sleep.

"You've been out for about a week. Lockonis wasn't exaggerating when she said you drained yourself completely. For your first field assignment, that was hell. Good job managing to scare all of us half to death with your last stunt," Vince said and bookmarked his place as he stood up. "Let me go notify the hospital staff you're awake."

Once he left, I turned my head to look out the window, or at least what I thought was the window - it was dark. I vaguely wondered what time it was, but could not seem to find a clock. I had a hard time focusing on anything.

Something reddish laying on me caught my attention. I moved an arm to grab it, but ended up groaning as pain shot through me instead.

"You won't want to move for a bit." This time it was a voice I did not recognize and I turned to look at the new person.

It was an Elven man. White hair? The lighting and my poor vision made it difficult.

He said, "I'll talk to the doctor on duty about upping the levels of your pain medication. You were so weak we didn't want to harm your system. We also didn't want to shock your system by using any healing spells. You are certainly one lucky lady, Miss."

He walked around while he talked, checking this and that, writing on his clipboard. Did he have a clipboard when he came in?

He departed quickly.

"Where?" I asked, my voice hoarse and it took more effort than it should - the attempt made my eyes water.

Vince returned to his chair and said, "You're in the hospital in Ocean's Edge - they didn't want to risk moving you any further. I've already gotten an earful from Kitteren so you should expect the same."

I would more than happily sit through one of my sister's lectures right now - it was better than being dead. For being younger, she worried too much about me. I thought it was the older sibling's job to worry over the younger ones.

"One?" I asked - I needed to know. I only hoped he understood what I asked.

Vince said, "Yes. What we can gather from the footage is Brown only made the one to go off after he collected whatever it was he came for. He likely wanted to draw the attention of the city. With the number of dead, there would have been a lot of responders walking into the effect." I was glad Vince did not need me to elaborate further. "Now rest, you need to heal. I'll keep Kitteren off you until then."

Struggling to sit up, I needed to know more. I could not rest - there was work to do. Everything hurt and I considered giving up.

Vince pushed me back down and I mentally cursed him and his lack of effort to get me back in place. He hit a button on the side of the bed in the process. "I said you need rest. You'll do no one any good if you hurt yourself more."

The same Elven man came back in. "Please stay put, Miss. You're straining yourself too much," he said in a rush.

I refused to back down. "No," I said. I hurt everywhere, but the pain helped me focus. I needed to find out everything that happened. My vision blurred further and my cheeks felt wet.

Another came in, but between the two keeping me in place, I could not see who it was. The nurse accepted something and took my hand. "I'm sorry, Miss, but you need to rest."

The fog came back just before darkness greeted me once more.

THE SUN WAS up by the time I woke again. The pain was considerably lower and my vision cleared, but I felt drained. The reddish thing which had caught my attention before was my braided hair. It sat innocently on top of me over my right shoulder. Immediately it made me think of Silver.

The pain I felt then was not a physical one. He lost all of those he cared about. I fought against my eyes watering.

"He almost did." It was a different voice this time. I recognized Lockonis quickly.

Had I spoken aloud? I turned to look at her.

Lockonis shook her head and said, "Geez, Ket, can you not pull something like that? I'm supposed to be the crazy one, remember? And anyway, since when have you been able to teleport?"

I supposed I was in for a tongue lashing from a number of people. My mouth felt too dry to respond. Lockonis reached over and punched a button on the side of the bed.

"Hold those thoughts for when you don't look like Death warmed over," she said teasingly. "In any case, I should probably give you a rundown of what happened after you decided to play hero. But it can wait until the doctor looks at you."

She was looking over her shoulder toward the door when a couple of people came in - different than last night.

One of the new people came over and sat my bed up - she looked like she was a nurse. The other wore a white lab coat.

The doctor addressed me, "Miss Ketayl, you are certainly looking better. Your Director asked us not to restrain you. You certainly were determined last night even with the state you were in." She paused to read something on the computer in the corner of the room I had not noticed before. "I think you're through the worst of it. Your vitals have been looking good since you woke up last night, but I'll need your friend here to confirm your arcane levels are stable. A caster of your type makes things a little more interesting. I'm glad we had the help of the EAC to figure out how to care for you."

"Her arcane levels are stable. I've been here for a few hours and she's low, but she hasn't dipped back down again," Lockonis said.

What were they talking about? I dug into my mind for information, but gave up quickly, not wanting the headache threatening to come forth.

The doctor made a face. "Not quite what I hoped to hear, but we should be able to have some healing spells cast now. The rest will simply require time."

They bantered back and forth and I tuned them out. Taking the offered cup of water, I thought about everything that happened. The images were there and all I could see was the death and destruction. Looking at the cast on my left arm, I walked away relatively unscathed. So many... so many...

"Ketayl? Ketayl, look at me," Lockonis said and was practically on top of me, trying to get my attention. Her face was too close for comfort. "You need to keep it together. Remember what you promised Silver."

I promised to play for the dead. Then I raised my cast-covered arm a bit, not trusting my voice to tell her I needed both hands.

"Soon," the doctor said and smiled at me, "He's usually here about this time to check on you. Actually, there he is now." The doctor looked out the door. My eyes went to the door, both wanting to see Silver and yet not wanting him to see me like this. His overprotective nature was not something I could deal with right now.

Why did I want to see Silver? I barely knew him. Or any of the others for that matter.

It was a few moments before Doc walked through the door and my heart sank. It was a new sensation and I filed it away for later contemplation. Perhaps I had simply gotten used to Silver's presence.

Doc said, "It is wonderful to see you awake, Ketayl. We've all been very worried." He accepted the clipboard from the doctor.

With four sets of eyes on me, the small room felt extremely crowded. The hospital doctor patted my foot and excused herself and the nurse.

Doc said, "I can heal your more severe injuries. You'll still need to stay here overnight for observation, but after that I don't see a reason you can't continue your recovery at the hotel. You will have to promise me to take it easy though."

He dug through his bag. "Paladin Blaise wanted to be here, but his order called him back to the church a couple of days ago. I offered to do this in his stead. The process is easier when it's someone you're at least familiar with." He moved quickly, checking vitals, and I was not ready for when he shined a light in my face.

Blinking to see straight again, I felt a little more confident in my voice. I managed to get out, "Didn't know... healer."

Doc laughed lightly, "Well, not many would. Most things can be cared for with modern medicine, which is preferred, but there is still a call on occasion for a bit of divine intervention. There are too few of us who practice both, but it has started becoming popular again among your generation. It's simply a matter of time before there are many who will be experienced enough."

He made small talk with me as he healed my injuries, explaining what he was about to do and what I was likely going to feel during it. By the end, I ached still, but I felt a lot better.

Lockonis left at one point and I heard her outside talking to someone. They spoke too low for me to hear or to make out who the other person was.

I felt better, but tired. My sister once explained to me that most healing magic amplified a body's natural healing ability. It was something she learned while training as a tracker.

Once Doc finished, he looked at the tube still stuck in my arm. He said, "Let's get that off you and remove this cast to make you more comfortable." I looked away before he pulled the needle out.

I found out upon coming to the TIO I disliked needles and would have to divert my attention. It still made me squirm as he gently removed the device, but once it was out and he placed a little square of gauze over where it had been, I was fine.

Lockonis poked her head in. "How's it going in here?"

Doc was still holding my arm, putting a blue medical wrap over the gauze. He answered, "Good. Just need to get this cast off and with overnight observation, she will be fine. And rest, don't forget plenty of rest."

"Great! I have a visitor for you," Lockonis said and smiled broadly. She came in, dragging someone behind her. That someone was Savanas who looked more than a little agitated at her former partner.

Yanking her arm away from Lockonis, Savanas said, "Well, you certainly look a lot better than when I was here yesterday." Her face changed to relief.

I simply nodded as the sound of velcro separating loudly claimed the room. Once the outer shell of the cast was removed, Doc set about cutting off the cloth wrappings.

"Ketayl, I need you to make a fist," Doc ordered gently.

The conversation paused for a bit. I made gestural responses to his questions about if something still hurt. I did not trust my voice after the effort it took to speak earlier.

Doc announced, "It looks like we're good here. Have them call me if you need me." He patted my leg as he stood up.

I nodded in response and then felt a bit of trepidation as he left, leaving me with two powerful TIO agents. Savanas crossed her arms over her chest and stared me down. She said harshly, "You have some explaining to do."

"No kidding," Lockonis jumped in excitedly. "I mean I didn't believe the footage when I saw it. And then that last stunt... you were running on empty when you teleported with the arcane bomb."

"That was a damn stupid fool thing you did, and hells if you didn't save all our asses with it," Savanas said, giving up her tough act and hugged me.

Lockonis chimed in, "You know that first part made no sense."

"Oh, shut up."

Since my voice was not the best, they spent the next while catching me up on what transpired. Which included that until he was ordered back to the church, Silver refused to leave my side. Lockonis seemed to think it was adorable.

Archmage Maewon and a couple of his highest-level mages set up a rotation with Lockonis to keep transferring arcane energy to me. My levels kept dropping and they worried what would happen if I drained completely again.

The others from the Ocean's Edge office had taken turns staying with me - apparently Rathal and Darius managed to hook up their game system to the screen in the room. Vince had been mostly busy dealing with Naval Command and the media, but would come in overnight.

They also told me of a memorial service was scheduled to take place in a couple of days. They spoke a little about the few people in the group they managed to take into custody. They left out important details like what the body count was because I was too slow to figure out Brown's true objective.

2 1

AFTER SPENDING another day resting in the hotel, I was restless - I needed something to do. I could not go very far since Retanei hid the keys. Or returned them - I forgot. Not to mention, she was out picking up something for us to eat. It was the first time since I returned that she let me out of her sight.

The well wishers continued to visit yesterday, but it was quiet today. It was only a hour until noon and I was ready to climb the walls. I understood the others had a lot of work which needed to be done and I would be inundated back at the lab, but I needed something to do now.

There was Silver's request. Testing the dexterity in my left hand as I walked, I pulled the case onto the bed with me and busied myself. I was about to play through pieces I thought might be appropriate when Retanei returned. She stood at the doorway with Artemis at her side. She said, "Oh, sorry. Are you sure you're up for that?"

Lowering the violin to my lap, I picked at a fuzzball on my sweater. I said, "I'm not sure, but I need to do something. Do you think we could go to the church later?"

The words were out before I filtered them again. I wanted to see how Silver was doing, that was all. Maybe see if I could lend a hand somehow. With the pain medication, I felt a bit off, but not so much that I could not contribute somehow.

Silence hung in the air long enough I knew something was wrong. Retanei said, "I'm afraid not. Once we concluded our investigation at the church grounds, the new paladins refused to let anyone not directly affiliated with the church onto the property. Brad took the news pretty hard. He hasn't been able to contact Silver since."

It made no sense. I looked to my friend for answers.

Retanei sighed, leaning against the door frame. She explained, "The best I can summarize is they're casting blanket judgment on everyone involved even if we were there to stop the people responsible. Vince has tried to talk to them, but they've isolated themselves. For the moment, they've even locked their doors to their remaining parishioners. I can understand a period of grieving, but something seems very off about the whole thing."

My attention went back to the violin on my lap. It was a favor I could not fulfill. Even though the circumstances were out of my control, I felt guilty all the same.

A sudden weight on the side of the bed made me look up. Retanei suggested, "I know it's not the same, but Savanas is making dinner tonight for everyone before the memorial service. I'm sure they would appreciate it. And Lou has been hoping you would come back."

I remembered something mentioned about a memorial service. I was uncertain I was ready for that large of an audience. I said, "Maybe? I don't know. I'm really no good with this stuff."

"This stuff" encompassing all the things I did not want to voice aloud: playing in front of others, choosing music, dealing with the horrors I kept seeing when I closed my eyes...

"You'll be fine. Let's eat and we can figure it out from there. Savanas wants us over at her house by 1600. Dinner will be roughly an hour later, which is why I picked up something light," Retanei said and headed for the common area.

Rushing to catch up, but not wanting to possibly break anything, I half-fell off of the bed. "Wait. What about the memorial service?"

Retanei pulled a couple of sandwiches out of the bag. She said solemnly, "It starts at 2000. With some help, they've been able to release the bodies from both crime scenes. Rathal lives near the water and arranged for us to have a spot on the pier to view the fires. It's a little different because there are so many whose ashes need to travel."

"What was the final count?" I needed to know. How many people had I failed?

I barely reacted in time to catch the wrapped sandwich tossed at me. I caught it clumsily with my forearms, hugging it to my chest.

Retanei snapped at me, "I'm not answering that. I won't let you torture yourself any more than you already have. Numbers don't matter. What matters is that these bastards will not be able to do this again."

My eyes went wide - I had never seen Retanei like this.

Her shoulders slumped. "Ket, I'm sorry. I... I've seen a lot. Dealt with a lot. But I keep seeing you lying almost dead on the beach. Why did you do it?"

It was a complex answer I had not the energy to tell so I went with a simpler explanation, "I could tell we didn't have a lot of time left before it went off. Not everyone would have gotten out. It was the quickest solution I could come up with."

Retanei pursed her lips and looked out the window. She said, "It was a good thing you didn't go far then. Lockonis about went into a panic when you disappeared. She ran outside, but couldn't locate you until the bomb went off. I can still hear your scream."

Ducking my head, I said, "I'm sorry."

"Don't be. You saved a lot of lives. I'm glad you blacked out before we got to you. Though, it made it worse dealing with Rathal and Silver - they were still suffering from the effects and we both know how extreme it made their personalities," Retanei said.

As much as I cringed to hear this, I needed to. I needed to know what happened.

Before I could push for more, Retanei's phone rang and she answered, ending our conversation.

Reluctantly I sat down at the counter and ate, not tasting anything over the bitterness of our barely won victory. And what kind of victory was it? There could be others out there still planning who knows what.

DINNER AT SAVANAS' house was a solemn affair. There were wonderful smells coming from the kitchen, but I feared it would only be the same as earlier. Even Rathal and Darius did not argue with each other over the video game as last time.

Melody pet Artemis. Retanei said both of them still hurt from the loss of Big Black. I could only imagine how Savanas was handling it.

Doc sat quietly, contemplating the drink in his hands. Brad was in the kitchen with Savanas so I did not know how those two faired.

They all seemed so much stronger than me and the mood brought them a little more back down to Terra.

"Oh, this won't do at all," Lou said as he came into the common area, his arms laden with trays he placed on the low table in the center of the room. "I could tell the lot of you to cheer up, but it would be a wasted effort." His eyes roamed the room, searching for something until he got to me. "Ah, my dear, would you mind me accompanying you?" He pointed at the hard case tucked behind my legs.

Retanei insisted I bring my violin, but I had not the nerve to play around the others. I sat quietly for a moment, unsure what to say or do.

I finally said, "I'm not very good." The conversation got the attention of the others, making me more nervous. "Besides, it wouldn't do well against anything acoustic."

Lou came over to me and said, "Let me see." Pulling the case onto my lap, I unzipped it for him, suddenly embarrassed about the purple thing inside. "Oh, I can fix that." Then he left the room.

Closing the case once more, I slid it back down behind my legs. With it away the attention of the others was still on me. Even the game had ended and sat idly on the menu screen.

Sinking further into the plush chair, I wished it would swallow me.

Savanas and Brad came out to see what was going on as Lou bustled by them, his hands full. Out of the items he carried, I noticed the small amp. Mother made me hook up to hers when I was at her house, but I did not own one. He also carried a larger case and some cables.

Lou admonished, "Well, it does no good to anyone in the case, get it out and tuned up."

Slowly pulling the case back out, I looked to Savanas who appeared as solemn as the rest of us. She said, "Too late to back out now, Ket."

Shyly, I checked the tune, which it kept from earlier. I had taken my boots off at the door as requested since they were soaked from the fresh snowfall. I tucked my feet underneath me, making myself smaller yet more upright. Lou tossed me the end of a cable.

Then I sat and waited as Lou tuned the guitar he pulled out, which was also electric, and adjusted the volume on the amp. He said as he worked, "I give music lessons to some of the kids who frequent the bakery so I keep a few things around. They get practice, I get free entertainment." He smiled at me. "Just play and I'll follow."

I sat silent. I did not know what to play. Everything coming to mind was sorrowful and I did not think it was what Lou aimed for. I said, "I'm sorry, anything uplifting is escaping me at the moment."

"It's fine. I think everyone needs to get it out of their systems at this point," Lou said.

Raising the violin to my shoulder, I mentally searched for the one which felt the most right and began. In time, I was able to move to lighter pieces. Only Savanas ushering us off to eat was what ended the music. Everyone's mood had lightened. Even Darius and Rathal argued about their last game.

After the meal ended, we returned to the common room, Brad insisted Savanas leave the clean up to him. It surprised me neither Vince nor Lockonis were here.

Lou convinced me to keep playing and the others returned to their normal activities, or at least as how Melody described them. Doc told a story to Savanas, Retanei, and Melody. Melody's attention was more on Artemis, playing tug of war with her with a knotted rope that had belonged to Big Black. Darius and Rathal threw insults between their button mashing.

I contemplated Lou's wisdom. He knew something about how they would react to the music and it was almost like magic. I remembered Mother having a similar talent. It was something I wished to learn.

We kept it going until Savanas announced we needed to get down to the pier for the memorial service.

<hr>

CROWDS GATHERED along the shoreline as we drove. The particular pier in question was just ahead and I could see a small crowd already there.

Getting out, I shivered against the cold wind coming in off the water. The others headed toward a small tower leading to a skywalk over the road below. Once we got to the top, Vince and Lockonis were there with others who responded at the church.

Lockonis came over to us, greeting people as she went until she got to myself and Retanei. She said, "Heya, Ket. We're leaving after this so we'll take you back to the hotel to get your stuff."

I did not understand. I asked, "Tonight?"

"Yeah, Tanei is staying here for the Winter Solstice. Well, sort of," Lockonis said and looked at Retanei.

The Winter Solstice was in a few days - I had forgotten about it.

Retanei rolled her eyes and explained, "My village is a couple hours away. You're going back with them."

I opened my mouth to protest, but Lockonis cut me off, "Don't worry, Tanei will be fine flying back. Come on, we should catch up with the others. They're going to light the fires soon."

Standing near the railing of the tower, overlooking the water, I curled into myself for warmth. Perhaps it was a last minute thing about wanting to leave tonight.

I heard Lockonis talking to Retanei, "You heading out after this to go pick up the package?"

"Yeah, Brad gave me the meeting location and time earlier. Are you sure you don't want to..."

Lockonis cut her off, "No, just as the big guy said. I've learned to trust his judgment."

Rathal stood at my side and commented, "Never did get to take you out, did I?"

"It's okay," I faked a smile for him. I did not deserve anything after my failure.

"Next time you happen to be this way then," Rathal said and smiled at me. Then he turned his attention back out over the water where the light from the fires started to spread. Each little raft was chained to another - I could not count the number of bodies being burned.

Turning off the part of my mind that started to become too emotional, I stared blankly ahead, focusing on the fire itself. Their ashes would fall into the ocean and travel the world - their souls already having moved on to wherever it is they go. Wherever that was, I hoped they found peace.

EPILOGUE

Due to the medications Doc insisted I take, I slept through most of the flight back. I found the experience more disorienting than teleporting.

I wanted to stay behind so Retanei would not fly back by herself. I would have been content to remain alone in the hotel so I would not intrude upon her family time, but I was sure the others would not have let me be. At least back at the main office most people would ignore me and I could hide in either my quarters or the lab.

My sister left to go spend time with our parents in Great Tree before I returned. She had not thought I would be back before the Winter Solstice. While I could have gone and joined them, I was not feeling up to the drive.

Kitteren would have returned for me if I had not conceded to a video call. As soon as the call connected, she started to cry. I could not remember the last time I saw Kitteren shed tears. I could not seem to reassure her enough that I was fine. We spent a while talking, but avoided the case. It was something I knew she was going to want to talk about when she returned.

It was good to speak with Mother and Father. Father and I rarely had anything to talk about - he and Mother had become mates after I had gone to the Arcane College so I did not know him well. He still said little, but even over the video feed, I could sense his concern.

The Winter Solstice was this evening. I overheard talk in the dining hall of a party being planned for those remaining on the grounds. It was impressive I heard anything about it given I avoided people by taking either early or late meals - if I took them at all. My appetite was simply gone.

Cadwr chided me every time I skipped a meal. I would tell him I lost track of time in the lab again. It was still the truth in a sense - there was a lot of work to do and I had been known to do it before. Lockonis dealt with most of the backlog while I was away, but there was still more than enough to keep me busy.

While I was told repeatedly to take it easy, I hid myself in the lab. I avoided watching the footage of the fight, especially the copy Retanei rigged up with the arcane filter. I saw the events enough every time I closed my eyes. My brain simply could not process a different perspective right now. I refused to see myself on screen.

It was enough I had all of the paperwork from Brown I still needed to finish analyzing. I did not know how I would handle the divine text. I would need to inquire if there was someone who could help.

Both Vince and Lockonis seemed to be giving me space - there had been no requests for updates from either one. No one visited the lab. Admittedly, I was starting to get lonely and with only my thoughts to accompany me. My daily conversations with Doc were not enough because they were always focused on my physical well being.

Doc made me promise not to push it while I worked. The doctors here wanted to schedule psychological evaluations, but Doc assured me they would only do so if absolutely necessary. I was not so ignorant I did not notice the mental health questions he snuck into our conversations.

What I did not tell him or anyone else was I still struggled with my control. Hopefully once Lockonis lifted her order against any casting, I could get back to normal. The daily routine of using my power to do simple things like dry my hair had been interrupted and it was as useful to help maintain my balance as the arcane combat training sessions with Lockonis.

A knock on the glass of the lab door startled me. I turned around and saw Retanei letting herself in. She said, "I had a feeling you wouldn't listen to the doctors."

I managed to plaster a small smile on my face for her before saying, "Too much work to do. I thought you were spending the holiday with your family."

"Yeah, well, I wanted to beat the storm system coming through tonight and I can only take so much of them at a time. Plus Vince requested an important delivery," Retanei explained. She came around to my left and leaned her hip against the station I worked at.

Artemis sat at her side and whined at me, which caught Retanei's attention. She rubbed the wolf's head, murmuring something too softly for me to hear.

I went back to transcribing my notes into the computer. I was not a part of their conversation. My mind going to other questions I needed to answer while my fingers copied what was written down. How did Brown know where he was teleporting and how did he get through the barrier? His teleports were too perfect to be working off just maps. There had to be something else. Maybe the clue was in Silver's notes. Where did those end up again?

"If you're avoiding thinking about what happened this is a really bad way of doing it," Retanei said.

I paused briefly in my typing. "I need to do something - I can't just sit around."

Retanei put her hand on the notebook I was transcribing into the report and said, "There is a limit. Come on, let's go get ready for the party. Cadwr is still here so you know there's going to be an amazing spread at dinner."

I pulled the notebook out from under her hand. "I'm not hungry and I don't feel like celebrating."

"Too bad, you're not going to have much say in the matter," Lockonis said, making me jump. When had she come into the lab?

I turned to see Lockonis with Vince standing behind her - both were dressed for the evening's celebrations. He wore a black suit while Lockonis had donned a very shiny blue dress that clung to her. It was far from her usual attire, but it was the Winter Solstice. I thought of the lavender dress Kitteren bought and put in my closet while I was away. It was not going to get worn - at least not this year.

Vince's arms were crossed and his face neutral. "It's time we talked," he said and signaled toward my office. Lockonis moved ahead, holding open the glass door.

I glanced at Retanei who shrugged. Well, she did just get back. Though I hoped if she knew something she would have warned me.

Nervously, I slid off of my stool and went where I was told. Not knowing what to do, I stood in the middle of my office. It was sparse and held another desk on the opposite side that Lockonis used when she worked in the lab.

Lockonis came in, closing the door behind her. Vince took a seat at my desk looking more like he belonged there than I ever did.

Vince sat back in my chair and watched me for a moment.

I fidgeted.

Picking up a pen to play with, Vince finally spoke, "If I had known what this assignment was going to lead to, I wouldn't have sent you. But I also would have been wrong not to send you because no one else has your abilities or knowledge. Not to mention the ability to work in conjunction with a paladin. So you see the dilemma I'm facing. The others are also having a hard time coping. They're tough, but this is something none of them have seen before. Almost losing you on top of it really pushed their limits."

"I'm sorry, sir." I was not sure what else to say. I clasped my hands together, unsure of what to do. This was awkward. Lockonis stood on the other side of my desk, watching me. Her silence told me something was wrong, but I had no idea what.

I fidgeted with my hands, unsure what they wanted from me. Too many thoughts hit me at the same time to parse them into any semblance of order.

Vince tossed the pen back onto my desk and said sharply, "I've held this off so you could heal, but it's far past time we talked. What I want to know is about you and teleporting. Last I knew, the only people the Arcane College allowed to learn that spell were Magisters and higher."

I jumped at the movement and the sharp tone. This was a question I should have expected. For some reason I had filed it away as forgotten about.

It struck me for a moment Vince knew so much about the Arcane College. Taking a deep breath, I quickly glanced at Lockonis before I said, "I am classified as a Researcher - I can pull up my records in the library if you need me to."

"Yeah, I double-checked that. Wanted to make sure I read it right," Lockonis chimed in. Her voice was even, giving me not a clue as to her thoughts. "And where Donovan had been ranting about you 'only being a Researcher' I'm positive the records weren't falsified. Not that you've ever given me a reason to doubt you."

I bit my lower lip for a moment before continuing, "I had access to the information about teleportation and taught myself. When no one was around, I would use it to get the books and scrolls too high up for me to reach. Flight spells are easier, but were too obvious with the amount of dust they kicked up. No one ever commented about seeing teleport lines."

There was silence for a moment and then Lockonis snorted before laughing hard. Vince shook his head for a moment - an amused expression on his face.

Vince looked at me and said, "That is certainly original. And perhaps the most mundane use of teleport I have ever heard. I believe you, but you have to understand my questioning after finding out Brown's rank wasn't as advertised. I'm going to contact Magus Engelil after the first of the Terran year and ask the EAC reevaluate you for rank. After this latest debacle with the Arcane College, I would like to keep them out of this process."

"Why have they been trying to recall me?" I asked. The question was out and I covered my mouth. I should not question those above me. I could only imagine the repercussions for this.

The look on Lockonis' face told me she had not been prepared for my sudden question.

"I'm so sorry, sir, I didn't mean..."

Vince held up a hand for me to stop. His face went hard. He said, "It is a question I don't fully have the answer to myself. Lockonis informed me of your conversation. You've certainly been more vocal lately, which is a good thing. You are harder to read than the others because you've kept yourself closed off."

I fidgeted with my hands again, unsure of where I stood with the heads of the TIO. Lockonis crossed her arms over her chest, sizing me up. Even in a shiny blue dress, she still came across as intimidating.

Vince changed the subject, "I'm wondering about the issues with your Arcane College pin Savanas described. Any ideas?"

I shook my head and told him, "There was a thread between me and the pin that broke during the last conference call, but I don't know what the connection was. I never encountered anything while I was storing information in it." There was no point to keeping it to myself. "The first time I saw it was after Silver held it."

I refused to go into what it felt like when I pulled against the thread. I suppressed a shudder at the memory. Feeling like I could not breath and something tightening around my chest would have had me keeping my distance from my pin if it had not been taken away. I felt stupid about being afraid of a pin.

Vince sighed and leaned forward, obviously not happy with the answer. He looked to Lockonis for a moment who shrugged. She said, "I've got both pins and will process them myself to avoid exposing Ket to further possible danger."

I thought about my student pin, which I kept in a box in the bottom of my closet. "I have one more pin if it would help you have a reference."

Lockonis raised an eyebrow at me.

"My student pin - it's in my quarters. I almost forgot about it," I said quietly. It had not crossed my mind for a while now.

"I'll get it from you tomorrow," Lockonis' face softened a bit. "And then we'll talk."

I nodded and rubbed my left arm where it had been broken. It was still sore and I refused to take the pain killers. I did not know if I should be looking forward to the talk with Lockonis. At least I would get some questions answered.

Vince glanced out the door and waited a moment to see if we were done. I mentally cursed having my back mostly to the door.

Vince said, "There is another reason I called you in here. As much as I would like to spare you from potentially dealing with another situation like this, I need a team dedicated to finding and bringing this group down. I will be assigning you a partner and you will have access to others as needed. You'll continue your work in the lab for now until we can find someone else."

"A partner?" I asked. I doubted he would break up any of the other current teams and those who ran solo were typically specialists - filling in on different teams as needed as Retanei and I had done. Though Retanei was not normally pulled like this - she usually worked with Ted only or they would form with a larger team if needed.

Vince waved to someone outside of my office door.

I turned toward the door and I was not sure I was seeing right.

Silver opened the door quickly and pulled me into a tight hug before I could decide if this was real or not. He said, "The Gods only know how truly grateful I am to see you well again."

Lockonis snickered from her spot, but said nothing.

I did not have a chance to react before he released me. I asked, "How?" I backed up a step to regain some personal space, pulling my lab coat tighter around myself.

I looked at him, still not entirely certain this was real. He wore different clothes, but his long silver braid still hung over his right shoulder. He wore a black jacket over a light blue dress shirt, khaki pants, and black boots. He retained the circlet, belt, and gloves. I figured the metal bracers were hidden under the jacket.

Ironic now that I was the one wearing white.

Vince stepped back into the conversation, "Silver has agreed to join the TIO full time as a free paladin, which means he has no affiliation with any particular church. He will have a lot of training to catch up on, but I needed someone well versed in the divine and who can work closely with an Arcane Investigator."

When did all of this happen? Apparently there was more I missed and no one thought to fill me in.

"Silver will spend a couple of weeks here while we get him processed. Then he'll return to Ocean's Edge for training. During this transition time, Lockonis has offered the assistance of the cyber team to help get the two of you started," Vince elaborated.

"Not that they have any say in the matter," Lockonis spoke again, grinning broadly.

Vince looked up at her with slight annoyance. "I'll let the two of you catch up and I expect to see both of you at the celebration this evening."

As soon as they were gone, Silver picked up my hand, kissing the back of it. I quickly pulled away from his touch. "Please don't scare me like that again. I thought I may have lost you."

My mind rolled its eyes at yet another person with a similar statement, but I pushed it back. I said, "I don't understand, I thought you went back to your church."

"I had, and I'm so sorry I wasn't there when you woke. They ordered me back to help clean up and prepare the funerals for those few who were to be buried." Silver said solemnly.

Silver brushed a stray lock of hair out of my face and I resisted the urge to bat his hand away. I had a feeling we were going to be talking about not touching me again very soon.

He explained, "The Director proposed the position to me shortly after we got you to the hospital. He insisted I take time to think about it. It took me a while because I was kept busy, but once I learned the new paladins cast such an unfair judgment, knowing the circumstances..." he trailed off. "I spent time in meditation and found the path the God of the Sun wanted me to walk was here, with you. I managed to contact Brad to make arrangements and, well, here I am. Retanei was kind enough to pick me up on the evening you departed."

I backed up another step, to get some space again. I apologized, "I'm sorry I wasn't able to fulfill your request."

Silver smiled gently and said, "You did. Retanei showed me a video of the music you played along with the other gentleman on the flight here. Thank you."

I saw Retanei was still in the main part of the lab. Her attention was on Artemis. Guess I was not getting help from her for this awkward situation.

Finding something to do, I picked up the pen Vince had tossed across my desk and put it away.

"So this is your domain, huh?" Silver asked, looking around the office.

I fidgeted. "I'm usually in the main part of the lab, but I guess." I rubbed my left arm where it had been broken. I hated taking the pain killers because they messed with my head and my control was lacking enough as it was.

Silver came over and put his hand over the area on my arm. It felt warm for a moment before the pain dissipated. "You should still be recovering from your injuries, not working."

I glared up at him, folding my arms over my chest. I did not care how ridiculous it might look, given our height difference. "Look, I can't just sit around. There's a lot of work to do and it won't process itself." Why was my stubborn streak coming out full force now? "Besides, no magic in the lab."

"Someone needs to put up a sign. Come on, it's the Winter Solstice."

"So?" I asked, my tone confrontational. I struggled with my control, but I should not be giving in. Sighing, I walked over to the office door. "Sorry, I'm just... This hasn't been..." Why could I not find the words to explain? "You should probably go. I need to get some work done."

"Ketayl," Silver put his hand on the door to keep me from opening it and said, "You're still dealing with what happened, but you can't do it alone. I can't promise I can make things better, but I can at least listen."

I could not look up at him. I moved away from the door, needing space. I sat down at my desk and stared at the blank screen. The real truth had been in the back of my mind as much as I ignored it. Why did I want to tell him about what I hid from everyone else?

After several moments, I admitted, "It was my fault I didn't figure out Brown's goal sooner."

"That's crap and you know it," Silver said sharply. I looked up at him, not expecting his tone.

Silver moved to stand over me, anger plain on his face. I was not about to back down though, not without a good reason why I should. I adjusted my lab coat. This was my domain, as he said, and I wanted to remind him of it.

"I didn't figure it out either and I feel like the answer was right in front of me. Retanei couldn't track down the group without your help. Savanas and her team would have been running in circles if you hadn't been there to at least point them in the right direction," Silver's voice was sharp, but not loud. At least not enough to get Retanei's attention.

I remained silent. I would let Silver speak his peace, but Brown was an Archmage from the same school I came from. Someone I had done some of the research for that he then used to trap and murder all of those people.

Silver's face softened, resigned. "And yes, I wish everyday we had gotten to them sooner. That all of those lives could have been spared. I have forever lost those I counted as brothers and sisters, other people of the community I had come to care for deeply, but I can't change what happened."

I stared at my partner, trying to process what he said. The logical side of me told me he was right. I did not want to be logical right now.

Silver squatted down next to me, his face serious. "All I can do is work toward the next sunrise and try to make sure this doesn't happen again. But I'm going to need the help of my partner."

I stared at him for a few moments longer, still attempting to understand what he was saying. I nodded and said, "Okay." Even if I could not accept his words right now, in time I would. I knew he was right, as much as I refused to admit it.

Silver's face changed to a mischievous grin. "Good. Now I saw them setting up a dance floor while I was being given a quick tour. Would you do me the honor of one dance?"

I forced down the heat I could feel rising to my face. "I'm sorry, but I don't know how to dance." I still did not understand my own reactions to him sometimes.

The smirk had not left Silver's face. "I shall have to teach you then." He tugged me out of my chair.

"I don't think it's a good idea…"

The look I got told me I was about to eat my words. Silver said, "Of course it isn't, but you seem to like bad ideas. This won't be nearly as bad as teleporting yourself with an arcane bomb into freezing ocean water."

Silver would make light of that particular event, but the strange part was I found it amusing.

We were in the main part of the lab before Retanei rescued me - only to drag me off to get ready for the evening's festivities. Apparently Kitteren told her about the dress.

ACKNOWLEDGMENTS

Joshua Jackson for encouraging me along an indulging me in this crazy adventure. Also for dragging me down the path of publishing.

My local critique group: Brandi Burns, Kenneth Jorgenson, Skip Knox, and Rick Just. Brandi put up with my insistent messaging and the others indulged me on this weird adventure. Most of them also were subjected to being beta readers as well. Without you I would not have learned as much as I have and ever put this out.

Loni Townsend for both beta reading and putting up with my many questions.

My gaming groups for giving me space to develop a few of the characters that appear in this book.

And all of my friends and family who have been cheering me along.

ABOUT THE AUTHOR

J.C. Jackson is originally from New England and currently lives in southwestern Idaho with her husband and daughter.

On top of writing, she enjoys gaming whether that is picking up a controller or throwing down some dice in a tabletop RPG (as well as other board games). She has also been a fan of science fiction and fantasy since she was little.

9 781732 283510